Praise for the Cyd

Lost Luggage
Macavity Award and Lefty nominee for Best Debut Novel 2018

Drowned Under
Anthony nominee Best Paperback Original and
Lefty nominee Best Humorous Mystery 2020

Fogged Off
Lefty nominee for Best Humorous Mystery 2022

"*Cheap Trills* is strikingly original, brightly inventive, masterfully plotted and, on occasion, truly hilarious. To say this seasoned travel agent is a cynic would be an understatement. But she's *our* kind of cynic: world-wise, sharp-witted, undeterred and with a heart that bleeds compassion. Equipped with her trusty Balenciaga purse, there's no danger she can't handle, no mystery she won't tackle, no bloody wound she can't patch up. Brilliant writing, engaging reading!" —Stephen Mack Jones, author of the award winning August Snow thriller novels

"Bali High! Cyd Redondo is at her charming, quirky, and determined best in *Cheap Trills*. Thomas's tight, clever, and witty writing has never been better!" —Matt Coyle, award-winning author of the bestselling Rick Cahill series

"Thomas has created a sidesplittingly hilarious heroine without rival. *Cheap Thrills* is a nonstop laugh adventure." —James L'Etoile, award-winning author of *Dead Drop* and the Detective Emily Hunter series

"Cyd Redondo puts the fun in funicular. Sparkling, witty, delightful. I laughed on every single page." —Lou Diamond Phillips, actor, director, and bestselling author of *The Tinderbox: Soldier of Indira*

"I love, love, love this book . . . screwball comedy mystery at its best." —*Dru's Book Musings*

"These books are wonderfully outrageous, consistently surprising, and totally hilarious—instant escape, instant entertainment, and diabolically clever. I would follow the fab Cyd Redondo anywhere." —Hank Phillippi Ryan, *USA Today* bestselling author

More Praise for the Cyd Redondo Mysteries

"Thomas makes a rollicking debut with this comic mystery featuring an unconventional protagonist who proves to have the skills of MacGyver. With its sexy overtones, this fun, character-driven novel will appeal to Janet Evanovich fans." —*Library Journal* (starred review)

"*Fogged Off* is what the world needs right now . . . truly laugh-out-loud, coffee-down-your-shirt, don't-read-it-on-the-bus hilarious. The sheer joyful ass-kickery of this terrific heroine is second to none." —Catriona McPherson multi-award winning author of the Last Ditch Motel mysteries

"Laugh-out-loud funny and enchantingly ridiculous . . . highly entertaining." —*Shelf Awareness*

"Brilliant, hilarious, and surprising from start to finish, Wendall Thomas's new mystery is a screwball delight . . . If Preston Sturges and Janet Evanovich had a baby, she would be Cyd Redondo." —Haris Orkin, award-winning author of *You Only Live Once* and *Goldhamme*

"I loved *Lost Luggage* . . . Great combination of humor, social satire, espionage, gender politics, and animal trafficking. Cyd Redondo is smart, sexy, and wonderfully dented." —Tom DiCillo, writer/director of *Living in Oblivion* and *Delirious*

"Thank heavens! I've been waiting for years to find a successor to Janet Evanovich, and I've finally found one." —Cathy G. Cole for Kittling Books

"Fans of Janet Evanovich's Stephanie Plum will cotton to Cyd." —*Publishers Weekly*

"A hilarious book . . . Ms. Thomas has an absolutely lunatic talent for plot and one of the funniest first-person voices I've read in years." —Timothy Hallinan, Lefty winner and Edgar and Macavity Award-nominated author of the Junior Bender and Poke Rafferty novels

"*Drowned Under* puts Thomas in a class with Carl Hiassen . . ." —Nancy Tingley, Lefty-nominated author of the Jenna Murphy Mysteries

"Cyd's Balenciaga bag deserves to become as legendary as Sherlock Holmes's deerstalker and magnifying glass." —James W. Ziskin, Anthony, Barry, and Macavity Award-winning author of the Ellie Stone mysteries

"A breath of fresh air in a world gone mad. Has my vote for one of the best new characters in mystery/crime." —*The Reading Room*

"You will laugh from the very first page. I love every single book in this series. Don't miss any of them." —*New York Times* best-selling author Paige Shelton

"What a heroine for the modern age. Do not miss this!" —Daryl Wood Gerber, Agatha Award-winning national bestselling author of the Cookbook Nook and French Bistro Mysteries

"Thomas packs a whole franchise's worth of adventures into her heroine's debut . . ." —*Kirkus Reviews*

"*Fogged Off* has suspense, murders, international scandals, backstabbing . . . humor, frivolity, light-hearted conflict, and most of all it has Cyd . . . she is the plot, the plan, the problem, and the solution." —*Looks at Books*

Books by Wendall Thomas

Cyd Redondo Mysteries

Lost Luggage
Drowned Under
Fogged Off
Cheap Trills

CHEAP TRILLS

A Cyd Redondo Mystery

Wendall Thomas

Cheap Trills
Wendall Thomas

Cover design Dar Albert, Wicked Smart Designs
The map of Bali featured on the cover is from a painting by Miguel Covarrubias

Beyond the Page Books
are published by
Beyond the Page Publishing
www.beyondthepagepub.com

ISBN: 978-1-960511-20-1

Author's Note

It was a privilege and a challenge to write this novel.

Bali is an extraordinary, gorgeous, complicated, sacred place and by far the most fascinating location I've ever researched. To me, the way the Balinese people are able to weave their religion and culture through every aspect of their daily lives is astounding and completely unique.

The book also required extensive research into endangered Indonesian songbirds, the criminals who poach and traffic them, and the heroes who work tirelessly to save them. This is also a compelling and heartbreaking world, with many moving parts.

Because this is a comic novel, and because everything in it is filtered through Cyd Redondo's first person narration and her Bay Ridge upbringing, I wasn't able to delve as deeply or as seriously into these subjects as they deserve.

I hope perhaps some of you will. And if Cyd inspires you to explore Bali, I have faith you'll respect its rich culture and leave the island the way you found it.

Acknowledgments

Writing a travel book during the pandemic, especially one about the new-to-me world of endangered songbirds, would never have been possible without the wonderful people who took time out of their busy schedules to help and advise me.

First, Dr. Chris R. Shepherd of the Conservation Monitor Research Society has been so generous with his time, stories, and research. He was the one who pointed me in the direction of the bird markets and songbird competitions in Indonesia and their effect on the native bird populations. He has spent his whole life in the service of endangered species. I admire him tremendously and am so grateful for his help. Thanks to Loretta Shepherd of CMRS as well.

Lori Rogalski has traveled to Bali to work on starling conservation, and also helped to hand-raise two clutches of starling chicks at the Los Angeles Zoo's Avian Conservation Center. When she assured me it wasn't impossible for Cyd to keep the newborn birds alive in her purse, I knew I had a book. I owe all the details on the habits, care, and feeding of these extraordinary creatures to her. She is another person doing so much good in the world.

Sincere thanks also to Jan Mantjika—a travel agent in Bali for fifty years—for her kindness. Her heartbreaking and occasionally hilarious memoir, *Bali 1964 to 2009: The Shadows that Dance in and out of My Memory*, was of immeasurable help in my understanding of Bali and of the challenges visitors face there, and I was thrilled to find, in her, Cyd's real-life doppelgänger.

Nancy Tingley also served as an advisor on Bali, as well as offering smart text edits.

Everyone's advice and information has been impeccable. Any errors are completely my own.

I have the kindest, speediest beta readers on the planet in my husband, James Bartlett, my sister, Kim Stout, and my friend Daryl Wood Gerber. Thanks also to Rochelle Staab for her notes on the early pages, and to Catriona McPherson, who always answers emails promptly, with exactly the right advice. My deepest gratitude to James L'Etoile, Matt Coyle, Hank Phillippi Ryan, Lou Diamond Phillips, Tom DiCillo, and Stephen Mack Jones, for their generosity.

So many friends and family members supplied moral support as well, so thanks to all, but especially to Ray Stout, Carol Bartlett, Carolyn Thomas, Rick and Carter McGarry, Smith Richardson, Keith Sears, Nancy Cole

Silverman, Baron R. Birtcher, Wyatt Easterling, Debbie Clark Kaiser, and Karin Altmann (for the Balenciaga!).

Thanks also to the lovely Beatrice Ann North, whose generous donation to the Anaheim Public Library Foundation landed her namesake in the soup with Cyd.

My editor and publisher, Bill Harris, was, as always, a huge support and a delight to work with. Hats off to artist and designer Dar Albert for the cover, and belatedly, for her gorgeous work on *Fogged Off* as well.

And finally, thanks to all the librarians, booksellers, reviewers, and bloggers who have been so kind to Cyd over the years, I can never thank you enough.

Chapter One

Eat. Pray. Barf.

Elizabeth Gilbert's pert best-seller was ruining 2007, and it wasn't even March. I should have known when my eighty-two-year-old lapsed nun assistant asked "How much could an ashram really cost?" I was in trouble. I just didn't know how much.

Eat, Pray, Love featured three locations: Italy, India, and Bali. Italy could be expensive, and, for some women raised on chuck roast, Catholicism, and coffee klatches, the book's promised "vegetarian vow of silence" version of India was a stretch. That left Bali, which was gorgeous, affordable, and (erroneously) associated with *South Pacific*, as the hands-down winner for recent inquiries at Redondo Travel.

Because of the complicated travel logistics alone, I'd tried to steer any Rodgers and Hammerstein fans to Fiji instead. For my clients, rumors of a 2008 Broadway revival of the fan favorite musical, paired with the book's promise of sexy, single Brazilian lovers at every seaside bar, trumped my expertise, which, let's face it, was completely theoretical anyway.

I had nothing against Bali, personally. In fact, I was fascinated by everything the guidebooks said about it. It had Kermit-green terraced rice fields, crowd-pleasing interactive monkey forests, mesmerizing and astonishingly accessorized traditional dances, over ten thousand Hindu temples, volcanic lakes, stunning cliffs, coves, and both white and black beaches. For those who cared, the surfing was world-class, though I'd read the locals mostly stayed away from the sea, which they believed was full of demons. Apparently, the Balinese thought the whole world was an ongoing fight between gods and demons—kind of like Bay Ridge, Brooklyn.

So, I could understand the attraction. If someone was forty, sporty, and had alimony to burn, Bali made sense. And it was a nice change to have a few clients who were more interested in massages than Metamucil. I kept the fact I considered them book club delusionals to myself.

Nobody loved to read more than I did. I spent half my childhood—and huge chunks since—at the Bay Ridge Branch of the Brooklyn Public Library reading everything Head Librarian Bea Ann North recommended. Books were one thing. Book clubs were another. Anyone who believed a book club was anything more than an excuse to drink wine and try out appetizer recipes was a donut short of a baker's dozen. Still, in moments of quiet desperation, or overwhelming peer pressure, we'd all succumbed to some boozy book club or other. Even my hermit mom, Bridget Mary Colleen Colleary Redondo, had given one a whirl.

Before now, I'd only had a sprinkling of book club–inspired travelers—a widower headed for the Louvre after *The Da Vinci Code*, a sentimental retiree headed for the Carolinas after *The Notebook* or *The Prince of Tides*, a mother/daughter rehab trip to Malibu after *Postcards From the Edge*—but suddenly, *Eat, Pray, Love* freaks were calling daily for their shot at tropical self-realization. That was fine until Gilbert's book made its way into local thrift stores and library book sales and my regular clients started to inquire about Bali, too.

For the last ten years, in order to survive, our family business had specialized in senior citizen travel. At the advanced age of thirty-two, I was the queen of destinations with wheelchair ramps, Flying Doctors, and AARP discounts. My clients, however young they felt, had specific requirements, which I didn't mention, but always catered to. Not only did Bali lack most senior amenities, it had additional risk factors.

The island might qualify as one of the most beautiful and exotic places on earth, but it had suffered two terrorist attacks in the last five years, had a serious drink spiking problem, and had three active volcanoes. Three. The island, which resembled a veal chop, was barely the size of Delaware. Imagine three active volcanoes nestled around I-95 in the Diamond State. Would you risk your retirement savings for three days and two nights at a Marriot there, however good the crab cakes?

Although I appreciated that many of my older clients would be happy to go out doing something they loved, I'm not sure that included melting. Or standing before a firing squad. Bali had the death penalty for even minor drug smugglers and jail time for all sorts of contraband, from undeclared cash to racy magazines. After my experience in Tanzania, I was particularly nervous about smugglers taking advantage of my senior clients' gullibility—or their luggage. I was just checking into Bali's 2006 tourist arrests when the phone rang.

"Cyd Redondo, Redondo Travel."

"Cyd, it's Madge Dupree." Madge's voice reeked of forty years of Virginia Slims, bought one carton at a time. I used to babysit for her four rug rats when I was eleven. I think her oldest was about a communion wafer younger than I was. Her husband had developed a sudden interest in the strippers of Fort Hamilton six years ago. Honestly, why does anyone get married? I'd tried to send her to Fiji, but she'd been adamant about Bali, so I assumed she was calling back to book her trip.

"I've changed my mind."

"About Bali?"

"About my plans."

"Oh. Okay. Where would you like to go instead?"

"Still Bali. I found a package tour that doesn't require all those shots."

I didn't want to lose the booking by explaining that Bali travelers risked malaria, dengue fever, and Japanese encephalitis, all three transmitted by mosquitoes, which, by all accounts, were the size of hand puppets and which you couldn't avoid, since some buildings didn't have walls. This also allowed access for pythons, which the Balinese welcomed, since it helped to control the rat population.

"It's not about the tours, Madge, the country requires those shots for entry."

"I think that's incorrect."

Two other clients had bailed, citing the same incorrect information, last week.

"I'll be happy to readjust the itinerary. Did you book it yourself?"

There was a long silence. "No."

"Right. Okay. Well, I hope you have an amazing trip and please call me if for any reason you change your mind."

I was getting a horrible feeling. I let it burble in my brain while I checked on a few clients who were mid-trip.

Pete and Hattie Murphy were doing the Plantains Eating Tour of Miami, before their arteries gave out altogether, while the Olafsons were on one of the increasingly popular Naturist (i.e., nudist) tours of the Bahamas. Of course, they insisted on sending videos of themselves playing golf, which gave a whole new meaning to the term "swing." When I'd asked if they were ever self-conscious, they said, "At our age, who gives a flying fudge?" I could see their point. Sadly, I couldn't unsee it.

The neon lights of Third Avenue started to flicker on. Time to go. As I locked up, I noticed a few pieces of mail lodged under the welcome mat.

On top was an oversized cream-colored envelope addressed to "Sid Redundo," in calligraphy. To my mind, nothing good ever arrived in calligraphy. The return address on the back was The Manzonis. I didn't want to open it, but sometimes you just had to rip the Band-Aid off. I should have left it on.

Chapter Two

It was an invitation to Angela Hepler Manzoni's baby shower. The theme was "Diapers and Such!!"

Barry Manzoni and I had been friends since elementary school. One weekend when we were both approaching thirty, I saw him at the top of an escalator in Atlantic City, wearing a pirate outfit. In a moment of temporary lust and matrimonial panic, we'd gotten married in one of the more reasonably priced wedding chapels. It didn't take. Six months later, we'd gotten an annulment and Barry had married Angela Hepler, a *Desperate Housewives* wannabe who'd tried to take me out with a sandbag during high school auditions for *Macbeth.*

It was bad enough she was having what should have been my baby. Did she have to rub my nose in it? Christ on a bike. To add insult to injury, the slot for "Your Guest" had been scratched out with a Sharpie.

Of course, I could say I was busy, but everyone in the neighborhood would think I was a coward or worse, not over Barry. I wasn't giving Angela, or anyone else, that satisfaction.

I reached down for the rest of the mail and noticed a glossy, tri-color pamphlet with a fold-out section the most expensive kind. I almost threw up.

"Patriot Travel announces their 'Eat, Stay, Fall in Love!' tours to Bali. Visit the unspoiled paradise that changed Elizabeth Gilbert's life. Find your own bliss in one of these Bali package tours, all-inclusive and designed for every budget." And the final death knell: "Special Senior Discount!"

Peggy Newsome. My nemesis. Madge Dupree had left me for Peggy fricking Newsome.

This was war. I grabbed my red vintage Balenciaga bag and headed for the door.

The ten-minute walk home, down Third Avenue and onto 77th Street, usually cheered me up and cleared my head. Something about waving at fellow members of the Third Avenue Businessperson's Association as they shut their lights and clanked their security gates always gave me a peaceful feeling.

Not tonight. Maybe it was Angela's invitation. It was definitely Peggy Newsome's bitch slap Bali pamphlet. But it felt like more than that. As Valentine's Day loomed, there was something strange going on at home, too.

Let's face it, a day devoted to happy couples and obligatory cards/

flowers/candy can be a polarizing event—like making you want to flee to the South Pole kind of polarizing. Penguins mate for life. People, not so much. And when it comes around and you're not in a relationship, the look on people's faces is the same scrunched, tilted one they have when pets die.

I'd had one really good Valentine's Day in my thirty-two years. It was when I was four and my dad and mom filled up my room with paper hearts while I was sleeping. My dad died two weeks later.

When I was eleven, not a single person in my class gave me a card. Barry Manzoni ran to the deli and bought me a jar of artichoke hearts. That's probably why I married him. When I was fifteen Mark, my former boyfriend and current mechanic, was on the outs with his girlfriend and brought me to the Valentine's Dance. They made up on the dance floor, leaving me to walk home, slip on black ice, and break my foot in five places.

For all the others, my mother and I had kept a standing date at New Corners, where the owners always gave us two red roses and extra garlic bread. My mom would tell me how much she loved me and how happy she was that I was her date. But, no matter how hard she tried, at some point the loss of my dad took over her face. She never quite finished her ziti and mainly gulped through dessert to keep from crying. So, I grew up associating Valentine's Day with gulping and plaster casts.

This year I was actually looking forward to going out with Mom. But a couple of days before the holiday, she started avoiding me, leaving the house before me in the morning, or closing her bedroom door when I got home. I finally cornered her on the stairs.

"Are we dressing up or going business casual on Friday?"

"For what?"

"For what? New Corners. Valentine's Day."

She leaned against the wall, her long, reddish-gray braid swinging, and looked up at me. She was paler than usual, which was saying something for a woman whose baseline skin tone was "starched dinner napkin."

"What? Are you okay? If you aren't feeling well, we can stay home and just have pizza with a Pepto-Bismol chaser. That's plenty festive. I don't mind."

"No. It's not that." She just kept looking at me. Oh no.

"You don't have cancer, do you?"

"No. No, I have . . ."

"Oh God, leukemia? Not leukemia! I'll get my bone marrow checked. I could be a match."

"No! I don't have cancer or leukemia." She sighed. "I have plans."

I clutched the handrail and sank to the fifth step.

"Plans? You never have plans."

She sat down beside me. "Exactly. So I figured you wouldn't mind."

"Right. That's why you gave me so much advanced notice."

Her arctic cheeks turned pink. "Cyd Elizabeth Madonna Redondo, are you saying I'm not allowed to have plans? Have I raised someone that selfish?"

"Sorry! Sorry, I didn't mean it that way. Of course you're allowed. That's great. That's really great. I'm happy you have a date." I kissed her on the cheek and pulled myself up.

"Cyd?"

"Yeah."

"It's not a date. I'm going into Williamsburg with a few of the single girls from my book club."

"That sounds like fun."

"Yeah. It does. You'll be okay?"

"Of course I will."

"Good. Sleep well, sweetheart."

"You, too. Night, Mom."

When I got to my room I realized it was only seven thirty, but it was too humiliating to go back downstairs now. I grabbed an airline bottle of Jack Daniel's out of my Balenciaga—I always had one, as it doubled for hand sanitizer in a pinch—then ordered a pizza from Dino's. Their guys were willing to climb the fire escape as long as I paid cash.

Chapter Three

So, for the first time in my life, I was on my own for Valentine's Day. I considered myself brave, but not brave enough to go solo to the most popular Italian restaurant in the neighborhood. Just the act of cancelling our reservation involved being questioned for half an hour by the owner, with additional questions from the waitstaff, on speaker phone. Within an hour, I was getting looks at the post office, One-Hour Martinizing, and Food World.

On the dreaded day, I focused my energy on sending Valentine messages to all my clients, memorizing visa requirements for Bali and Ghana, and waiting for a call from my sometimes boyfriend, Roger Claymore, which never came.

I arrived home that night to find a card from Mom beside a piece of cheesecake with a heart made of Red Hots. I wrapped it up, filled one of Uncle Leon's flasks with two shots of Jack Daniel's, and drove my emerald green 1965 Ford Galaxie 500 to the Cruise Terminal parking lot in Red Hook.

The place was deserted. Even the parking attendant kiosk was empty. My high school buddy Lou, who usually manned it, must be overcompensating for his failures as a husband at New Corners, along with everyone else. Still, with no ship docked in the way, it was a great place to watch the red heart pulsing on the Empire State Building.

I thought of all the clients I'd seen off for Silver Wedding cruises on the *Queen Mary 2*. Those memories made the parking lot one of my favorite places in Brooklyn. Also, I'd been shot here.

I watched the sparkly red heart and thought about the scar from my bullet wound, which had, on the plus side, taken a half inch off my waist. This made me think about Roger, who'd rushed me to the emergency room and pulled a Shirley MacLaine in *Terms of Endearment* until a surgeon looked at me. I was pretty sure I was in love with him, but I didn't trust him and most of the time he was unreachable, which didn't make him a great candidate as a plus one for regular life.

I toasted him with the Jack Daniel's, finished the Red Hots, and was just about to head home to an empty house when my phone rang.

"Cyd Redondo, Redondo Travel."

"Cyd?"

Roger. I felt a twinge in my bullet wound. We'd been together a month before, briefly, in London, but hadn't talked about the future.

I tried to be as cheerfully insouciant as possible. "Hiya."

"Hi. Happy Valentine's Day. It's still Valentine's there, right?"

"For another hour."

"Did I interrupt something?"

I'd been too flummoxed to lie. "Not really. I'm in the Red Hook parking lot."

He was quiet for a minute. "Does it sound crazy that I think that's romantic?"

"Yes." I looked across the river. "No. Where are you?"

"Jakarta. On the way to Malaysia."

"Work?"

"Yeah. Cyd, look, when I realized what day it was, all I could think about was you. I mean, if I was going to talk to anyone today, I wanted it to be you."

For us, this was uncharted territory. I wasn't sure we could navigate the landmine of Valentine's Day, so I asked him if he'd seen our mutual acquaintance, Grey Hazelnut.

"Not since London," he said. "You?"

"No, I only see him accidentally."

Roger laughed. "Welcome to the club." He asked after my Aunt Helen and Uncle Leon. As usual, he couldn't tell me anything about his undercover job for Interpol in the South Pacific.

After an awkward pause, he cleared his throat. "I might be passing through Paris in April. Any chance you want to meet me there?"

I tried to sound blasé and keep the exclamation point out of my "Yes!" but I totally failed. After all, I had enough frequent flyer miles for the trip and could always change my mind.

"Okay. Great. Okay. Until then, we'll always have Atlantic City," Roger said.

"Now that's romantic." Just thinking about our first night together gave me tremors—in a good way.

"Yes. Yes it is. Bye, Cyd. See you in Paris."

This wasn't exactly a vow of undying love, but given the week I'd had, I'd take it. At least I could drive home without the desire to veer into oncoming traffic.

• • •

Three weeks after my solo Valentine's Day, I'd lost four more Bali clients and still wasn't sure what I would or would not find at home. I turned onto 77th Street, famous for its year-round holiday decorations. It was strangely unfestooned—although the Stewarts did have four uninflated leprechauns scattered face down on their lawn, arms and legs akimbo. It looked like a crime scene.

I stared up at our house. It was a three story red brick affair on a long narrow lot, with a bricked-in sun room on the left side and a bay window on the right, separated by a heavy oak door that had withstood a lot of slamming. My tiny attic window was like an exclamation point at the top.

Tonight, there were only two lights on, which was about thirty too few. If you couldn't see our house glowing like a nuclear plant from a block away, something was very, very wrong. Where was everybody?

I unlocked the front door and called out. No Uncle Leon watching PBS. No Aunt Helen losing control of the electric mixer. The kitchen was clean and empty. All I could hear was the hum of the fridge. I headed up the stairs to my mom's room and knocked on the door. Nothing.

My mother was not a loud person, but like anyone, she made noises—the splash of water on her face as she got ready for bed, the flap of her slippers skipping up the stairs, jazz radio late at night, the pop of cereal pouring into a china bowl. I hadn't realized how much those sounds were part of my life until I couldn't hear them.

When I was growing up, the only "girlchild" in the extended Redondo family, surrounded by aunts, uncles, and all my male cousins, not to mention a clutch of Little League coaches, and a few itinerate Avon ladies, I used to fantasize about having the house to myself—just a few hours when I wasn't under surveillance. The imaginary me would turn the heat above sixty-eight degrees, blare Linda Ronstadt, dance up and down the stairs naked, and leave casseroles on the counter without trivets.

I looked around one more time, turned on a dozen lights, and headed for Chadwick's.

Chapter Four

Chadwick's on Third Avenue was my favorite restaurant in Bay Ridge. I'd fought hard to get exclusive drinking rights there in my annulment agreement. Barry had only violated our deal once, when his parents went missing on a cruise to Australia. Now it was officially back in force, so I hoped to have my usual double shot of Jack Daniel's and three crab cakes in peace.

I opened the padded green door to the scent of martinis, rib eyes, and melted butter, with a note of clams casino. My favorite bartender, Tim, was working. He loved extreme winter sports vacations, surfing in Santa Cruz, and adding the maximum medical and accident insurance. I grinned at him. He leaned his head to the left.

I froze.

It wasn't possible. There was no way that the woman who'd abandoned my former in-laws in Australia, who'd tried to bankrupt Redondo Travel, who'd outspent me on pamphlets, was sitting on my stool, clinking glasses with Merv Stone, my most trusted United States Postal Service connection.

I gestured at Tim and mouthed, "Why didn't you call me?" He threw up his hands.

This was serious. Service businesses are all about relationships—mine more than most. To assure the best prices and service for my clients, I needed more than a village. I needed something the size of a mid-range college town. In addition to hundreds of "sister" travel agencies, foreign currency agents, tour operators, limo and bus companies, concierges and cleaners, and airline and airport personnel, I needed tons of last-minute help with passports, visas, and vaccinations. But most of all, I needed new clients.

That's why Merv, Supervisor at the Bay Ridge Post Office #3, was vital. Not only did he ensure that any expedited passports and visas arrived safely, he tipped me off whenever there was a new invitation to join AARP, so I could send out mailers with senior travel discounts before anyone else.

In exchange, I made sure he, his wife Annie, and his four children had annual passes to Dollywood (his wife loved Dolly, but who doesn't?), six annual seats for *The Nutcracker* at Lincoln Center, and lifetime passes for The Cyclone at Coney Island, along with just about anything else he asked for. How could he be fraternizing with Peggy fricking Newsome?

Although she'd violated many neighborhood rules in the year since she'd opened the corporate Patriot Travel office, as far as I knew, this was the first time she'd breached my personal culinary sanctuary. As usual, she was "dressed for camera," since she considered herself a combo of the Dianas—Sawyer and Princess. Her blonde wedge haircut fell perfectly around her face and her mauve silk blouse was unbuttoned to the "I'm a professional but this is happy hour" level.

If the restaurant had been quieter, I would have thrown my drink in her face, but three of my clients were mid–beef Wellington. Plus, I figured she was baiting me on purpose. But for what? It didn't matter, I wouldn't give her the satisfaction. I had a long history of dealing with bullies, and not just by landing a kitten heel in their balls.

I waited until I'd rearranged my "rage" face into an "I don't have a care in the world" face, then walked to the bar and pulled out a stool.

"Hey, Tim," I said, my voice steady as a Tilt-a-Whirl.

"Hey, Squid! The usual?"

Honestly. Did he have to use my childhood nickname? His tip took a dive to twenty-five percent. Merv turned around and went white, spilling half of his Manhattan onto his khakis.

Peggy didn't even blink. She pursed her lips around her olive and slid it off the toothpick, then recrossed her legs to make sure I could see the red bottoms of her Laboutin heels.

I turned to Tim. "Another round for my friends, please. Peggy. What are you, slumming today? I thought you didn't drink anywhere south of Cobble Hill."

"Well, it depends on the company," she said, patting Merv's extensive, stained thigh. "And don't you look cute! I love that you always have one of those nineties throwback outfits."

"Well, the nineties haircuts were already taken. Are you in touch with Chip?"

Peggy and my old high school friend Chip Jessup had been involved in a corporate money laundering scheme involving international coffins. He was currently somewhere that didn't have an extradition treaty with the United States.

"Hi, Merv! How's Annie?" I figured it was fair enough to mention his wife.

Merv winced and stared at me. "She left me."

"What? Oh my God, Merv. I am so sorry. When?"

"Monday."

"Holy crap. She adores you, it must just be a blip."

"I don't think so. She took the kids. Peggy thought I needed some cheering up."

How had I not heard this? Though I wanted to punch Peggy, I couldn't make things worse for Merv. "That was really kind of her." I got up and gave him a quick hug. "It looks like Peggy has you covered for company, but the rest of the drinks are on me." I looked at Tim, he nodded. "And if you need anything at all, will you let me know?"

"Sure, Cyd." He turned back to Peggy, who gave me a combination hair flip/evil look worthy of Alan Rickman in *Robin Hood: Prince of Thieves*.

I shot my drink, took my crab cakes to go, and let the air out of the rear passenger side tire of Peggy's BMW. The one with the TRVLBABE plates.

Chapter Five

I didn't want to go back to an empty house, so I headed the two blocks to the office and pulled down the Venetian blinds. The whole neighborhood didn't need to see me swig an airline bottle of Jack Daniel's with my takeout crab cakes.

I pulled up all my Bali files and printed several airline timetables and routes. I had to figure out a trip that rivaled Peggy's that wouldn't kill or bankrupt my fixed-income clients. They didn't know Elizabeth Gilbert's self-help journey had the non-self-help of a two hundred thousand dollar advance from her publisher. That covered a lot of ashram.

Right now, the flight in most of my clients' price range took fifty-one hours. I didn't want to do fifty-one hours of anything, and I imagined they wouldn't either, especially in coach, with arthritis or an enlarged prostate.

Even the most expensive flights had at least two plane changes. With every change, the odds of a missed connection or lost luggage went up exponentially. And the closer you got to Bali, the fewer flights were available to rebook if you did miss one. A client could wind up in the Perth, Jakarta, or Singapore airport for days. Who would do that to their grandmother?

I was cataloguing Indonesian air disasters in the last two months (three!) and Bali's venomous snake species (six!)—which included a deadly sea serpent whose salient characteristics were "speed and curiosity"— as well as available snake-specific anti-venoms (one!), when I heard Sister Ellery sneak upstairs.

She'd been my eighth-grade teacher at Xaverian Middle School until she abandoned the Church for tantric sex. In the years since then, she'd been my client and friend. I was the one who suggested she retire on a series of cruise ships, which landed us both in the middle of a shipboard murder. After that, I'd made her come home for a while and offered her my pending apartment upstairs.

She'd been helping with the office, but had also gone behind my back and used my credit card to book a flight for one of my relatives, so I had to keep an eye on her. I noticed the time. It was two in the morning—too late to walk home.

I hadn't stayed here overnight since my Uncle Ray had turned the business over to me. Technically, as the head of Redondo Travel, his office in the back was mine. But I'd left it locked and undisturbed since he'd been arraigned because I missed him too much.

I opened the door and looked at the massive mahogany desk where, five months ago, I'd found a bright blue parrot skewered with a steak knife. I grabbed an Army/Navy blanket and a blow-up travel pillow from the storeroom and lay down on my uncle's black leather Ethan Allan couch.

I woke at five in the morning, wearing my travel pillow backward, like a whiplash collar. A quick date with a double espresso, my toothbrush, and a swipe of Responsible Raisin lipstick had me back at my desk in thirty minutes.

By seven, I'd booked one trip to the Kentucky Derby, mint juleps and ribs included, and one to Colonial Williamsburg, where I assured Mrs. Thompkins that yes, she and her daughter could make their own tallow candles and that I, too, had heard the peanut soup was a must-try. I turned back to my Eat, Stay, Safe project, which I'd named "Bali, Hi!"

The Bali research paid off when Patty Sims, three years divorced and one year Botoxed, dropped in, requesting information on various packages, with and without scuba diving.

Patty had just left when the front door blew open and in came Sister Ellery, her short, spiky white hair anchored with gravity-defying gel and wearing something that made her look like a half-melted Creamsicle.

I stared at her. "How come I didn't know Annie had left Merv?"

"You're losing it, is why."

"I beg your pardon!"

"You've been gone too much, you're distracted."

"Yeah, well, whose fault is that? Everywhere I've gone has been about getting someone else out of trouble."

"Has it?"

"Yes. Are you trying to get thrown out of your free apartment?"

"You don't have the guts. What did you get Angela for the shower?"

"What are you getting her?"

"I wasn't invited. Plus, somebody has to hold down the office." She peered at me. "Did you sleep here?"

"No comment. I'm going to run some errands." I handed her the mock-up of our new brochure. "Could you double-check the Bali emergency kits and make sure we have enough extra Avon bug spray if we get more bookings?"

"Roger."

"Please don't say that. I'll be back."

By the end of the day I'd delivered a freezer-friendly tray of lasagna to

Merv at Postal Office #3, my Bali brochures were being printed, and Angela's present was wrapped in my trunk.

I pulled into our driveway and saw a light on in the den. The knot that had been in my stomach for days eased a little. Uncle Leon was in his forest green Barcalounger, watching PBS, so at least something was right with the world.

As usual, he was dressed like a mod from 1963—tight suit and pants, silk socks, and pointy shoes, shiny enough to be visible from Queens.

"Hey." I poured myself a shot of Jack Daniel's and sat down beside him. "Have you seen Mom?"

"She's out with your Aunt. Book club thingy."

"Since when does Aunt Helen belong to a book club?"

"Your mother talked her into it. Apparently there's sherry." Aunt Helen was forever sending me for "cooking sherry," which disappeared at the rate of a six-pack of Tab.

"What on earth are they reading?"

"Girl stuff." He had one eye on *Nova* and one on the *Daily Racing Form*.

"How'd you do?"

He shrugged. Meaning, he'd lost. After I got up, I would drop forty bucks on the floor in the hallway, which he'd pick up and forget to give back to me.

"Have you eaten?"

"Had a bratwurst at the track."

I glanced at the TV and saw a crocodile headed for a water buffalo. I fled before the serious thrashing began. I decided to heat up some eggplant, which didn't scream in its death throes, at least not at a frequency I could hear.

Afterward, I headed upstairs. It was quiet. Too quiet. Because we were so surrounded and outnumbered, my mother and I had always given each other as much privacy as we could. I never went into her room unless invited. I knocked three times.

"Mom?" I opened the door and stopped. The "early Virgin Mary" decor I remembered, anchored by a white chenille bedspread, had been replaced by a red and gold batik coverlet and four square, silk pillows. Over her bed was a print of what I knew from my Bali research was the Hindu elephant god, Ganesh. What the hell was going on?

First, why hadn't Aunt Helen told me about this? And second, how had Mom gotten this stuff into the house? If there'd been deliveries from Pier One I would have seen the boxes—I was in charge of recycling. And, I couldn't even ask about it, because then I'd have to admit I'd violated the sanctity of our unspoken agreement. Needless to say, I didn't sleep. I would have bags under my eyes for Angela's shower.

Chapter Six

I don't know why the idea of Angela's baby shower bothered me so much, but it did. Plus, I had no idea what to wear. A shroud? In the end, I settled on a royal blue Eva Marie Saint in *North by Northwest* style dress, with a V-neck, V-back, and a tight waist—the only thing I had that Angela Hepler didn't. I added a tiny patent-leather belt and matching Charles David Mary-Jane stilettos.

Of course, gift-giving had been another landmine. Diapers were not my forte and I had no clue what the "such" was supposed to be. I tried making a diaper bouquet and wound up with what could charitably be called a wad. A wad might be better than Angela deserved, but half the neighborhood would be there and they'd tell the other half about it, so, for the sake of the business, I had to deliver something impressive.

In the end, in addition to a gift from Angela's Teeny Tots registry, I found a baker in Williamsburg who made diaper cupcakes, with marzipan pins. I bartered a baker's dozen of the overpriced confections for three free bus rides to Atlantic City.

Even armed with a killer dress and designer cupcakes, I didn't want to leave the house. I popped my head into the kitchen. Aunt Helen was pounding veal.

She didn't even turn around. "You're due at the shower. What's wrong with you?"

"I don't know if I can handle it. Why would I do this to myself?"

Aunt Helen turned around, mallet in hand. "You have to go and show that witch that you're the bigger person."

"Actually, right now, she's the bigger person."

"Fine, be a smart aleck. You need clients, don't you? And you might meet a nice man."

"At a baby shower?"

She turned back to hammering the cutlets.

"Where's Mom?"

"Went to the store, I think."

"Okay. I'm sure I'll be home soon."

"No hurry."

I'd considered walking the five blocks, but I might need to make a quick getaway. I circled past Barry and Angela's house, then parked one street over so I had an escape route through the Talberts' yard. They had a Tuff Shed I could use for cover.

I sat in my Galaxie for a few minutes to gather myself, then grabbed my offerings and headed over Barry's perfect lawn. This would be the first time I'd seen Angela since she'd threatened me with a nine iron. At least today, at this female-only event, I wouldn't have to see Barry, too.

Until he answered the door.

He went pale, then jerked down his diamond-patterned "Almost Dad" sweater over the slight pooch he'd developed under Angela's watch.

I backed up. "What the hell are you doing here?"

"I don't know, Cyd. I live here? And hey, nice to see you, Barry, congratulations on the baby."

I hung my head. "Sorry. Congratulations on the baby, of course." I looked up. "Nice sweater."

"Screw you."

We both laughed. I held up the gift and cupcake box.

"Do I need to check these for explosives?"

"Emotional landmines, maybe. Seriously, I thought husbands weren't allowed."

"Apparently, it's a new trend. You can imagine how thrilled we all are." His shrug was the same one he gave me when we decided on our annulment. Basically, it meant, "I give up."

He let me in. "Exhibit A." He pointed toward what could only be called an "unhappiness" of husbands.

Sister Ellery had taught me this collective noun when I was in junior high. I can't say it really encouraged me in a matrimonial direction. The spouses, in their dress shirts and too-tight sports coats, were huddled so close together around the punch bowl, they reminded me of a sweaty package of all-beef franks.

Unfortunately, I walked right into my former mother-in-law's sights. As usual, she was wearing something that made her look like a human tostada. She came ruffling toward me, her undercooked bingo wings flapping.

"My favorite daughter-in-law!"

The whole room turned my way, including Angela who, to my delight, currently resembled an Orca, shrink-wrapped in fuchsia. I guess she hadn't gotten the memo that fuchsia was usually best as an accent, but to each expectant mother their own.

I didn't mind if she hated me. But I couldn't lose a whole split-level house full of clients.

"Oh, I'm sure you mean your favorite ex-daughter-in-law. Look how lovely all this is. What a wonderful way to celebrate Angela and your coming grandchild. Congratulations!" I kissed her on the cheek. "And aren't you glowing, Angela? You look so fetching!"

I smiled, then backed away, shoving my cupcakes on an empty serving plate, then skedaddling down to the end of the couch to join someone who hated Angela Hepler as much as I did—my best friend, Debbie Pinkowski. She'd gone for full-on black in solidarity.

"Nice belt." She handed me a glass of wine.

Angela was encircled by the high school friends who had baby advice, and judgment, at the ready. I actually felt for her. Momentarily. Those women would never let up. Debbie and I, of course, only had advice we'd seen via *Look Who's Talking*. We decided to keep it to ourselves and finish the bottle of Chardonnay, which was not buttery, at all.

Debbie and I walked to the "diaperama" gift table. There were live flowers at each end, but otherwise, it resembled a laundromat massacre. In addition to all the diaper bouquets, there were diaper quilts, diaper throw pillows, diaper head bands and, in a show of questionable safety, a diaper candlestick holder.

Debbie pointed to what looked like a fully used diaper, featured in the middle of the buffet table. We watched in horror as one of the hotdog husbands dipped his finger into the brown substance inside, then ingested it.

"Eck. What the hell is that?"

Debbie snorted. "According to *New Mommy* magazine, it's the height of shit, I mean *chic*." She grinned at me. "All indications to the contrary, it's chocolate."

"Well, I am not partaking of that, even if it's seventy percent cacao!"

We moved into the living room just as the shower games began.

There was a diaper pin race, an origin of baby names quiz (apparently Cyneburg is an actual name) and a "famous babies in the movies" challenge. My brousin Frank, a tough guy detective for the 68th Precinct, was here with his wife and currently hanging his manhood on the name of the children in *Honey I Shrunk the Kids*. If they'd asked the name of the baby being christened in *The Godfather*, he'd have had better odds.

I wondered why he hadn't said hi. Seeing all these men forced to play baby shower games just seemed sad. I'd bowled enough with Barry to know when his ears looked disheartened. I went over to cheer him up, but Angela shot between us.

"Cyd! Still wearing your dress from Shep Helnikov's funeral, I see."

"Well, I am still mourning Shep, but actually, I wanted to make sure I wore something that would make you pop out." I'm not sure she appreciated the word pop.

"Oh, well, I guess you're not really dressing for anyone. It must be so much easier, being single," she said.

"It is a lot easier than being married to Barry, anyway. No offense, Barry." He shrugged. "I'm sure you're just a walk in the park next to me, Angela." I raised my glass and clinked it with a decorative diaper spoon. "To Angela, in her full pregnant glory! May she, someday. . ." I looked at Debbie, who gave me a thumbs up. ". . . return to a size twelve!"

The first cupcake brushed my bangs. The second smacked me right on the nose. Angela licked the icing off her fingers. "Get her out of here! Now!"

Barry put a hand on his wife's arm. "Angie! Calm down. Come on. Cyd saved my parents' lives. For free!"

"Well, I wish you'd paid her, so you would shut up about it."

"At least she cares about my parents."

As much as I loved this, it was time to go. "Thank you, Angela and Sandra, for the lovely party." I started for the door.

"Ha! You're not getting off that easy, you desperate, interfering, dried-up spinster."

I wanted to take the high road. I really did. "I think interfering first wife, as in the one he chose first, is the phrase you're looking for."

She towered above me. "Ha! You don't even know what's going on in your own house."

I heard a few people gasp, which was weird. Then complete silence. What the hell? "What is it that I don't know, Angela? Please enlighten me."

I saw Barry draw his finger across his throat, about seven times. Angela responded with a one finger gesture of her own, then laughed. "Your mother's on a flight to Bali."

"What did you say?" I got directly in her slightly puffy face.

"Your own mother's on Peggy Newsome's 'Eat, Stay, Fall in Love!' tour. Because you suck as a travel agent."

If Angela hadn't been pregnant, she would have been on the floor.

"That's not possible."

"It is when everyone in Bay Ridge helped her trick you."

I looked at the faces in the room, ending with Frank. His face said everything. It was true.

"Those stretch marks are never going away," I yelled, as I sprinted for the door.

On my way to the street, all I could think about were hordes of rat-sized mosquitoes, pythons the size of air ducts, and armed Customs Agents, all closing in on my kind, pale, naive, under-vaccinated, and probably uninsured mother.

A series of things started to add up—Aunt Helen's uncharacteristic cheerfulness, Sister Ellery's insistence it was good for the business for me to attend the shower. Had Barry been in on it, too? After all I'd done for his parents? Wow.

And my mother. How could she? I veered between the gut punch of her betrayal and an urge to strangle her. But I could only kill her if she were alive. In Peggy Newsome's hands, that was a crapshoot.

I was so distracted thinking of my mosquito magnet mother wracked with dengue fever, I boinked straight into one of those stupid "Baby Manzoni!" mylar balloons flapping above the Colonial blue mailbox. Remembering they were the number two cause of power outages in the U.S., and that party-givers could be held financially responsible for the damage, I whipped my travel nail clippers out of the side pocket of my Balenciaga, made a snip here and a snip there, and released five of them right under the electric lines for the north Fort Hamilton grid.

I saw sparks, then the domino effect of a two block, "take that Angela Hepler," blackout in my rearview mirror, as I headed for Third Avenue. Aside from the day I shared a truck bed with an incensed warthog, it was the longest ride of my life.

Chapter Seven

I slammed my Galaxie sideways into the "Reserved for Employees of Redondo Travel" parking space behind our building and ran inside.

"Get the hell off my computer. Never touch it again."

Sister Ellery, overexposed in a burnt orange tank top, flapped her scrawny arms up in the air. "I can explain."

"I don't care. Out. Seriously."

She tried the look that had worked on me in eighth grade. Not anymore.

"Lurch over, you lying sack of nun!"

I think it was the first time I'd ever said anything mean to one of my elders. I felt like throwing up. But this was the second time she'd betrayed me "for my own good." Plus, I was tired, I was angry, and I hadn't had enough finger food. "Get out!"

Finally, I heard the door slam. I leaned forward and saw the computer screen.

No. Mom was booked on Adam Air. They'd had two crashes already this year. And she'd left last night. Had Uncle Leon lied to me, too?

The phone rang. "Cyd Redondo, Redondo Travel."

"Don't hate her too much," Sister Ellery said. "She won the trip. In the Catholic Woman's League raffle. You know she never wins anything." It was true, not even Scrabble. "You have to let her walk on her own, even if she falls. It's not like she doesn't know she can call you."

"She should feel too guilty to call me. Plus, she doesn't even have a cell phone."

Christ on a bike, my mother didn't have a cell phone. I started to hyperventilate. I put Sister Ellery on speaker, dumped the sandwich she'd left out on the desk, and breathed into the empty paper bag. Nothing like the stench of liverwurst on rye in a crisis.

"Don't worry. I gave her your standard emergency bag and instructions with the burner phone and your number on speed dial. Whatever is happening, she can deal with it. She's dealt with you for thirty-two years and you're no picnic."

"Thanks a lot." I hung up on her, changed my computer password and shut the server down. I picked up my Balenciaga, but where could I go?

Not home. My sneaky aunt was there. Not Chadwick's. There weren't any fifty percent off or more sales this weekend, and Debbie was probably still at Angela's shower, which I hope had descended into a non-refrigerated melee.

I considered the Verrazano-Narrows Bridge. When I was tiny, my Uncle Ray told me I'd always be safe if I kept the bridge in my sights. But if everyone in town, including my own mother, was willing to conspire against me, maybe I couldn't trust the bridge anymore. It was one thing to be a fish out of water in Tanzania or Tasmania. It was another to be a fish out of water on Third Avenue. I wished I could go to Uncle Ray for advice, but that required a visitor's pass and was only possible on Tuesdays and Thursdays, between twelve and two.

The phone rang again. I was not in the mood.

"What?"

"Cyd? Oh thank God. It's Mom. Do you speak Jakartan?"

Chapter Eight

"Jakartan? There is no Jakartan. Are you in Jakarta? Why are you calling?"

If she wanted help, she was going to have to ask for it.

"Cyd, your father's been dead for twenty-eight years."

"I know! What does that have to do with anything?"

I heard a scuffle, then a Virginia Slims voice. "Cyd Elizabeth Madonna Redondo, your mother has just been roughed up by Customs in a foreign language. Get your travel agent ass over here."

"Madge?" I remembered that Madge had thrown her mid-sixties divorce rage into a series of wine-soaked, self-help-themed book clubs. And she'd gone over to the Newsome dark side. This was probably her fault.

"Are you just winding me up? Because they execute people there."

"Don't be ridiculous."

"I'm not. Look it up!"

"She's fine."

I tried to calm myself. "Are there any more traitors with you?"

"Bea Ann is here."

"Bea Ann North is with you?" So much for a lifetime of loyalty to the Brooklyn Public Library system. I'd have expected better from the woman who introduced me to *Harriet the Spy*.

"Call Peggy Newsome. Isn't she your travel professional?"

"We tried. She's at an ashram and has taken a vow of silence. She can't be disturbed."

Holy Mother of God, I thought. "Okay, start from the beginning."

• • •

From what I could decipher, Peggy had booked them with impossibly tight connections, so of course they had missed their second and third flights. Madge, afraid to call me, had managed to get them onto alternate flights as far as Jakarta. But there were no flights to Bali for four days on the death-watch airline Peggy had used. Plus, their luggage was nowhere to be found.

"Put my mom back on."

More scuffling. "Hi."

"Do I go on a spiritual journey when I have a tour in progress, full of women who've never been abroad before? No, I do not. And even if I did, I would check in on everyone online, since it would not violate ashram rules. Put Madge back on."

"Madge here."

"You will pay for this. But right now, I need all your ticket numbers, the names as they appear on your passports, your credit card numbers, with expiration dates and security codes, and cell phone numbers. I will try to rebook you on the earliest possible flight to Denpasar. Do you have reservations once you're there?"

"Absolutely. Peggy took care of everything."

"Well, yes. Everything but this. Do you have roaming set up on your phone?"

"Yes."

"Good. You're going to arrive late at your hotel, so you need to call and let them know. Can you do that while I sort out the flights?"

"Yes."

"Madge? Take care of my mom. And tell Bea Ann I'm very disappointed in her."

"I'll look after your mom. But I'm going to put the Bea Ann thing on hold. Humidity makes her cranky."

"Fine." I hung up.

Before I hacked into the Patriot Travel computer system, I called Peggy's office to see if there was anyone there. It went to the answering service.

"Patriot Travel. Travel better."

"Jen?"

"What is it, Cyd?"

Jennifer Hedges and I took Shop together. She worked for three answering services and had always sounded as much like Betty Boop as she did now.

"Peggy has stranded my mother, Madge Dupree, and Bea Ann North in Indonesia. They were told she was in the midst of a vow of silence?"

"That's what she told us to tell everyone."

"So where is she, really?" Another long silence. "Jennifer. How many people know about your suspended sentence for shoplifting?"

"Cyd! You wouldn't!"

"This is my mother and our childhood librarian she's screwing with."

"Okay, fine." It turned out Peggy—surprise, surprise—was not at an ashram. She was at a spa resort on the west coast of Bali. She was actually in Bali and wouldn't help my mom. This time I was going to do more than flatten her tire.

"Jen, give me the info!" She did. "Thanks. Your Kate Spade bag is safe."

My favorite IT guy had given me Peggy's login codes in exchange for a four day/three night "raclette" tour to Montreal. He'd wanted to practice his French.

I found Mom's reservations under a file labeled "Eat, Pray, Losers."

I called the Indonesian airline and used a combination of Bahasa Indonesian and English to explain the situation to a clerk—who was using a similar language combo. I negotiated a refund by threatening to have them put the three women up in what I knew was an expensive hotel. At least, I think that's what I did. It was the first time I'd had to use the language with another person, as opposed to my cassette player.

I made new round trip reservations for the three woman, Jakarta to Bali, on a safer airline. I couldn't find their checked luggage, yet, though. That was a headache for later.

I called Madge back. "Your flight to Bali is on time and departs in an hour."

"An hour? That's not much time."

"What didn't I understand about stranded? You need to check in at the Eva Air desk and get your boarding passes, okay? The airport code is D as in despicable, P as in Peggy fricking Newsome, and S as in son of a bitch. DPS. Got it?"

"Yep." She hesitated. "Thank you."

"Mom should have a Bahasa Indonesian phrase book in her emergency kit if you need it. Did you get through to the hotel?"

"Not yet."

"Okay, give me the info, I'll do it from here."

I reached for my last two pieces of Bazooka Joe. This was a double-bubble situation.

I opened the files again and almost sucked the gum down my throat. I stopped myself just in time, since there was no one to perform the Heimlich maneuver and I was too tired to hurl myself against the back of my chair.

Mom, Madge, and Bea Ann didn't have any reservations in Bali—at all.

Chapter Nine

There are a few basic things you should expect from your travel professional. We should be familiar with destination time zones, understand the international date line, and know each country's national or religious holidays and any other quirks in their calendars before making reservations, booking connections, etc. There are a million things that can go wrong if we don't.

If Peggy had done more than read the back cover blurb of *Eat, Pray, Love*, she would have known that the Balinese operate on three separate calendars. Their most important one, in terms of their day-to-day lives, has 210 days in a year rather than 365. And, since Peggy didn't know the difference, or care, she'd failed to check the box for the Gregorian calendar, and booked her clients' reservations according to the wrong one, like the over-coiffed and irresponsible half-wit that she was. She was probably the only travel agent on earth who could have screwed this up.

So, my mother's reservations were for over two weeks ago, as were all their prepaid tours to the volcanoes, ceremonial dancing performances, snorkeling in the coral reefs, trips to three temples—complimentary sarongs included—and a half day in the Ubud Monkey Forest. And per the fine print, there were no refunds if they were no-shows. On top of that, the Bay Ridge matrons were landing in an airport where lying about your accommodations had serious consequences. With the image of the three of them standing in ill-fitting sundresses in front of a tropical firing squad burned in my brain, I called their original hotel. They were completely full, with a long waiting list.

At least I'd recently reconnected with the one person who might be able to help me—the queen of Bali travel, Jill of Jill's Adventures.

Jill was an Aussie who'd come to Bali to surf in the early seventies, fallen for a Balinese man, and never left. She'd had her agency for over thirty years. We'd shared horror stories at a "Rehabilitating the 777" convention at Madison Square Garden after 9/11.

With the exception of Peggy Newsome, travel agents are the best. They are calm, practical, well-educated, curious, and tech-savvy. And the ones in Southeast Asia regularly had to navigate airport shutdowns, monsoons, plane crashes, the occasional political coup, and death by firing squad if their clients were caught smuggling drugs, animals, or large amounts of cash. I thought my job was tough, but Jill was a study in badass.

"Jill's Travel, Jill speaking."

"Jill! Cyd Redondo, Redondo Travel. I'm so glad you're there."

"Cyd! Glad you caught me. I'm off on holiday in three days. What can I do for you?"

"Three words. Peggy fricking Newsome."

"No! What is it this time?"

I told her. She said there was a small but comfortable hotel near Denpasar with rooms she kept reserved for emergencies like this. I could hear Jill's keyboard clicking over the line. "Do all their tour arrangements need to be rescheduled as well?"

"Yes. Please. I trust whatever you'd suggest. I really owe you for this one, Jill."

"Nope, I'm still paying you back for front-row seats to Lord of the Dance, 2003." She paused. "Customs is very strict. They'll penalize you for an overstay. I'll send my second in command, Lu, to pick them up. Should I add a fourth reservation? You want to come over? It's ceremony season."

My mother might resent it. But if Jill was leaving the country, at least I'd be on the ground for any other emergencies. There was another good reason. Peggy was there and not expecting me, which put me in a power position, for once. As ever, I erred on the side of responsibility. And revenge. "Yes. I'd better. I'll let you know when I'm arriving."

"Do you want to give me a credit card for the rooms?"

I'd have to lock the office and put the calls on forward. I called my former high school lab partner and current owner of Lockness Monster Key Service for an emergency lock change for the office. While I waited for him, I called in a couple of favors and cashed in some miles on Singapore and Eva air. My flight left in five hours. It would be tight, but at least all my shots were up to date.

I grabbed my vaccination records, forwarded the office phone to my "client emergency" cell and backed up all my client files onto a flash drive, which I put inside two ziplocks, inside a small pink Tupperware container, inside one of the padded pockets of my purse. Finally, I shoved a set of the new keys into a prepaid envelope addressed to Debbie Pinkowski and patted the office door for luck.

Our house was dark except for the light in the foyer. There was no drone of *Nova* in the den. If my Aunt Helen and Uncle Leon were home, they were upstairs in their room.

For the twenty years when I'd barely left the neighborhood, my emergency travel bag had been ready for all time zones and climates. Ironically, now that I'd actually been somewhere, my trusty prepacked carry-on was missing vital items.

I pulled out my laminated "tropical locations" list and added three-ounce containers of industrial-strength antiperspirant, Avon bug spray, anti-frizz hair serum, 55 SPF sunscreen, and waterproof mascara to my quart-sized "liquids" ziplock. They just fit.

I checked that I had water purifying tablets, cornstarch, a crushable sun hat, two pairs of high-heeled sandals and a few scrunchies. My Balenciaga was up to date.

As I'd be going through airports in two Muslim countries, a miniskirt—my preferred travel uniform—wouldn't work. I crept down to my mother's room. I remembered she had a flowy red knit maxi skirt that would be modest, but not dull. I added a black silk boatneck shirt with my beloved Hermès scarf, and a pair of nude Charles David patent-leather heels.

I triple-checked everything, zipped up my carry-on, weighed it on the bathroom scale by subtracting what I hoped was still my current weight, and carried it all to the landing.

I stood for a minute outside Uncle Leon and Aunt Helen's door. You never know what's going to happen on a trip. Even though I was furious with them, I didn't want to leave without saying goodbye. I knocked and cracked the door.

"What is it, Squid?" Uncle Leon sat up. His nightcap was positively Dickensian.

"I'm going to Bali. Just wanted you to know that, even though you betrayed me after I saved both your lives, I love you anyway." I blew him a kiss and heard a groan from Aunt Helen.

Her hairnet twinkled as she turned over. "Everybody deserves a vacation."

Chapter Ten

I'd split the difference between the easiest and the cheapest trip, finding flights that had the best on-time and safety records. I needed to get there fast, but I wasn't going to help Mom, or anyone else, if I missed two connections, or careened off a runway. I'd managed to get all bulkhead seats. My maxi skirt was wide enough to hide my Balenciaga from the flight attendants and I'd be first in my section to get off the plane, which would help if the flights were delayed.

Which, of course, they were. I was due to have a two-hour layover in Qatar, but our late departure sliced it to thirty minutes. I'd run through the Doha airport, holding up Mom's skirt, my Hermès headscarf slipping over my eyes, to catch the plane to Jakarta. At least I'd been prescient enough to wear stilettos for balance and speed. I made it onto the jetway just before they closed the gate. Then waited on the tarmac for forty-five minutes. So we were late arriving in Indonesia, but that was all right, as my Eva Air flight from Jakarta to Bali was delayed, too.

My experience with the Jakarta airport was limited to multiple viewings of the movie *The Year of Living Dangerously*, so I was happy to take the time to explore, keeping my eyes modestly low and my headscarf modestly high.

Now that I was at least in striking distance of Bali, I found the closest thing I could to a quiet corner and checked my messages. So far, all my current travelers were okay. Why was there nothing from Mom? Or Jill? Were they trying to give me a stroke?

To distract myself, I decided to practice more Bahasa Indonesian. Indonesia had over seven hundred indigenous languages, but most inhabitants, especially officials and locals who dealt with tourists, could use and understand this standardized form of the language. Of course, when I'd tried all the pronunciation sites online, every one of them pronounced the words differently, so I had no idea whether I was even close to correct. Which is why I was drinking Schnapps instead of Scotch with my satay.

I wasn't really supposed to have alcohol with my malaria pills, but no one else was doing what they were supposed to, so why should I?

Then, I couldn't put it off any longer. I had to use the bathroom. I knew that most of Indonesia used squat toilets. I had used them in East Africa, but not in a maxi skirt.

I clutched my bag and carry-on. According to my phrase book, there were three different ways to ask for the ladies' room, so I used the one I was least likely to mispronounce. It worked, as a kind person directed me to the *waysay.*

I was a bit thrown once I made it into the small tiled room with a sign in four languages that read "Do Not Put Paper Products in Toilet!"

This became even more puzzling since there were no "paper products" in sight—just a trash can and a hose with a nozzle big enough to spray an Escalade. This must be one of the "wet clean" bathrooms that were conveniently never mentioned in *Eat, Pray, Love.* That explained the water all over the floor, which I didn't want to think about. I looked for a nonexistent purse hook for my Balenciaga and carry-on.

At least it was a rolling bag. I reached one-handed into my purse and dug out a handful of safety pins, then secured my purse around my neck, backward, and pinned the long skirt up as high as I could all the way around. At least my stilettos were waterproof and would make squatting easier. I pitied all women travelers who opted for the comfort of leggings or palazzo pants. Nightmare.

I pulled down my La Perla "ocean" thong, pulled up as much of my skirt as I could into my lap, and squatted over the toilet, slipping my heels into what I hoped were footholds. When I was done, I reached for the hose, positioned it, gently pressed the lever, and received my first ever travel enema.

Although my feet stayed put, the force of the water and the weight of my bag pulled the rest of me into the world's least attractive backbend. The waterproofed bag hit the floor pretty hard, but protected my skull, which was not waterproofed.

I was grateful for my kickboxing workouts, which meant my core could actually pull me back up into the squatting position. By the time I'd grabbed the squiggling hose to turn it off, it had sprayed the entire room at least three times and everything I owned, or was wearing, was soaked.

There was a lot of banging from outside. It appeared my fire hose stream had breached the door. I managed to pull up my damp underwear, lift my soaked skirt, and dismount. I removed my bag from around my neck and reached in for my packet of travel tissues, although what I really needed was a Sam's Club lot of Bounty. Once I'd I dried and hand-sanitized everything I could, I put the disintegrating tissues in the trash can provided, and for the five millionth time, cursed Peggy Newsome.

When I opened the door, there were twenty women and one armed guard outside.

I smiled at the women as I rolled my damp carry-on past them. They were giggling at me. I looked down and saw that I still had my skirt pinned up.

Two doors down I saw two Dallas housewife types coming out of a door with another bathroom sign. In English. I took advantage of the stocked paper towels and unpinned my skirt, which now dragged about an inch and a half on the floor, even with my heels.

I tiptoed into the nearest airport store. Fifty thousand rupiahs later, having cleaned out their tissue and hand sanitizer supplies, I headed for the gate to try to dry my skirt with the dual-current hair dryer in my carry-on. Unfortunately, all the electric outlets I tried were dead.

I only tripped twice going up the steps to the aircraft and once in the aisles.

I had to make a few ballerina-level leg adjustments when the flight attendants checked the cabin, as the wet skirt allowed the outline of my Balenciaga to show through. It was staying with me. Period. Putting the carry-on up was bad enough on this final flight, where the risk of smugglers sneaking drugs into tourist luggage was the highest. No one was safe.

The flight was bumpy, but short, and even from my aisle seat, included a few glimpses of blue-green ocean and distant volcanoes. No matter how much trouble I was landing into, I gave myself a minute to appreciate that I was flying over the Java Sea. Could anything be more romantic? Or less Brooklyn-esque?

At least, until we landed. The moment I stepped out onto the jet's roll-away stairs, my hair exploded. I may as well pour what was left of my overpriced anti-frizz serum on a bowl of cornflakes. No gel in the world was going to contain my hair at eighty-seven degrees and ninety-six percent humidity. At least my face would look gaunt. Relatively. I couldn't see an upside to the flop sweat.

The damp breeze was heavy with some kind of herbal cigarettes, diesel, coconut, and an unrecognizable thick floral perfume.

I stepped onto the tarmac, where my stilettos sunk all the way up the four-inch heels. I gripped the handrail and hefted my carry-on onto my hip, before its wheels suffered the same fate. I sucked my shoes out of the melted runway, step by step, and lurched my way into the terminal, my skirt a tarred train behind me.

Welcome to Bali. If this really was, as they claimed, "the dawn of the world," it was going to be a long day.

Chapter Eleven

I joined my second Indonesian Customs line, hoping the thirty-day tourist visa from a new vendor would work. I took comfort in knowing I could honestly say my bags had been in my possession for the entire journey. I had one moment of panic, wondering whether Tylenol PMs counted as narcotics in Bali, since all the agents were staring at me.

Finally, I was through the line and into Arrivals. I spotted my name on a poster board, held by a woman with a gleaming black ponytail, huge dark eyes, a perfect nose, and the best posture I had ever seen. She was wearing an ocean blue shirt with "Jill's Adventures" on the pocket, and frowning. I inched toward her.

"*Halo*. Cyd Redondo, Redondo Travel. Did Jill send you?"

"Cyd Redondo?" She continued to stare at me.

"Is something wrong?"

"No, do not worry," she said, finally giving me a smile that revealed startling white teeth. "Jill did not warn me. I am Lu. Welcome to Bali."

"Thank you so much for picking me up. Didn't warn you about what?"

"Your hair. Would you like help with your bags?"

"No, I'm fine, thanks. My hair? Does it look that awful? God, it probably does."

"Follow me."

"Okay. Did my mother and her friends get here okay?"

"Yes, I'm taking you to them now."

"Thank you. Now I can breathe."

She led me through throngs of travelers, vendors and drivers toward the street. As we got closer to the exit, every time the doors opened, I got that same heady whiff. Then, finally, we were on the curb.

I started to step into the street. Lu jerked me back as a scooter, driven by a small man with two children on his shoulders and two more on his lap, shot out from our left. The scooter drivers dodged between and around women in tight sarongs, with baskets of ornate floral arrangements stacked on their heads. They didn't even blink. Wow.

The street itself was littered with crushed flower petals and halves of coconuts. Oh God, were we going to navigate all this, my carry-ons, and both of us on a scooter? I almost collapsed in relief when Lu gestured to a square dark blue vehicle with "Jill's Adventures" painted on the side. It didn't look like the standard *bemos* I'd read about—minivans with benches on each side.

"It's a Kijang. Toyota," Lu said. "Jill's customers go in style."

I put my carry-on on the floorboard, held my Balenciaga on my lap with one hand and grabbed onto the door with the other, as Lu navigated the moving traffic to pull out in the road, which we shared with scooters, bicycles, pedestrians, potholes, and the occasional animal. Lu managed a remarkably smooth ride, considering.

"Great driving. Are you from here, Lu?"

"I was born here, yes. I lost my parents when I was young."

"I'm so sorry."

"I was lucky. Jill and her husband raised me. And sent me to school in Melbourne."

As we slowed down for a brief traffic jam, I watched a man buy a bottle of vodka from a roadside stand, then pour it into his gas tank. If that worked here, I had a few distant cousins who were going to thrive in the Apocalypse.

"How about you?" Lu sped up a bit. "New York travel agent. You must have been everywhere."

"You'd be surprised."

Before I had to explain, the stop and go became a full stop. Lu pulled to the side and everyone, even the pedestrians, made space for a large procession headed our way down the middle of the road.

A group of bare-chested men in black and white-checked sarongs and what looked like white kerchiefs around their heads, walked in front. Behind them, more men carried a huge red, blue, and black papier-mâché bull with canary yellow horns. When it got closer, I noticed it was on a platform decorated with flowers and glowing sticks of incense.

Behind the bull, women and girls in white lace shirts over corsets, wide sashes, and brightly colored silk sarongs, moved with stacks of flower baskets on their heads. They wore glittery makeup, had flowers woven into their hair, and danced in golden sandals. It was the most beautiful thing I'd ever seen.

I turned to Lu. "Is it a holiday?"

"Cremation," she said.

"Oh."

"It's the most important ceremony for us. For the dead and for those they leave behind. This one is for a Brahmin."

How did she know that? I had so many questions, but saved them for later, out of respect.

As the mourners got closer, I could see they were followed by a second procession. This group accompanied an oversized lion in colors of red, black, and gold.

Lu saw my double take. "That one's a warrior."

"Are they related?"

"Maybe. Maybe not. Families always choose an auspicious day. So, often there are multiple ceremonies on the same day."

"So I guess sometimes they have to wait a few days."

"Or two years."

"What?"

As the first platform neared us, she put her hand on my shoulder. "Duck, please." I slid down in the seat and stared at her.

"To us, red-haired women are demons. No one wants to see one on their way to a cremation."

"I'm a demon? So, not auspicious."

"No, you are not. I apologize if I was rude at the airport, but carrying two red-haired women in one week is what Americans call a high-stress gig." Ah, my mother looked like a demon, too. I wondered how that was going.

Staying low, I reached into my Balenciaga, semi-contained my disco ball of hair with a scrunchie, and slammed my sun hat over it. I looked up at Lu, who tucked in a stray hair and smiled, then pulled me up. We waited until the trails of incense were well in the rearview mirror, then Lu restarted the car.

I couldn't stop thinking about the funeral processions, filled with color and glorious smells and dancing. Every funeral I'd ever been to was pure black and gray, with the occasional washed-out lily. They were grim and heartbreaking. This was more like a Mardi Gras parade, but better, and much more of what I would want if anything happened to me. My mother had never talked about my father's funeral and I could only remember tiny snatches of it. I wondered what she would think of this. And how awkward it was going to be when we saw each other.

Chapter Twelve

Lu had swerved to miss so many chickens, food stands, *bemos*, and packs of dogs, I didn't even realize we'd turned off the main street until frothy, sea green trees with fronds big as surfboards closed off the sky.

There was less traffic on this small road, but it was just as unusual, as a man passed us with a twenty-gallon aquarium full of tropical fish balanced on his scooter.

The soundtrack was pure David Attenborough—chirrups and squeaks, punctuated by clackety, piercing birdcalls, stranger even than the ones I'd heard in Africa. The air was pure Mounds Bar. I think Americans—especially from my parents' and grandparents' generation—associate the smell of coconut with Pepperidge Farm cakes and Hawaiian Tropic lotion and so, with a holiday.

I took a deep breath of paradise. Lu told me the flowers I smelled were frangipanis. I mean, the name alone made me swoon. Underneath, I noted the metallic scent of a recent thunderstorm, an overripe prom corsage, a hint of animal droppings, and the salty, mildew smell that haunts any beach house, anywhere.

I breathed it all in and, despite everything, my shoulders lowered a quarter inch. I forgot about Peggy Newsome and my mother for a minute as a tiny monkey swung over the road from tree to tree, followed by a bird so electric blue it looked animated. Uncle Leon, PBS aficionado and master taxidermist, would have had a conniption.

I returned to reality just in time to find us turning down another, smaller road and headed straight into an enormous tree. Its roots alone put our boxwoods to shame. At the very last minute, Lu swerved and I saw the road had been carefully built around it. That would never happen in Brooklyn.

I looked at Lu. "What is that?"

"Banyan tree. Sacred to us. Our ancestors are protected inside them after death."

"That must be wonderful, to feel them that close to you."

"Yes. It is. The trees bring luck and prosperity to all who stay here."

"I could use some of that."

"The luck is in your hands. After all, the fruits of life fall into the hands of those who climb the tree and pick them."

I turned to Lu so fast my head almost swiveled off my neck. I'd used that quote on a hundred women, but no one had ever used it on me. And then I remembered that an orange and white object on Lu's keychain looked strangely familiar.

"Is that a Tupperware Tiniest Treasures key chain?"

"The Mix & Store Batter Bowl. Limited edition."

"Wasn't that a dealer gift only? Holy crap, do you sell Tupperware?"

She went quiet, then looked around to make sure no one was near the moving car. "Yes. But I don't want anyone to know, yet. You, too?"

"Yes. Now I mainly give it away to my clients, as an added bonus. Of course, it's perfect here, isn't it, given the weather?"

"Yes. The carrots never rot."

I snorted. "Brownie Wise was a genius."

"Yes. My idol."

In the early fifties, Brownie, the Queen of Tupperware party planning, made dealers leave a sealed bowl with one carrot inside and asked potential clients to also leave one carrot in the regular crisper for a week. The Tupperware always won. Wise called it "carrot calling." She was also the first person to fill a Tupperware bowl with water, burp the top, then toss it across the room as a selling technique.

"I'm going to have to see your catalogue. Any parties on the calendar?" Given my carry-on allowance, I'd have to limit myself to lightweight, nesting items.

"We'll speak of it later. Ah, we are here."

We pulled up in front of a building open on three sides, with a thatched roof that formed a gentle, mushroom-shaped wave over the dark, carved columns of the structure. The threatening figures cut into them were beautiful and terrifying at once. They were echoed on the reception desk, which was adorned on both sides with ceramic fountains filled with flower petals. If this was Jill's idea of a budget Mom and Pop establishment, I had sold Bali short.

"You are expected. Jill was able to arrange for the four of you to attend a local dance performance tonight. I will be back at seven to retrieve you." She reached into the backseat and handed me a beautifully wrapped package, with flowers and curled bits of banana leaf on the top. "Sarongs required," she said. "One size fits all."

"Wow. How incredibly kind! Are these ceremonial ones? Are they just for the temple?"

"No, these are for every day. You may wear them anytime."

"Thank you, Lu. Really. May I ask, would you prefer one tip at the end of our trip, or per journey?"

"Per journey. You never know what will happen in Bali."

The first thing I'd done after the bathroom at Jakarta was to check the exchange rate. At the moment, one U.S. dollar was worth just over 9,000 rupiah, and I guessed Madge Dupree, a woman who haggled over babysitting fees, had underdone it with Lu. So I counted out the equivalent of fifty U.S. dollars—which was 450,000 rupiahs—and tried not to pass out.

Lu got out and opened my door. I anchored my Balenciaga on my shoulder, grabbed the package, and lugged my carry-on up the broad wooden steps, trying to keep the wheels up so they wouldn't scratch the wood.

Inside a smallish man in a white shirt and dark orange sarong placed his hands together in front of his chest and bowed. "Welcome! I am Ketut Nyoman Suardika, but you may call me Burung Ketut. Or just Burung."

I put down my bags and returned the gesture as best I could. "Cyd Redondo, Redondo Travel. I think Jill's Adventures arranged for me to stay with my mother and her friends. I'd like to check in and go to the room, please."

There was a tiny frown line between his eyebrows before he smiled. "Would you like some cucumber water?" He handed me perhaps the most beautiful drink I'd ever seen, and it was water. I'd only been in Bali for one hour and I could already see the incredible care they took with everything they made and did. Americans were known for 7-Elevens. I felt like crying.

"We are having brief work done on your lodging."

Before I could answer, I was distracted by a sudden operatic trilling. I turned to see a gray-white bird sitting on a perch in a huge turquoise cage. Burung did a series of whistles. The bird answered back in an elaborate series of warbles and squeaks.

"What a gorgeous bird! What kind is it?"

"Spotted dove. Mitzi. She is my heart," he said. "Champion. Three times." He gestured to several trophies sitting behind him.

I nodded and smiled, having no clue what he was talking about. "A champion? Congratulations!"

"Yes. We prepare for the songbird competition in Ubud, in a few days. We have commenced our final training." He whistled again and the bird answered.

I listened to them for a few moments, then asked Burung if I could at least put my things in our room and rest a bit.

"It would be better if you wait. There is a removal man there."

"I promise I won't get in his way. It's just, I've been traveling now for about forty hours."

"If you wish it. I will call for someone to take your bags and show you the way."

"That's not necessary. If you can just give me directions, I would like to walk."

"And you are American?"

"Yes. Maybe not typical."

He drew me a small map. "Please stay on the path."

"I will."

Over the tap, tap, drag of my carry-on wheels on the stone pathway, I heard a child laughing, running water, clicking sounds, and leaves flapping overhead in the wind. The pathway was strewn with a preppy palette of pink fallen flowers and bright green leaves.

As I turned a sharp corner, I looked up to find a bat hanging head-down on a branch five inches from my face. In broad daylight. The fact that it was asleep didn't help. I don't think I've ever wanted to scream so much, but that seemed ill-advised, under the circumstances.

My cousin Jimmy had instilled my lifelong fear of bats by telling me they always get stuck in curly hair and would suck all the blood out of me before I could untangle them. Honestly. Who does that to a five-year-old?

I stayed as still as I could until I was sure it was still sleeping, then ducked and walked around it. I'd seen on PBS that fruit bats could be active during the day, but I hoped it was an urban myth. It wasn't. There was a whoosh and the bat swooped over me, then hung itself back upside down in a nearby tree. I didn't stop slapping my head and flailing my arms around for about two minutes. I might have handled it better if I hadn't been jet-lagged. I was already almost in tears when I heard drawers opening and slamming, then a crash.

"Bloody Americans!"

The British accent was so exaggerated and clichéd, I wondered whether I had stumbled upon my old frenemy, Grey Hazelnut, aka Ron Brazil, aka Pete Stacio. But Hazelnut's toupees were better than the one atop the gangly man in the worn navy blue jumpsuit, reeking of Brut cologne and throwing my mother's Lantz nightgown across the room.

His oblong, acne-scarred face was a collision between James Woods and Klaus Kinski. He was whipping and poking some kind of metal rod around.

None of these things boded well, but our family motto is, it's better to be angry than scared, so I went with that.

"Hey!" I stamped my carry-on down, hard, and gripped the specially made plastic mace container that my brousin Frank had made for me to get through security. "What the hell are you doing with my mother's lingerie?"

He rolled his eyes. "My job, madam."

"Don't madam me. You can't possibly have any reason to be going through these women's bags. Burung said there would be a removal man, not a thief."

"Are you calling me a common thief?"

"I don't know if you're common or not. I just got here."

"And why, pray, are you here?"

"I'm staying in this room." I started to roll my bag in toward the three gorgeous four-poster beds with mosquito netting overhead.

"I wouldn't do that."

"Why the heck not?"

"Because I haven't caught the cobra yet."

Chapter Thirteen

My mind stayed where I was, but my body decided to inch backward. Into Batland. In terms of which was worse, it was pretty much a tie.

"Wait, what?"

"Alistair Brush. Snake removal. Someone reported an intruder."

"A reptilian intruder?"

He gave a patronizing sigh. "Yes. Obviously a reptilian intruder. And I have more clients I need to assist today, so I need to get on with it. Burung assured me the room would be empty so I could work." He flailed his metal rod around and I finally realized why it looked familiar. It was a snake hook, a reptile accessory I'd become familiar with at my last unintentional herpetology convention. So he might be a snake man. But that didn't excuse going through my mother's bags.

"And you haven't found it?"

"I didn't say that. I said I hadn't caught it." He poked the hook into a wad of tropically themed Chico tunics on the floor. I clutched my Balenciaga harder and inched my carry-on down the first step.

"Does my mother know about this? I mean about the cobra?"

"I don't know. Who is your mother?"

"Bridget Redondo."

The rod went still. "Redondo? You are a Redondo, too?"

I didn't really want to shake his hand, but as an ad hoc ambassador for international relations, I held mine out. "Cyd Redondo, Redondo Travel."

He had a Uriah Heep kind of handshake, slippery and damp.

"You may leave your bags here, but otherwise, you need to vacate and let me perform my duties."

"No, thank you, I'll keep them with me for now."

He stared at me for a moment. "As you like." He picked up a pet carrier. The logo on the side was a coiled snake that resembled the *Jungle Book*'s Ka with bulging eyes and its head in a noose. "If you could let me continue?"

"How long do you think you'll be?"

"No idea."

He turned away, headed into the bathroom, and closed the door.

I thought I heard the clunk of a toilet tank. I hoped that meant there was an actual toilet in the room, as opposed to the whole dancing colonoscopy situation at the airport.

I hated leaving him there, as he was clearly not respectful of anyone's property, and I also wanted to make sure he got the snake. I backed up and stood a few feet outside the door. I was so exhausted I wanted to lean against a tree, but the whole bat/snake combo kept me upright.

He opened the bathroom door and looked out. I waved. He gave the equivalent of my Aunt Helen's harrumph and slammed it again.

I heard a faint "Ha!" and something jangling. When he came out, I could see a snake coiled in the carrier.

"They like drains," he said, snickering, which was creepy. I don't know why I got such a suspicious vibe about him. In general, I liked Englishmen and I definitely liked people who saved me from snakes. I didn't like him. He stomped past me, then looked back.

"You never know what is going to happen in Bali," he said, lifting up the carrier.

"Thank you, I think."

I looked into the room, which was a mess. I couldn't face it. I decided to wheel everything down to the pool and rest for just a minute.

I followed the sound of running water and came around another corner to find two huge, elaborately carved stone fish heads spouting water into an impossibly turquoise pool, which eased up over the edge to lap to under the bamboo lounge chairs.

Ordinarily I would love this, but in the maxi skirt, not so much. As I got closer I heard a familiar smoker's cough.

I spotted Madge and Bea Ann under an umbrella, in matching Ann Cole one-piece bathing suits. We were all suckers for the Loehmann's eighty-five percent off sale. Even without the sale suits, I would have known that Bay Ridge sickly white winter skin anywhere. Nothing like red and orange to set it off. The two traitors were splashing their feet in the water below their chairs and talking, so I held back to eavesdrop.

Madge took a long draw on her cigarette. Smoking wasn't shamed here. She must be in heaven. She leaned toward Bea Ann. "I was really hoping he would call her."

"Well, if he'd lived, he probably would have." Bea Ann sipped another drink festooned with exotic plant life.

I shifted and the wheels on my carry-on gave me away. They both whipped around. I kept my distance to keep my skirt out of the lapping water.

"Hi, ladies."

"Cyd?" Bea Ann became even paler than a Bay Ridge librarian, if that was possible.

"What are you doing here?" Madge stood up, splashing water on my skirt.

"Jill insisted I come and join you. Didn't Lu tell you I was coming?"

They both shook their heads.

"Well, I'm glad she found you somewhere so lovely." I waited for them to mention the snake. If they didn't, I wasn't going to.

"Shouldn't you be in the office?" Madge accidentally-on-purpose splashed me again.

"Where's my mom?"

There was a long silence.

"Bea Ann?"

"The police came and got her."

Chapter Fourteen

I lowered myself onto a lounge chair. Since it was the closest thing I had to a paper bag, I opened my Balenciaga, and put my head inside. I sucked in the curiously strong peppermint scent of a couple of stray Altoids until my eyes stung.

"Don't worry, Cyd. They said they'd bring her back." Bea Ann leaned toward me and patted my shoulder, the reading glasses around her neck bumping me gently.

I took my head out of the bag. "Right."

"Jill said she'd meet her there." The idea that Jill was there helped a little, but not enough. And why hadn't Jill told them I was coming? Or called me? And why did the police want Mom, anyway?

"Here." I put the package of sarongs down on the table. "We're going to a traditional dance ceremony tonight. We need to wear these. Leave me the shortest one. Lu's picking us up at seven. If I'm not back, just go without us."

I zipped my purse and rolled my carry-on behind me as I headed to reception, where I watched Alistair Brush get into his rusting blue "Brush Your Reptiles Away" Kijang and head down the winding road. I asked if Burung could put my carry-on luggage behind the counter for a little while and if he would call me a ride to the police station.

Then I spotted a rusted blue-and-white scooter leaning against the side of the building. That would be faster.

"Burung, may I please borrow your scooter?"

"I will call someone to take you if you wish. You will never find the police station on your own."

"I will if you draw me a map."

He shook his head, but I finally convinced him to give me the keys and a helmet. I tried not to think about the fifteen thousand accidents and fifteen hundred motorbike and scooter deaths in Bali every year (this apparently averaged out to about five a day), and kept my thoughts on the amazing man who'd driven past us on a scooter, carrying an aquarium. If he could do that, I could surely manage my Balenciaga. Whether I could navigate around Denpasar traffic remained to be seen, but when I stacked it against my mother's being imprisoned, it was worth a try.

I had enough balance from kickboxing and ballet with Madame Rushka to keep the scooter steady when it was going straight. Power to the core! And happily, I, like every woman from Eve through *Grease*, had fallen for a motorcycle bad boy, so I understood "the lean." Even though the scooters were lower and lighter than a motorcycle, the move still came in handy, when the wheels slipped on a few petals or needed to shove around a wobbly American tourist on a bicycle. It was pretty easy to spot them—they were the only ones wearing helmets. I only had one real blip, when I had to let go of the maxi skirt to signal and it wound around one of the wheels and sent me veering off the road. I caught myself before I fell over completely, jerked the skirt out, placed it firmly between my legs, and kept going.

Finally, I spotted the oversized neon sign for the Denpasar police station. The building itself was built in a more traditional Balinese style.

I got a few laughs from various drivers and passersby as I careened into a space between two parked cars, startling a man with a rooster in his lap. He almost lost his grip on it and made a rude gesture, then stroked the bird until it was calm. His teeth were bright red, I assumed from eating betelnut, which I'd read about in *National Geographic.*

I was afraid to think about how I looked at this point. I was going to be dealing with officials. I should check. I leaned toward the scooter mirror, jerked off my helmet and watched my scrunchie fly off into the road and under a truck.

My reddish, impossibly frizzy hair had expanded to "double demon" status. And that wasn't all. Layers of mud and grease had created a zigzag pattern on Mom's skirt.

With some relief, I saw one of the "Jill's Adventures" Toyota Kijangs in the lot. Still, I needed to hurry, so I used emergency bobby pins to tame my hair and covered it with the helmet. I had no idea whether wearing a helmet inside was considered rude in Bali, but it had to be better than demonhood.

Even after a few Handi Wipes, some neutral lipstick, and a brush-off of my clothing, I still looked like a lunatic. I straightened up, moved toward the door, and took a minute to breathe and remember how to address the police in their own language.

I managed to stammer out that I'd come to see my mother, Bridget Redondo. She'd been brought in this afternoon? The man behind the desk kept his eyes on my helmet and said I would have to wait.

"But she's not under arrest? She's not in trouble?"

He shook his head, continued to stare at the helmet, then said something in Indonesian. When I sat down, I looked it up in my phrasebook and it seemed he'd said "witness." Witness of what? Christ on a bike. I let her out of my sight for two days.

"Sit. Wait," the clerk said again. I sloshed my trailing skirt around another officer, then sat down to wait with the same mix of criminals, freaked-out family members, and irate victims that populate every police station on earth.

I heard voices raised behind a door. That was my mom's voice. I jumped up, stepping on my skirt and pitching forward.

A smallish man with heart-shaped cheekbones and thick black hair caught my arm before I did a complete face-plant, then grinned at me. He looked familiar. I put my hands together in front of my chest and gave him a short bow, then gathered my skirt and moved toward the voice. I looked back at him. He was staring at me, too. He headed out. I couldn't know him, that was crazy.

I turned back and there was my mother, her long red hair unbraided and nearly as frizzy as mine. She was deep in conversation with Jill, who was just as statuesque as I remembered. She was wearing white pants and a blue batik tunic with a subtle "Jill's Adventures" logo where the pocket would be. Also, heels, God love her. I recognized her stance—travel agent damage control.

Finally Jill noticed me. She shook her head, no.

I was just backing up when Mom turned and saw me, too. "Cyd? What are you doing here? I told you I'd be fine." She looked me up and down. "Is that my skirt? What have you done to it?"

Chapter Fifteen

I looked down at the damp, trailing, grease-stained maxi-mess. "Mom. I am so sorry. It was a modesty thing, and then a toilet thing, then a scooter thing and, well, long story. I'll get you a new one."

Jill stepped in between us and threw her arms open. "Cyd! You got here in one piece!" She backed up, still holding my shoulders. "You look great." She knocked on the helmet. "Very wise, considering. Here, let's get you back to the hotel." She handed Mom a handkerchief, put her arms around both of us, and nodded at the clerk, who leaned over the counter.

"Your son came by. He said safe travels if he doesn't get to see you."

She thanked him and turned to me. "How did you get here?"

"Burung let me borrow his scooter."

"We can throw it in the back. Bridget, why don't you jump in while we grab it?"

Jill walked with me to the scooter. "Sorry. I thought your mother would be excited to have you here. No worries, it's sorted out. I'm leaving in the morning, but Lu and my staff will make sure you have a wonderful time."

"What did the police want?"

"I'll let your mother tell you. For now, everything is as okay as it can be here. Don't worry. We can talk more after the performance tonight. I hope you like it. It's always a thrill for me to introduce people I like to the real Bali."

We got the scooter in and I climbed into the back.

Jill turned on the Kijang. "I was just telling Bridget how lovely you were to me when I was in Manhattan. And that I've been able to comp you at the Hanging Vines just outside Ubud. They're so happy to host you, Cyd, so you can give firsthand recommendations to your clients." She shot me a look I didn't understand, but heeded, keeping my mouth shut.

Jill was a bit more erratic than Lu in traffic. At one point, I yelped and Mom actually gave me a sympathetic look, which heartened me. Then, we veered right and around the banyan tree and were back at the hotel. Jill got out and helped me with the scooter.

She looked at her watch. "Lu is very prompt. That gives you an hour."

I retrieved the scooter and put it back in its place, then held out my hand to Mom. I was honestly afraid she wouldn't take it, but she did, and we walked into reception.

I bowed to Burung, thanked him for the use of the scooter and asked for my carry-on.

"Listen," he said. He had added a rose-colored birdcage that housed another, less exotic-looking bird, but its trilling was equally as beautiful and unique as the other. He tapped on Mitzi's cage and she echoed the other bird, almost perfectly.

"She's mimicking it?"

"She is an angel."

Mom stared at me.

"Burung is taking Mitzi to a songbird competition in Ubud. Isn't that incredible?"

She gave an enthusiastic if befuddled nod. "It is." We all shared a moment of silent wonder as the birds sang back and forth.

Mom turned to Burung. "How does the competition work? An award for the loveliest song?"

"That is part. Originality, also. Strength of voice. And dancing."

"Dancing?"

"Yes, Mrs. Redondo, the performance. It is a wonderful thing to see." He called out to Mitzi, who gave three little hops and a spin. "You should come, also."

I noticed the time. "Burung, I'm sorry. We have to get ready. Thank you again." I took my carry-on and Mom and I headed down the path. "You go ahead," I said, as I tried to wrangle all my gear.

"Do you need help?"

"No, it's fine." We looked at each other. "I've made it this far."

"Me, too. Cyd? You have to remember, I'm not Shirley MacLaine, I'm Debra Winger. I'm not a senior yet."

"I know. Sorry. Force of habit."

She reached over and kissed me on the head, but didn't say anything else. I was dying to ask her what had happened, but I was afraid to destroy our partial *detente*. And I was on high hanging bat alert.

We arrived at the room to find Madge and Bea Ann looking as Balinese as two women who were raised on raspberry congealed salad with walnuts could be. They had chosen blue and turquoise sarongs, with contrasting sashes, and they had frangipani flowers sprouting from their Bay Ridge perms. Their only Western fashion concessions were white linen long-sleeve shirts and flip-flops. Madge's had rhinestones, I think from the J. Jill catalogue. They were so ugly I really hoped they'd been on sale.

They ran to Mom and all hugged each other as I looked on.

"Do they know anything else?" Madge let out the mouthful of cigarette smoke she'd been holding in during the hug.

Mom just shook her head. "We need to get ready. Cyd, you go ahead."

"No, please, you go. If I'm not ready in time, I can always borrow Burung's scooter again. Seriously, you've had the harder day." It was a battle of wills, as we both wanted Madge and Bea Ann to ourselves. I handed her a sarong and won. As she closed the bathroom door, I hoped it wasn't still a revolving reptile hotel.

"Okay, what the heck is going on?"

"We'll let your mother tell you when she's ready."

"What does that mean?"

"Cyd. We love you, but this is your mother's story to tell. It will be all right." As old as I was now and as long as we'd known each other, Bea Ann was still my childhood librarian, so hugging wasn't in the cards. There were some lines you couldn't cross.

I distracted myself by making sure there were enough mosquito coils and nets for later. I wondered if they made cobra coils? I still found it strange none of them had mentioned the whole snake removal thing. Who'd reported the snake to Alistair Brush?

"Are you happy with the room?"

"We love everything about it. Peggy was right, it's the perfect place."

I suppressed the urge to throw my carry-on at them, since Peggy had nothing to do with this, except indirectly by leaving me and Jill to rescue them.

Instead, I sat down on a carved coffee table, went through my Balenciaga to retrieve my cosmetics ziplock, and put it into a sturdier makeup bag for the remainder of my trip. While I did that, I imagined Peggy Newsome's perfect forearms with multiple cobra puncture marks.

Mom emerged, looking even younger than she had before, despite some circles under her eyes. Her sarong was a deep pink, with a blue sash. Madge came forward and hooked a pink frangipani flower in her hair.

I headed into the bathroom. It took a while to get clean and to try to rinse out Mom's skirt. I got most of the grease and mud out, and was able to lay it out flat to dry. But the odds of it ever drying in this humidity were slim.

My sarong was the same color as Mom's, but too long. I was able to do a couple of folds at the waist and anchor them with a mint-colored sash. I wished I had one of those corset shirts I'd seen during the cremation march. Since I didn't think my black La Perla bustier was appropriate, I stuck with a white silk DKNY wraparound blouse from six seasons ago. At least here, you sweated everywhere, not just under your arms, so the "wet look" would be consistent.

I checked myself out in the mirror. Suddenly, I got sarongs. They hid a lot of problems. My experiences with long skirts, including the most recent, had been horrible, which is why I stuck with short or pencil skirts. Also, because I felt my legs were all I had. But these long "skirts" were different—they were slimming and not too restrictive if you kept the slit in front. My stilettos were still covered in tar—I'd have to deal with them later—but my Stuart Weitzman black kitten heels set off the hot pink and they were already tar-colored, in case I encountered more melting pavement.

I tied my hair up into an updo, using about fifty bobby pins, so that as little of it showed as possible, then hid the rest with the biggest, brightest flower I could find in the bathroom arrangement. I locked my carry-on for snake protection, hid it behind the shower curtain, and tucked the key in my bag. Normally, I would leave a TV on and put a Do Not Disturb sign on the room door to deter break-ins, but here, leaving a light on in the bathroom with the door closed was the best I could do.

I could hear my three roommates talking. When I came out, they stopped. Honestly, what was going on and did everyone hate me?

Mom gave me the look she used to give me when we were late for mass. "Ready?"

"Yep. Thanks for waiting."

I gave them as much of a smile as I had in me, grabbed my Balenciaga, and followed them. The birds and monkeys seemed louder than before. Maybe that was just something that happened here at dusk. Oh no, dusk. Or as I thought of it now, batwing hour. I kept my head down.

Madge's cigarette smoke veered my way. "How was Angela's shower?"

"Class all the way. She had a serving dish shaped like a diaper filled with light brown chocolate mousse," I said. "I heard the power went out, later, though."

Bea Ann snorted and, suddenly, I felt better. It was great to see these women who had shaped my whole life all dressed up and on vacation. This was the point of a travel agency, so it was nice to remember that for a minute.

Lu looked even more gorgeous in her traditional outfit. "Jill wanted me to give you these for the ride." She pulled out a Tupperware drink holder in a color I'd never seen, and handed us each something that looked like a Balinese version of Jell-O 1-2-3. The drinks had a deep green liquid on the bottom, a creamy, milky middle, and light green cubes that looked like lime gelatin floating on the top. The whole thing was topped off with a slice of lime on the rim and a bamboo straw. I took a sip. And almost died of delight.

"Lu, what is this?"

"It is called daluman."

"What's the green stuff?"

She laughed. "Jelly made from leaves of the *cincau.* plant. Very healthy. Has cooling properties."

It certainly did. We moaned in unison as we sucked down the icy coconut milk drink, then speared the tangy gelatin squares with our straws. It was strange how, every time I was frustrated by something about Bali, like snakes in the hotel, or the lack of traffic cops, something wonderful changed my mind.

After we'd all had a sip or two of the drinks, Lu showed us how to get in and out of a vehicle in a sarong. We eased into the Kijang and headed back down the long driveway. As we drove, we caught glimpses of an astonishing orange and aqua sunset through the trees. The roads got busier as we neared our destination.

I watched Lu maneuver around three unsteady scooter drivers. "Is the traffic this bad on inauspicious days?"

"Traffic is the same. Just more accidents."

Chapter Sixteen

I pulled out my notepad, wrote "check for auspicious days," and wondered whether the American equivalent of inauspicious ones was Mercury in retrograde, which I completely believed in.

As we drove, Bea Ann took my mother's hand and squeezed it. I still didn't know why she'd been at the police station, why she was suddenly weepy, or who would have called her if he'd lived?

I distracted myself watching women walking by with stacked baskets and even stacks of bricks on their heads. The nuns had made us walk carrying *Pride and Prejudice* for posture, but it would have taken the complete *Oxford English Dictionary*—the "don't need a magnifying glass edition"—to learn how to do this. How did their spines not completely compress? Or detach? It wasn't just the weight and height of their burdens, it was keeping your shoulders back and chin up. Navigating the potholes and debris without ever looking down. In flats!

Finally, we arrived at a white stone structure, decorated, like everything here, with elaborate carvings. It was the Pura Agung Jagatnatha temple, built in one of the city squares and, according to Lu, run entirely by volunteers, which gave it a lot in common with every Catholic church in Bay Ridge, and most animal rescues, anywhere.

Lu helped us navigate the entrance, where we gave a donation and moved past the sarong sellers. I'd already made a note to keep a sarong and headscarf in my Balenciaga, but it was good to know that in an emergency, they were available on-site.

We finally entered the grounds, filled with bright green lawns, fringed gold umbrellas, fountains, mini-moats, shrines covered in offerings, and statues everywhere. Some of the statues were wearing sarongs, too, in black and white check. I tried to imagine one of the stone eagles on the Bay Ridge overpass draped in an apron. Or a tutu. For some reason, it really cheered me up.

Lu explained a bit of the religious history behind the shadow puppet show and traditional dance we were about to see. Both were about the fight between good and evil, represented by Rangda, the child-eating widow demon, and Barong, the leader of all things good. She said the locals left offerings for the demons as well as the gods, to keep them happy and away. I saw Madge blanch.

"God is not plural," she hissed. She was divorced, and twenty years out from her last confession, so pretty selective in her adherence to Catholicism, but I guess the "one god" thing is where she drew the line. I was going to ask her about the Holy Trinity, but why spoil the evening?

I elbowed her instead. "Shhh! It's 'when in Rome,' not 'when in the Vatican.'"

Lu handed me a freshly folded banana leaf filled with colored rice formed into a face and garnished with flower petals.

"This is gorgeous. Where do these come from?"

"My sister and I made them."

"Are you kidding?"

"We all learn when we are very small. Everyone in Bali."

"Wow. Well, I bow to you. Again. I can't even string popcorn for Christmas without leaving half of it on the floor."

"I'll show you how at the Tupperware Party."

"I would love that. How much time do we have before the performance starts?"

She shrugged. "Time is relative in Bali."

I took my mother's arm. "Let's go sit down somewhere and catch up."

She came with me, which was something. We heard lots of atonal chimes and bangs while the orchestra warmed up. We sat on a rough sandstone wall.

"Mom? What happened?"

She shook her head and picked at her hem.

I gave her a minute, then tried again. "Okay. I know it's none of my business, but I hate your looking so sad."

She clasped her long fingers together. "Well, you know, you couldn't get us seats together on the plane."

"I know, I'm sorry. I really tried. It was just too last-minute."

"It turned out to be lucky. Or I thought it was. I wound up in a window seat beside a lovely man. Gerald."

I wondered whether I'd ever met a lovely man with the name Gerald. I thought not.

"He was traveling from Singapore. He was very handsome and polite. He helped me with my bags and even managed to find my aspirin. Anyway, we talked for the whole flight and just before we landed, he asked me out. Of course, I wouldn't have gone without Madge and Bea Ann. But it was just so great to talk to a man who wasn't from Bay Ridge, you know?"

"Yes, I do know."

"That's right. Of course you do. So he asked if I'd have dinner with him last night, and asked for my number and where we were staying."

How had my mother failed to learn the most basic tenets of traveling alone, like not giving anyone your hotel address? Maybe it was because she'd never actually traveled alone. I managed to hold in my scream, but some of it must have leaked onto my face.

"You have no room to talk, young lady. Besides, Bea Ann said she had a good feeling. And Madge was jealous, which usually means quality. We were all excited. For us, a date for one is a date for all. But he never called. And then today, when the phone finally rang, it was the police."

I put my hand over her wringing ones. "And?"

"They said he'd been murdered. Murdered, Cyd! I mean, he'd just kissed me on the cheek the day before. Is every man I meet going to wind up dead?"

"Oh, Mom." I put my arm around her. "Of course not. For the love of God, no! It's just terrible, terrible luck. Please don't think this has anything to do with you. What did the police want?"

"They found my number in his jacket. They wanted to know what we talked about, if he'd said where he was going, or what he was doing here."

"Did he?"

"Not really, no. I mean, we talked about other things—movies and books. And surfing. He's a bit of surfer. That was one of the reasons he loves it here. Loved it here. I know it's stupid to cry, I didn't even know him, really."

I reached into my Balenciaga and found an emergency handkerchief. I didn't have a lot of experience trying to comfort my mother. I think I'd only semi-succeeded twice, when my grandfather Guido died, and when Uncle Ray got taken away. I kept real linen handkerchiefs, to make up for my lack of skill. She took it and wiped her eyes, then put it in her pocket.

No problem. I had three. I squeezed her hand. "It's not stupid. At all. It's awful for you and I'm so sorry."

"They asked me if he gave me anything. I showed them his card. They didn't seem to believe me. They asked me about that several times."

That wasn't good. "Do you still have it, the card?"

"I think they gave it back. Why?"

"No reason, just wondered if it said what he did for a living."

She dug in her purse and handed me a thick vellum card.

"Gerald Boynton, Esq. Was he a lawyer?"

"He said he was in real estate."

"Did they say what happened? How he died?"

"The detective just said it was a homicide. I just don't understand it, he was, well, he was as normal as your Uncle Ray. I really liked him, Cyd."

"I'm so sorry, Mom. Is there anything I can do?"

She looked down for a long time. I could hear the orchestra starting a more organized cacophony. I spotted Lu playing one of the instruments. What the hell?

Mom took my hand. "Could you find out what happened? You did that in London, didn't you?"

"That was an accident. But of course, if there's anything I can find out, I will. Do you know the name of the detective?"

"Detective Ketut." Great, one of the four names almost every Balinese native shared. This should be easy. I wrote it down and smiled.

She smiled back. "Thank you. There's one more thing."

"Okay."

"Can you please go away?"

Chapter Seventeen

"Go away? Right now?"

"No! No. Tomorrow morning would be okay."

Wow. "Oh. But I thought you wanted me to try to find out something about Gerald's murder?"

"I do. It's just, the three of us wanted a kind of girls' trip, you know, without children."

I guess, at thirty-two, I was considered children rather than one of the girls. Since I was finding it hard to control my face, I was relieved to see the performance was starting.

By the time we joined the others, the shadow puppets were already stabbing each other. I'd seen them online, but they were much more beautiful and terrifying in real life. Maybe it was because they were two-dimensional and super spikey, but there was a fierceness to the figures and a jerkiness in their movements that conveyed a malice I could feel on some primal level—currently for Peggy Newsome, who'd caused this rift with my mother.

I was still stinging from Mom's comments. Then I thought about how hard it must have been for someone who always went along with other people's plans to actually tell me to get lost. I wasn't sure she'd ever done it since she defied her parents to marry my dad.

She'd met him on the night James Taylor bombed at the Bitter End on Bleecker Street. They'd shared a mutual "let's get out of here" look and he'd taken her for her first cappuccino ever at Caffe Reggio. At the end of the night, he'd leaned in and kissed her through the cab window and that was pretty much it. She was seventeen. Her parents hadn't approved of my dad, so they'd had to wait until she was eighteen to get married. They'd had me twelve months later.

Then I realized, had she not had me, she would have been able to start over completely. She'd only been twenty-three when Dad died. He had been dead for twenty-eight years. I was a jerk.

Of course she deserved her own vacation.

And I would have mine—I just wished it didn't involve another murder investigation.

I didn't know everything about Bali, but I knew enough to know you didn't mess with local law enforcement. I would make a call to my old acquaintance at Interpol and that would be the end of it. Maybe this was a sign from the universe that I should track down Peggy fricking Newsome in her Balinese hideaway and kick her Pilatesized ass to Antarctica. That thought cheered me up until a group of shirtless men, holding very sharp daggers, jumped onto the stage and started to stab themselves. This must be the "trance dance" Lu had spoken about. It looked so real. Then came the main battle.

Lu had not completely prepared us for the sight of Rangda, who was mostly naked, with breasts that hung to her knees, claws, and a huge mask with bulging eyes and a protruding tongue. And, of course, bright red, frizzy hair, kind of a cross between Bozo and Swoosie Kurtz.

The Barong figure looked more like a lion, with lots of shiny gold in his mask and a long blond mane. It was an intricate and violent battle dance and I was caught up in the drama and the heady smells of frangipani, satay, incense, and damp until the good did, in fact, conquer evil and the performance was over.

Jill found us, after. "What do you think about Bali?"

I looked around. "I think this is probably the most beautiful place I've ever seen and it scares the bejesus out of me."

"That's about right," Jill said. "Bali is gorgeous and violent, both, sacred and profane, both. That's why it's so addictive, you never know what you're going to get."

"Speaking of hell, can you please tell me what went down at the police station? Mom was pretty vague."

"They just wanted to talk to her. I guess she and the man were carrying on a bit of a flirtation?"

It was still hard for me to imagine my mom flirting.

"Are you okay?" Jill stared at me.

"Fine. Just thinking about my mom. Do you think she's still in any trouble?"

"My son is in law enforcement and he smoothed things over. She should be able to carry on with her holiday. And you with yours. By the way, I got you a room in possibly the most unique hotel in Ubud. Maybe on the whole island. It even has a funicular railroad."

"Get out!"

"I remembered you'd never been on one and it was one of your dreams."

"I told you that?"

"I think tequila was involved."

"Ha! But I probably can't afford it."

"Comped. As soon as I told them you were a New York travel agent, they practically fell over themselves. I think you'll like Ubud. Lu has family there, so she will be around to help and my son may be there as well, if you decide you don't want to be completely on your own. There are tons of tours and hikes and there's the Monkey Forest, if you don't mind losing your sunglasses. Or, you can just spend your time having spa treatments by the pool."

"I can't thank you enough. Can you do one more thing? I know you were holding some things on my credit card. Mom and Madge don't want me with them, maybe you could switch those to Madge's so I'm not over my limit? Her alimony payments would fund a small principality."

"You've got it. Here's Lu's number in case you have any issues. As you've probably figured out, she is invaluable."

"Yeah. I got that."

I hugged her goodbye and we all piled into the Kijang and headed back. All I wanted to do was sleep. Since there were only three beds, I opted to bunk in one of the hanging bamboo chairs. I might have been more comfortable on the floor, but there was the whole "snakes can get in" thing. I lit some mosquito coils, lathered myself in Avon bug spray, then made an eggroll wrapper out of my mosquito net, chin to toes.

Bea Ann took one look at me and snorted. "'Extreme fear can neither fight nor fly.' Literally."

"Are you really going to bully me with Shakespeare?"

"It's always worked before," she said, then winked as she got into bed, so I guessed I was forgiven.

The next thing I knew, I heard a squawk, felt sun on my face, and sat up to see it was dawn and there was a monkey sitting in the windowsill. I wasn't in the mood.

"What?"

It hissed at me and jumped down.

I could hear Burung practicing with his birds.

It took me awhile to untangle myself from the mosquito net, as I was already drenched in sweat and it didn't want to let go. I briefly considered wearing the net for the day, as a bodysuit. That seemed like something only Madonna might pull off, ten years ago. Being so short, I'd just be Casper the Ghost, stripper. Maybe a cold shower would help. It did. For about thirty seconds. No sooner had I toweled off and applied my dual sunscreen/ moisturizer, than I watched about six dollars' worth of it drip onto the floor. Everything in this country was sticky—the rice, the air, and now, me.

Sticky was the mortal enemy of false eyelash preparation, since they were designed to cling to something moist, which was everything. I lost three pairs in about as many minutes. I thought I saw one winking in the mosquito netting, then squeaked when it moved. Finally, to save the ones I had left, I decided to keep my sunglasses on. I tucked my hair up under my sun hat—it would be cooler, and I wouldn't inspire as much fear—and put on a linen top. I figured I needed sarong practice, both tying and walking, so I put the one Lu had given me on under it, donned patent- leather kitten heel sandals, and I was ready for the day.

As I walked down the steps of the bungalow, I noticed a red betel nut atop a small ball of rice, laid out neatly on a banana leaf, with a yellow frangipani petal on top. What a lovely thing, I thought, as I walked through the property and saw one by every door. Were they for gods or demons? Or just for whichever one of them was hanging around? It didn't matter. It was a gorgeous way to start the day. I guess our Christmas decorations were a seasonal version of this. Year-round, I wasn't sure we had an equivalent—holiday-neutral decorative napkin rings? Here, there was beauty everywhere, every day.

I had a text from Lu, saying she would make sure I had a proper ride to Ubud. And a note from Mom saying they were having breakfast by the pool and then were off to Gunung Agung, the island's biggest volcano. I walked down to say goodbye. The three women were all in sundresses, laughing. In my thirty-two years of life, I had never seen any of them in a sundress.

"Morning," I said, and smiled. "I'm off. I'll be staying at the Hanging Vines in Ubud. And you have my cell if you need me." I grabbed a piece of fruit and headed toward reception, wondering if bats ever took a day off.

Burung was deeply engaged in his songbird training and didn't notice me for a minute. I told him I was flying to Ubud in the afternoon and he invited me to attend the songbird competition and see Mitzi in action. I wrote down all the details.

"You've inspired a bit of bird fever in me, I think." I leaned in to take a closer look at Mitzi, who pecked at me through her cage.

"Splendid! We have a wonderful bird market in Denpasar. You could visit this morning before you go to Ubud."

It felt impolite to say no, and I did want to see some of the city before I left, so I let him call a car for me. I couldn't take the stress of a scooter this early in the morning. This driver, yet another Ketut, took a different route, one that went past the dreaded Kerobokan prison—the one where the notorious Bali Nine drug smugglers had been sent and two had been executed. He told me it was surrounded by grasslands filled with cobras. I could understand why Alistair Brush had such a rousing business, and wondered whether the bird market was a kind of cobra Costco. I hoped not.

We turned a corner and the tang of birdcages won out over the frangipani. I recognized the smell, having worked beside Mrs. Barsky's Pet World for fifteen years. That particular perfume was eternally linked to finding her body. As it got stronger, I tried to focus on the market rather than the sense memory. We turned down a tree-lined street and on the left I could see intricately carved gates in a creamy orange. The driver let me out, then pointed to the place where he'd be waiting.

Remembering that Lu preferred her tips in increments, I gave him about fifty thousand rupiahs for the outbound trip, then anchored my Balenciaga across my chest and took a moment to organize my browsing strategy.

Chapter Eighteen

The first international market I'd been to had been in Dar es Salaam and had seemed to go on for acres. The one in Denpasar was built up rather than out. Instead of tables, the bird sellers sat in darkened nooks inside tall, narrow, open stalls. Each stall had empty cages in every shape and size in front. The rest of the space was stacked, floor to ceiling, with frantically full birdcages.

The sound of constant—and to me, exotic—birdcalls was punctuated by the more mundane cock-a-doodle-dos of plump roosters and the roar of motor scooters. With its squawks, low, bad engine rumbles, and high-pitched beeps, it was like nature's version of an Atlantic City casino floor. I'd just started down the alley when a thick trilling started on one side of the market and seemed to move to the other, back and forth, back and forth, in stereo, like five hundred Tweety Birds attempting their own version of "Bohemian Rhapsody."

The sound went straight to my breastbone and stopped me cold.

Then something crashed behind me.

"Keperat!"

I turned to see a man in a worn, light blue T-shirt, khaki cargo shorts, and dark sunglasses, trying to restack the cages scattered around him. He was tall, with sandy hair, a deep tan, and a baseball hat low on his forehead that proclaimed "I Support the Right to Arm Bears."

I hurried to help. "That was completely my fault. I am so sorry. I'll pay for any damage."

"Good." He held up a birdcage, formerly pagoda-shaped, which now resembled a picture frame. The man who owned the stall came forward and I handed him a wad of rupiahs.

The man in the bears hat was looking at me. "What made you stop?" He sounded Canadian.

"Those birdsongs going back and forth. What was that?"

"The song that takes off through the whole market?"

I nodded.

"Laughingthrushes. If one of them starts, they all join in, cage by cage. It is pretty spectacular."

"I've never heard anything like it. Sorry, how rude of me. Cyd Redondo, Redondo Travel." I held out my hand.

He put down the broken birdcage and shook back. "Stu Capistranis."

"Nice to meet you. I've never seen anything like this. Are you here to buy a bird?"

He frowned. "No. Just seeing what's here. Are you buying?"

"God, no. I can't keep a ficus tree alive. The man who owns my hotel has a couple of songbirds and when I was looking for something to do this morning, he suggested this."

"Ah. And what do you think?"

I looked around at the stacked and overstuffed cages, full of droppings and lost feathers. "Well, I've only seen a few stalls, but I have to say, it doesn't look ideal for the birds."

"No. It's not." He pointed to the ground. "See the ones on the bottom?"

I peered at the bottom cages. "Are those chickens?"

He nodded. "You've heard the expression shit rolls downhill?"

"Oh, I see what you mean. They're just for eggs, right? I mean, people don't eat those?"

"They absolutely do. It's amazing the whole world doesn't die of avian flu, isn't it?"

"As a travel agent, this is really concerning."

"It should be." He pointed to another stack of cages. "See these ones in front? They're mostly full of 'cut flowers.'"

"I beg your pardon?"

"Birds that are beautiful, but sick and destined to die in a day or two. I passed two plastic bags of dead birds in the alley an hour ago. It makes me crazy."

"Are you kidding? How awful! Isn't there any kind of regulation on that?"

He gave a sad laugh. "Not enough. And definitely not enforced." His eyes focused on something behind me. "Excuse me just a second."

He ducked into the back of the stall and peered at one of the higher cages. I saw his lips move.

He came out whispering, "Three twenty-eight. Two. Three eighty-seven. One."

"I beg your pardon?"

"Nothing." He noticed the seller staring at us and touched my arm to keep me moving. We passed a particularly sad baby monkey with dead eyes, chained to the top of a birdcage, and a small cat with stripes who was yowling.

"Is anybody trying to do anything about all this? Is there a group or something I could give money to?"

"American? Throwing money around?"

"You don't think Americans can do anything else?"

"Can they?" He seemed suddenly serious.

"I admit I used to be pretty oblivious, but I try now. I, well, I know an activist who's taught me a few things. This would really piss him off."

"I know a few of those. What's his name?"

I hesitated. Grey Hazelnut, aka the UnaVet, occasionally my nemesis, but also my compatriot, went by a series of fake names. Which one should I use? Would I betray him if I used the real one?

"You know, he uses a lot of aliases and I feel like I shouldn't give any of them away. I know that sounds dumb."

"Actually, it sounds smart." He reassessed me. "Wait, did you say your name is Redondo?"

"Yes."

"Does your compatriot have bow legs?"

I grinned. "Like a wishbone."

"Are you AntiChristine? The one who was with him in Tasmania?"

"How do you know that?"

He looked around. "We go back. He helped us catch a few bird smugglers last year. And get money to chip some of the ones in the wild. He's a titan."

"He's a lunatic with a good heart. So are you trying to do something about this crappy situation."

"Yes." He looked all around him and leaned down closer. "I'm actually working now."

"Doing what?"

"There are hundreds of birds being sold here, illegally. Some are endangered, others are just protected, but we have to have numbers to try to get the government to do something. So I'm trying to count them."

I looked around. There were thousands upon thousands of birds. And so many of them, to be honest, looked exactly alike.

"How on earth do you know which ones are endangered."

"I identify them by their songs."

"Get out! You can tell these birdsongs apart?"

"Of course. They're very distinctive."

"So what just happened in there? You heard something and that's why you left?"

"I just heard what sounded like a couple of straw-headed bulbuls.

They're almost completely extinct in the wild, because of the poaching. There were two of them and two black-chinned monarchs."

"Do you have a favorite?"

"That's too hard."

I looked around. Even the awful conditions didn't diminish the beauty of these birds. "I can see that."

"The most beautiful, I guess, is the Bali starling. You might have seen it. It's on the two hundred rupiah coin. But its beauty is its downfall. They're always poached. There are fewer than ten in the wild right now."

"Ten! Christ on a bike! That's insane."

"There are more in captivity—zoos and private collectors—but they're indigenous to West Bali and here, in the forest, they're almost gone."

"There aren't any of those here, are there?"

"Not today."

"When you see an illegal bird, how do you keep track if you don't write anything down? Or take pictures?"

"If I did that, the sellers would know. There's so much money involved, it's dangerous if they know you." I had dealt with enough traffickers to know he was right.

"So what do you do? Were those numbers you were whispering?"

"They're the MacKinnon *Field Guide* designations. I know the field guide numbers of all the Indonesian birds, so I remember that and how many are for sale. I can do about seven shops at a time, then I need to write them down. In fact, I need to write them down now."

"Oh, God. I'm so sorry I interrupted you."

"It's all right, but I better keep on, on my own."

"I understand. Well, good luck."

He pulled out a card. "Here. Sometimes it helps to have a friend in Bali."

"Thanks." I gave him one of mine. He tucked it into his pocket, then waved and ducked into another stall. After what he'd told me, I felt too awful to walk around the market, so I went to the little park beside it for a moment. Then I found my driver and headed back to the hotel, working on the lies I'd have to tell Burung so he wouldn't feel bad.

Chapter Nineteen

The driver was quiet and polite and drove like a maniac. Once I'd gotten my carry-on from Burung, he took me to the airport. Our only conversation was about how dry it had been for the rainy season. There were no festivals or cremations to slow us down, which I hoped didn't mean it was an inauspicious day for a helicopter ride.

Magnum P.I. notwithstanding, I didn't really associate helicopters with paradise. Even if my last two experiences hadn't been humiliating enough, the NYPD, *Apocalypse Now,* and billionaires would probably have ruined the whole idea for me anyway.

Plus, I hated, hated, hated running under the blades. Just hearing the whomp, whomp as a chopper approached made me feel faint. Remembering my mother, Madge, and Bea Ann were flying over a volcano right now in one of these didn't help.

Plus, there was the tarmac anxiety. I'd already tried to use the usually reliable Vaseline to remove the sticky black gunk from one pair of shoes, to only medium results. Tarmac was obviously peskier than beach tar. I wasn't anxious to lose my strappy sandals, too. If anything, it was hotter, too hot to go barefoot without second-degree burns. While I was waiting for the chopper, I squatted down in the grass to search for anything in my Balenciaga I could sacrifice to the tar gods.

"Hey! Wonder Woman!"

I spotted a compact, black-haired man jogging toward me and waving. I recognized that wave. The last time I'd seen it I was falling off a rope onto the deck of a moving cruise ship. What was his name? Scott.

"Hi. You're Cyd Redondo, aren't you?"

"Yes. Redondo Travel. Were you at the police station yesterday?"

"Yes. I guess I didn't recognize you without your skirt over your head."

"Hey!"

We both laughed. He looked at my carry-on. "What are you doing here?"

"Waiting for a ride."

"To Ubud? For Jill's Adventures?"

"Yep. Why?"

"I'm your pilot. Must be kismet. Ready to go?"

I avoided eye contact by looking at the helicopter, which was on the other side of the runway. "Any advice how to get across this melted tar without ruining my shoes? Do you have a golf cart or something?"

"Are you willing to let go of your luggage for a second? I remember you're touchy about that."

"I'm not touchy."

"Oh, come on! I've seen people have less separation anxiety about a newborn."

There was no way I could say no, now. But I wasn't surrendering my purse. I secured it on my shoulder. He grinned, lifted my carry-on off the ground, and jogged to the copter. I was relieved to see him put it on the floor of the passenger seat, then jog back.

"Now what?"

He gave me a deliberate look up and down. "You're still about what, one-ten?"

"I beg your pardon?"

"A hundred and ten pounds. As a helicopter pilot, it's my job to know how much weight I'm carrying."

"Yes. Approximately." Approximately as in within ten or fifteen pounds.

Before I could object, one of his arms was under my thighs, one was around my back, and my Balenciaga and I were lifted up in an "over the threshold" carry. When Barry Manzoni had attempted this move on our wedding night, he'd tripped over a copy of *USA Today* and both of us had suffered rug burns for a week.

Scott was more surefooted, though I could hear and feel the suck of the tar on his army-style boots as he walked. I could also feel the heat of his arms under me and smell patchouli mixed with axle grease in his neck. In what seemed like seconds, he'd deposited me in my seat and reminded me to put on my seat belt. He took off his boots, threw them in the back, then put on another pair of shoes.

"Don't want the pedals to get stuck, do we?"

"No, we absolutely do not." I tried to breathe while he talked to what I hoped was some kind of air traffic control tower, then checked the weather.

"It's a very short trip," he said. "We should just about make it before the rain hits."

"Well, that's comforting. At least I know you can hover well."

"You have no idea."

I don't know what it is about a helicopter and flirting. Maybe it's the proximity. Maybe it's the threat of imminent death. Maybe it's because it's so loud, you can pretend not to hear what the other person is saying.

I could still feel his arms around me. What would Roger think? After all, wasn't I meeting him in Paris next month? But he'd ignored my last two calls. And in the end, had we ever been anything more than a series of one-night stands? Yes, once. But what about now?

I decided there was no harm in a little banter with Scott, since that's all it would be. He would drop me off and I'd probably never see him again.

"Do a lot of tourists travel by helicopter here?"

"Only the wealthy ones. It's not that common yet. I think it will be, though."

He was a natural tour guide, pointing out several temples, a famous bird sanctuary, and finally, the legendary rice fields. The brochures had hardly done justice to the scope or the color. The rice plantings seemed to go on forever, like the Lake of the Ozarks, but soylent green. Scott explained the Balinese had developed a complicated irrigation system that came all the way down from the volcanic lakes. Rice had kept the island alive.

I was about to ask him what he was doing in Bali when there was a boom, then a vibration that realigned my spine and, a second later, monsoon-level rain. We took a hard dip to the left. Scott righted the chopper, but not my digestive system. I didn't want to vomit all over my luggage, or Scott, but I also didn't want to upset our precarious balance by leaning out the window, especially since I hadn't been one hundred percent honest about my weight.

I guess he'd seen green faces before. He took one hand off the wheel, reached underneath the seat, and handed me an airline sick bag.

I smiled, weakly, used it, then resealed it tightly.

Scott took it and tossed it out the window. I looked at him in horror. He snorted. "It's biodegradable. You disappoint me. Given our history, I thought you had an iron stomach."

"Maybe it's Bali belly," I burped.

"That mostly comes out the other end. Here we are." Before I could deliver an appropriate retort, I saw a round, Gumby-green target on the ground in the middle of a huge thatched resort. Then we were on the ground, which was steaming from the shower. Scott turned the blades off and looked at me.

I looked down at the landing pad. "Is that Astroturf?"

"Not quite. More like the stuff they use in children's playgrounds now. Okay for your heels?"

"As long as you don't think they'll punch holes in it."

"Are you angling for another honeymoon carry?"

"Is that what that was?" I wondered why I was slightly disappointed I wasn't going to hitch another ride in Scott's arms.

"I'll come around to help you get your bags down."

"Where are we?"

"The pad belongs to the hotel, but they let other pilots use it when it's free. This is not where you're staying, though, because this one doesn't have a funicular railway. That's what you want, right?"

"Yes. I forgot. That sounds amazing." I adjusted my bag. "Will I see you again while I'm here?"

"Considering I'm your ride to the hotel, yes."

"What? You're just going to leave the helicopter here?"

"Nope. Handing it off." He waved to a guy in a jumpsuit. As we passed, Scott threw him some keys, then gestured me down a ramp into beautifully sculpted grounds and toward, of course, a scooter. This presented first, the dilemma of how tightly you put your arms and thighs around a stranger you'd been flirting with, and second, my luggage.

Happily, Scott had already considered number two, which also kind of helped with number one, as he helped me secure my Balenciaga on my chest and that kept me from getting too close to him. He hooked the carry-on in front of him. As Scott roared through the grounds of the hotel, my thighs still held on for dear life.

We headed down another long kind of driveway, and then out into a larger street.

"So this is downtown Ubud? Is the traffic like it is in Denpasar?"

"Not exactly."

"What does that mean?"

I heard a squawk and a hiss and felt something pulling on my hair.

"More monkeys."

Chapter Twenty

"Ahhh! Get it off!"

"Sit tight. If it doesn't find a banana in there, it will go elsewhere."

"You've got to be kidding." I could still feel little feet. "Did you put a banana in there?"

He laughed. I stayed as still as I could, telling myself over and over, at least it's not a bat, at least it's not a bat, and in a moment, my hair was quiet.

"Most Americans love it when the monkeys jump on them."

"Yes, well, I'm not a big one for the surprise jump."

"I'll keep that in mind."

I punched his arm. the scooter veered slightly, then vroomed around some slow cyclists.

I could hear monkeys everywhere. "Are we on Monkey Forest Road?"

"No, that's south of here. We're on the way to the jungle. Are you hungry? There's a good place on the way."

"That sounds great."

Five minutes later, we were seated on a bench in a small thatched restaurant, my bag and carry-on secured at my feet. Out of politeness, and exhaustion, I let Scott order for me. I'd been to enough bad potlucks to realize you could eat almost anything if you swallowed it whole, oyster-style.

"Can you take spicy?"

"Absolutely!" I always went all the way up to medium at our local Indian restaurant. "Do they have dalumans?"

"Ah, you know about dalumans," he said. "I'll see."

He sprinted to the counter and returned with my new favorite drink. I thought about the rice fields and the banyan trees and the helipad and the floating cubes in my drink and figured, if the Inuit people had a hundred words for snow, then the Balinese must have a hundred words for green. Scott was looking at me.

I blushed, which I don't think I'd done since Catholic school. "So I thought you worked for the police in Melbourne. What are you doing here?"

"Taking a break. Helping out the family." The policeman's union would have had a cow if my brousin Frank had ever done that. In Brooklyn, "taking a break" usually meant a suspension, but maybe things were different in Australia.

"You didn't take my mother and her friends up to the volcano this morning, did you?"

"No. They got the second best pilot."

"Did they get back okay?"

"Do you want me to check?"

"Actually, I do. Is that pathetic?"

"No. Give me a second."

He walked down the stairs and took out his phone. I sipped my drink and thought I heard something that sounded like Burung's training bird. What a delight to hear that every day.

Scott jogged back up the steps. "They're fine, just landed back in Denpasar. Their pilot said your mother asked if you'd found out anything about Gerald. Who's Gerald?"

"He's a man Mom sat next to on the plane. I guess he's been murdered. She asked me to find out what happened to him."

"Why you? Do you also make travel arrangements to Hell?"

"When necessary. No. It's just that I've been involved, accidentally, in a few murders."

"Oh, of course. Harriet. You're the one who figured it out."

"It was a group effort."

"That's not what I heard." He took a long sip of his drink, then looked me right in the eye. "I have a confession to make."

I braced myself.

"I knew you were the one I was picking up. I recognized the name and traded assignments with the other pilot."

"Really? Why?"

"Partly because I never got to say well done, about catching Harriet's killer. But also because I couldn't get that image out of my head—you twirling on the rope, that orange skirt blowing up, taking out that guy on the lounge chair with your luggage. You gave Marilyn in *The Seven Year Itch* a run for her money."

I didn't know how to respond to that, so I raised my glass. "To Harriet."

"To Harriet. At least you got the bastards," he said, raising his glass. "Well done."

I felt like slugging my drink. I sipped instead.

He slugged. "So what are you doing here? I thought you lived in the States."

"I do. My mother read *Eat, Pray, Love.*"

Scott snorted a white-green stream of daluman across two benches, just as the server arrived with our beautifully crafted lunch. I held in my laughter long enough to thank her.

I turned back to Scott, who was still coughing. "I take it you're familiar with the book?"

"Upside, tourist dollars. Downside, tourists. But we should eat while it's hot."

I looked down at my banana leaf plate and the mounds of unrecognizable, brightly colored dishes, fanned out from a perfectly round scoop of white rice.

"What is this called?"

"Nasi campur."

I searched in vain for some kind of utensil. I figured the chances of a fork were slim, but I had hoped for chopsticks. I died a little when I saw Scott wash his hand in a bowl of water and lime the server had left beside our plates, then reach with his right hand, take some rice, and use it to scoop up a bite of what looked like meat.

"Anything wrong?"

"You probably have to teach me how to do that. I come from a fork-dependent culture."

"That's right. Okay. First, you always, always use your right hand. It's rude to do almost anything, except wipe your arse, with your left."

"Geez, got it."

He laughed. "See, you make a tiny ladle with the rice, then you scoop a bit of the food into it. Like this."

Scooping up Ethiopian food with injera bread seemed delicate next to this. "Okay. Here goes nothing." I looked down at my food. It smelled amazing, with notes of chili, pork, and coconut. Something that looked like the fried onions we used for Thanksgiving green bean casserole was sprinkled on top.

I reached in and scooped up something red, then spit half of it out instantly, in some kind of tongue self-preservation. Holy Mother of God, I thought, as my lips were too burned to say anything out loud. Scott laughed.

My outfit would never be the same. I'd be finding grains of rice in every fold and crevice for days.

"I thought you said spicy was okay?"

"Cultural misunderstanding on what constitutes spicy," I mumbled.

"Ha. I did think it was pretty ballsy to take a mouthful of chilis first."

"Is that what that was?"

"Try this one." He scooped up something brown and held it out to me. Was he actually feeding me? I would have hesitated, but I was starving. I took a deep breath and accepted the mouthful. I have to admit, it was not unsexy.

"Okay. That's delicious. Or it will be once I can feel my tongue again."

After that we both dug in, washing down the chilis with the daluman and laughing.

Once I'd gotten over the initial shock, everything was crazy delicious. There were so many flavors going on—heat from the chilis, sweet from the coconut, fat and salt from the pork, tang from the ginger, crunch from the beans and onions, and all fresh as it comes. It made sense that the Balinese didn't need large portions, since after a couple of bites, you had to stop just to allow your senses to process what was going on. In terms of slowing down your consumption, it was a lot more fun than the American fad of chewing everything thirty-two times.

Scott looked at me. "Not bad for your first Balinese street food."

For me, street food meant a pepperoni slice or hot dogs that had been cooking for three days in the same water. This was a revelation. I just hoped it didn't provoke honest to God Bali belly, since I had to get back on the motorbike.

The rest of the ride was littered with temples, more rice terraces, and after we took a turn, an increasingly dense forest on either side. We climbed for a while, finally arriving at a long entrance to a massive thatched building, tucked right into the mountain itself.

"Welcome to Hanging Vines," Scott said, helping me off and depositing my luggage beside the scooter.

"Wow." On closer inspection, I could see buildings above and below. Down the hill, I spotted what looked like a waterfall pouring over a cliff. "Is there anything I need to do or say to keep Jill in their good graces?"

"Just take notes and pictures. They want to cash in on the *Eat, Pray, Love* thing, but they're pricey."

"Most of my clients are on a fixed income."

"But the hotel doesn't need to know that, right?" He mounted the scooter.

"Right. Got it. Are you off, then?"

"I have another appointment, but Reggie is great and he always treats the agency's clients well, so I'm leaving you in good hands. Not as good as mine, of course."

"It's so sad that you lack confidence. Do some women find that attractive?"

"Some women don't concern me. Speaking of, watch out for ex-pats here. They will definitely put the moves on you."

"Well, forewarned is forearmed."

"I'm usually only an hour away if you need anything. There are more villains in Bali than you might think." And in Bay Ridge, too. I thought about Peggy fricking Newsome, smug in her western Bali resort.

"Do you ever fly to the west of the island? To the Java end?"

"I can."

"How much do you charge?"

"I'm open to the barter system."

"Oh my God. Really?"

"Can't blame a guy for trying. But seriously, if you'll pay for the fuel, you can have me for free. Give me your phone." He punched numbers in and smiled. "This will be easier than digging a business card out of that storage unit of a purse."

"It's very organized in there."

"I bet. Still." He started up the scooter. I touched his shoulder. "Hey. I just remembered that message from my mom. About that murdered guy, Gerald. Since you're Australian law enforcement, do you know anyone here I might be able to talk to about the case?"

"Probably. Let me see what I can find out."

He handed my phone back and looked at me too long, then kissed me on the cheek, hopped on the scooter, and headed out. He turned back once, to wave. The last time he'd done that, I'd been half an hour away from finding a dead body.

Chapter Twenty-one

I walked down the pathway to the entrance, where I saw a tall, elegant man with a touch of white in his sleek black hair and a perfectly tailored dress shirt and pants, standing in the carved doorway.

I smiled and held out my hand. "Cyd Redondo, Redondo Travel. Jill arranged my reservations?"

"Of course! Welcome, Ms. Redondo. I'm Reggie Punjabi, the manager. Lovely to meet you. We're delighted you could join us."

It was Bali, so he handed me a drink that looked like a statue. I wondered whether American life would be happier if everyone carried one of these around, if instead of Smart Water, we drank Beautiful Water. It's not like Smart Water ever looked smart. Neither did the people schilling it. Here, Reggie and the water were in complete sync.

"Thank you. I'm so happy to be here."

"We have a message for you from Lu at Jill's Adventures." He handed me an embossed envelope. It looked like it had been opened. "You know Lu?"

"Yes, she's been showing me around."

"She is a very accomplished woman. With many talents. I hope we will have the pleasure of seeing her while you are here. If you will just sign the register, we will take you to your quarters."

"Don't you need a credit card for incidentals?"

"We are happy to host you. Jill speaks highly of your agency and your discretion and we hope you will be happy enough here to suggest it to others."

My discretion? What did that mean? "I'm sure I will. Thank you very much."

Reggie nodded to a waiting staff member, then came out from behind the desk and gestured me toward the terrace. "Please follow me. You need a proper tour." The staff member took my carry-on and followed us.

The minute I walked out of reception, I forgot everything but what was in front of me.

Past the gorgeous open-aired bar, the hotel seemed to go on as far as I could see. The property was half Hanging Gardens of Babylon and half *Swiss Family Robinson* luxury retirement community. Either way, it felt like the Eighth Wonder of the World. The individual villas were built on descending terraces, above and below the main building, and looked out over a ravine and the jungle behind it. There were walkways and stairs to reach each lodging, but I was only interested in the other option.

Right there, in front of me, as promised, was the most beautiful funicular railway I'd ever seen. Not that I'd ever seen a real one, but I'd researched them like crazy, from England to Chile to Nepal. They'd been invented by the Swiss, of course.

This one looked anything but European. It had been carved with elaborate figures, and painted in so many coats of red and turquoise that the wood shone like glass. It was open on three sides, with a sliding, see-through entrance and a set of controls attached to metal gears.

Reggie nodded to the man in traditional dress who was manning the tram. "Good afternoon, Wayan."

The man bowed to me, then slid open the glass door. I bowed back, then followed Reggie into the tiny carriage. There was a lovely carved bench to sit on, but I wanted to stand at the front as I went down. It felt like flying. It was hard not to throw out my arms like Kate Winslet in *Titanic*. I loved being inside something that worked by counterbalances. I mean, you hardly ever get that in life.

If I hadn't been absolutely dripping in flop sweat, I don't think I could have been any happier.

As the car descended, I spied level after level of half-hidden, thatched structures, surrounded by elaborate tiles, stones, flowers, and fountains. Each unit had a patio, and many had private pools. Most were separated by steep steps. I decided to stop obsessing about the total lack of ADA ramps and figured, at Bali prices, if you couldn't use the railway car, you could afford to hire someone to carry you up and down the stairs. Preferably Scott.

Finally, jutting out into the forest itself was the falling water I'd seen before. It was actually two infinity pools, one cantilevered above the other. Each pool ended in an oblong section shaped like the head in Edward Munch's *The Scream*, which is how I felt when I saw that the top pool gushed into the lower one, which in turn gushed into the ravine below. This was clearly the centerpiece of the resort and a definite plus—for people who could swim.

Reggie stopped the carriage a few levels above the pool. I turned to him. "So, is this your own place?"

"It belongs to my family. I've come over to help modernize it just enough to compete with the new market, while making sure it isn't ruined. We were worried if we hired an outside firm, they might upgrade and destroy."

"There's a lot of that going around. Well, I'm very glad you are here to save it. It is, and I never use this word, breathtaking."

"Well, I hope you feel the same way about your villa. Here we are."

As a travel agent, I was always suspicious of the word "villa," which often meant "with rollaway bed." But not this time. I had my own private patio with a swinging bamboo chair, a small dipping pool, a huge bed covered in white linen, with a natural colored mosquito net and plenty of coils. In other words, perfect. And in terms of snake protection, it had walls and a door.

Flowers cascaded out of vases onto tables, desks, and beside the reading chair. Reggie opened a few doors and I glimpsed a round bathtub full of flower petals in the shape of a heart. As gorgeous and obviously labor-intensive as this was, the thing I was most excited about, delight of delights, was a flushing toilet. With toilet paper. I guess they had gone a bit Western, after all, but this part I didn't mind.

"Is it to your liking, Ms. Redondo?"

"Cyd, please. Very much so."

"Excellent. I will give you your privacy." He turned to go.

I walked him to the door. "May I ask you a personal question?"

"Certainly."

"Did you come here from London?"

"What makes you say that?"

"Your clothes are very Jermyn Street."

"Ah. Very astute of you to notice. In fact, they were made here. Copied from a suit my father bought in Savile Row years ago. I have the jacket, too, but it is too hot to wear it here. Hong Kong is always mentioned as the place for bespoke tailoring, but I would put Bali up against any tailor there. And it isn't just for clothes. Everyone here is an artisan, everyone can copy. They can create almost anything. Even your Balenciaga."

A man who recognized a Balenciaga—I really was in paradise. "Seriously?"

"Ask Lu about it, she knows everyone. May I offer some advice?"

"Absolutely."

"I often find our guests forget to breathe. They don't want to waste a minute, so they hurtle from one destination and event to another, but if they don't give themselves time to rest and settle into the place, to just sit in the landscape, they never really see Bali. The real Bali. Americans have a hard time with *jam karat*. You know about that? Elastic time?"

"Yes. It seems great in theory, but in reality, the idea completely stresses me out."

He laughed. "Yes, Jill said you were a highly responsible and competent person. Which I appreciate, having spent time in England and traveled by train. But here, time is more fluid. More relative. It might be rude in the States to be late, but it's considered rude here to expect anyone to be on time. It takes a while for Westerners to get used to this. That being the case, you might want to give yourself the rest of the day and night to relax, take advantage of our pools, our spa, or sleep. I don't know what brought you to Bali, but there is always a reason any traveler lands here. Sometimes you must allow yourself to be quiet to understand that reason." He pulled out a card. "Here is my private line if you need anything at all."

"Thank you, Reggie."

"Of course."

If his family owned the hotel, tipping was inappropriate, but I would definitely get the hotel a thank you gift before I left. He jogged up the stairs and his footsteps faded away.

Chapter Twenty-two

I could hear the slip and creak of the funicular and birdsongs that went straight to my breastbone. I hated to say anything negative about Bay Ridge, but robins, bluebirds, and sparrows just seemed like "roadies" for real songbirds now.

I had a momentary flash of the skewered blue parrot that I'd found months ago on my Uncle Ray's desk, then tried to put it out of my mind. I wondered how Burung's training was going and had to admit, I was excited to see all these amazing birds and their songs in one place. I guess my brousin Jimmy had been right about one thing—I was a birdbrain.

Then I thought about Stu Capistranis risking his life to count endangered birds. I felt like I hadn't done anything at all with my life. I just sent people to ruin wonderful places, where they might get hurt or arrested. Everyone in Bay Ridge was laughing at me and my mother couldn't bear to eat a mango with me. What was I doing to save the world?

Just then, a bird with a long black-striped tail stopped on a branch just out of reach and started a kind of hiccupping trill. I took in a deep breath of frangipani and decided it didn't matter that I'd come here to save someone who didn't want saving. At the moment I was staying at the Hanging Vines and I needed to be grateful for that and for the wild coincidence of seeing Scott again. Bless Jill. That reminded me to dig Lu's message out of my purse.

Cyd. Today is yours. I'll be by around ten to take you "carrot calling." It will be our secret. Lu.

Okay. I would take Reggie's advice and just try to be here. I took a minute to explore my terrace, swinging in my hanging chair and dipping a toe into my private pool. My view was just high enough to see past the ravine, where there were banyan trees and flowering vines and I glimpsed snatches of yet another lichen-slathered sandstone temple. I could even see a bridge over the river, which appeared, at least from this angle, impossibly narrow. My stomach flipped just looking at it.

I was ready for a bath, but remembering the noises I'd heard Alistair Brush make in my mother's bathroom, I was a bit afraid of what might be under those flower petals. I dug out my folding hairbrush and threw it with a crash against the side of the tub, just to see if anything surfaced. The heart-shaped design bobbed and blurred slightly, but I couldn't see any slithering. I figured the tiles and fixtures were such a gleaming white, a python or cobra would stand out.

To be honest, I didn't know how to take a bath in these petals. I dipped my finger in. The water wasn't hot. Was this like so many things I had seen already in Bali—there just for the beauty itself? I mean, someone had gone to a lot of trouble here. I appreciated that but, practically, what was I supposed to do with the petals? Drain them? That couldn't be good for the plumbing. Scoop them out? What a waste.

I locked the villa door, grabbed a towel and fluffy white robe, and prepared to desecrate this elaborate piece of bathroom art. As I looked down, my senior citizen travel agent-self noted the lack of handles on the tub. Stop it, I thought, you're only thirty-two. I stepped, hands-free, into the tub and sunk in until the petals brushed my chin and the scent overwhelmed me.

The water was full of scented oil, which left me refreshed, slick, and covered in petals in certain bodily orifices that I wasn't that comfortable "adorning." Rough toweling removed them, eventually.

I took a pitcher from the living room and scooped as many petals out as I could, then walked onto the patio and tossed them out into the massive compost heap of the jungle. I could spot tiny candles filling up the staircase to the hotel entrance. A woman in a sarong had a tray of them she was laying out, one by one.

I considered ordering room service, but the place was too beautiful and I could see better from the main building, which was higher up. I slipped on a knee-length sundress in Tiffany blue and my kitten heel sandals. Having learned my lesson about trying to apply false eyelashes in the tropics when jet-lagged, I headed out, bare-eyed, for the bar.

Who was I kidding? I just wanted to ride the funicular railway at night.

The whole complex flickered and glowed. I summoned the railway, and in a moment, Wayan welcomed me on. I put my hands together, lowered my head, and greeted him in my horrible misrepresentation of his language. He smiled anyway.

I asked him to show me how the levers worked. He did. In English. Some people are just kind by nature. It was a simple mechanism and my delight in using it made him laugh. He let me run it up to the main building and, even though I didn't know whether it was appropriate, I gave him a huge tip as I got out.

The open-air restaurant and lounge sat halfway down the property, with views of the pools below and villas above. Even the bar itself was see-through—bits of fountains and torches gleamed between the jewel-colored liquor bottles and sparkling glassware. I hiked up on a teak stool, crossed my legs, hooked my Balenciaga over my knee and leaned onto the bar. As I ordered a drink, I stared at the thousand tiny flames flickering down the steps and around the overlapping pools.

I asked the bartender if it was possible to eat at the bar and within moments I had another plate of fruit, chilis, and minced pork. This time, I staggered the chilis and washed it all down with a rum drink that could have wound up in the Guggenheim.

I was just taking in the amazing aroma of the drink, when it was marred by an overdose of cheap aftershave. A balding man in unfortunate shorts sat down next to me. He pushed the stool out a little to accommodate his basketball-sized gut.

"Get her another of what she's having. Better yet, a bottle of arak." He had a Dutch accent.

The bartender looked at me. "We don't have arak, sir."

"Vodka then." Was this a tourist, or one of the ex-pats Scott had warned me about? It didn't matter. I was not in the mood.

"No, thank you. I don't want another drink. In fact, I was just leaving."

"American. Nice."

I placed some rupiahs under my plate. I didn't want to leave a tab with my room number on the bar. I nodded to the bartender. "Thank you and good night."

The Dutchman put his hand on my arm. "Aw, don't be that way. Come on. Don't walk away from me. I thought American women came here for love."

I slung my purse over my shoulder, and jumped down from the stool. "Some of them might, but that fantasy involves abs. And hair."

By the time I reached the exit, he'd pulled out his phone and was coming after me.

Honestly, was I going to have to kick a stranger in the balls on this vacation, too?

"Hey. Hey you, Redondo!"

How the hell did he know my name? I sped up. If I took the funicular down to my villa, he'd know where I was staying. If I took the stairs, I might confuse him, but face snakes or bats in the process. How could I be in a situation where snakes and bats were looking good?

In the end, I split the difference. Wayan and the car were waiting by the restaurant. When I explained the situation to him, he started the car upward right away, took me to the top of the property, and handed me a map to get back down, via the stairs, proving once again, that tipping always pays off. I tipped him again, and got out at the top. I could see the Dutchman below, waiting for the car to return.

I started down the stone stairs, but my kitten heels seemed to echo through the property. I stopped, removed them, picked up one of the votive candles with my free hand, and headed down.

So did the funicular. It stopped yards from my villa.

Chapter Twenty-three

Had the fake-out failed? Or had Wayan betrayed me? Had I miscalculated the exchange rate? The man got out and looked up in my direction. Just at that moment, something crawled over my bare foot.

I slammed my hand over my mouth to stifle my scream, which I hoped was monkey-like. I was afraid to look down. Then I realized whatever it was had skittered, not slithered. My candle lit a gecko scampering into a bush. I breathed a sigh of relief. I decided to see this as a good omen. Barry the chameleon had sent friendly reptile backup.

I couldn't see the Dutchman, then he emerged from my walkway with a tall man in dark clothes and a black beanie. Who wore a beanie in Bali?

They boarded the funicular and Wayan took them to the pool level. I put my shoes back on and hurried to my villa, taking out the roll of quarters I always had on me, and tied it at the bottom of my "just in case" scarf, for a makeshift sap.

I held the sap in my right hand and fumbled the key with my left, eventually lurching inside. The bathroom and bedroom lights were on when I left. Different lights were on now. My carry-on was on the luggage holder. I had left it in the bathroom, like I did in every hotel until I was sure there weren't any bedbugs.

I returned it to the relative safety of the tiled bathroom floor. I had a laminated list of everything I'd packed, so I took that out. Before I had the heart to search, I checked the minibar to find a bottle of Jack Daniel's and shot it. I laid out each item on the floor and checked it against my list. It was all there.

Who were these guys? Inefficient burglars? Aspirational stalkers? They had known my name, though. That was the strange part. I pulled out Reggie's card and dialed, but it went to voice mail. I didn't want to risk heading back up to reception. I didn't think Reggie would give out personal information, but I guess you never knew. Who else knew I was here? Jill, Lu, Mom, Scott. I hoped it wasn't Scott. It wasn't going to be easy to sleep, but I did everything I could to secure the doors and window and I decided to sleep in my clothes, just in case I had to make a quick exit. People expected linen to be wrinkled anyway.

After I'd lit the mosquito coils, I slipped my personal alarm, my lipstick-shaped pepper spray, and my fashion-forward sap under my pillow, pulled the mosquito net down and tucked it under the mattress on all sides, then took out my phone and considered calling my mother.

I genuinely hoped she was having fun, though her rejection still hurt. Was I just a spoiled only child? I distracted myself by consulting my international time zone chart and checking on all the clients who were in places where it wasn't the middle of the night. No one was in the hospital or in jail, which I considered a personal triumph.

I was bone-tired and wide awake at the same time. Probably because it was only eleven in the morning in Brooklyn. I lay back and listened to the nighttime jungle chirps and screams, and waited for a rattling knob or the smash of a vase.

Instead, I woke up to a wall of warbling and the newly familiar smell of frangipani. I took a minute to appreciate the birdsongs, hoping I lived long enough to attend the competition and learn which bird was which.

I looked around and sighed. I hated to lose this room. Overzealous lotharios were one thing, but ones that knew my name, or broke into my room, were another. Should I even stay at this hotel? And if not, where could I go? I needed a new room, at the very least.

I ordered breakfast, then tried Reggie again. He was out, but the person at the front desk said she would find him. A bit later, or actually, quite a bit later—*à la jam karat*—I had the most beautiful room service meal I'd ever seen. Fruit carved into animals, tiny bubbles of rice, and all on a tray that would have given the *Antiques Roadshow* crew an embolism.

I stepped out on my terrace and looked down at the two pools on the edge of the cliff. As gorgeous as they were, I wasn't going to risk leaving my room unattended. It's not like I could really take advantage of the water, anyway. After my near-drowning in Australia, I'd promised Sister Ellery I'd take swimming lessons at the Y, but they didn't give them in the winter in Bay Ridge, so I remained a danger to myself and others. Especially in an infinity pool.

I figured I could sit on the edge of my small, private one, at least. I positioned myself with an intruder-convenient view of the path and lowered my calves into the water. Heaven. I heard a knock on the door and threw on my robe.

I slipped my pepper spray into the pocket and looked out the window. It was Reggie, this time in a fitted, light gray suit and a tasteful pink and turquoise striped tie.

I cracked the door open and pulled my robe tight against my neck. "Good morning. I'm not quite dressed."

"I won't disturb you then. I was just concerned, as you'd left several messages. I wanted to deal with any problems personally. What has happened?"

I told him as much as I knew.

"Cyd. I am horrified. Absolutely horrified. I apologize to you personally, and formally, on behalf of the Hanging Vines. I assure you, all guests' names and room numbers are private. I don't know how this could have happened." He asked me for a description of the men and said he would investigate.

"Do you think you can move me to a different room? Or a different level?"

"Of course. Allow me to return to the office and see what is available. Again, a million apologies. And of course I will put any new accommodation under an alias, just in case." He bowed and left.

I called Lu. "Should I wear my sarong to the party?"

"You haven't told anyone, have you? Some of the women don't want their husbands to know."

"Of course not."

"Good. I think everyone would love to see what you'd wear to one at home."

"Okay. I'll meet you at reception. Mum's the word."

At home, I might take hours choosing the best possible Tupperware outfit—cute, but not too cute, professional, but affordable, and loose enough not to be threatening. The most important thing was to make the other women feel good about themselves and about all the ways Tupperware was going to make their lives better. The last part was easy—it improved my life every day. The fashion part was harder. Bay Ridge was a tough crowd.

But at least at home, I had options. Given the demands of carry-on-only travel, my sixties hostess outfits were limited. I rarely wore black, but I was sweating through three outfits a day here and at least my black boatneck linen shift—which hit just below the elbow and kneecap—would camouflage the worst stains.

Normally, I'd wear it with a bright scarf, but here I would either suffocate from the heat or Isadora Duncan myself into an early death on the scooter, so I threw on the three turquoise necklaces my Uncle Ray and Aunt Noni had given me from my grandmother's closet, and my trusty nude patent-leather kitten heel sandals. I stuck a crushable sun hat in my purse, donned Jackie O sunglasses to hide my lash-deficient eyes, zipped up my carry-on, and rolled it out the door.

I looked both ways for the creepy duo from last night, then hurried to the funicular stop. I was ready to give Wayan a piece of my mind, but there was a different man running the railway today, so I merely smiled and bowed my head as I entered, and then exited just by the bar, where a Peggy Newsome-esque blonde was flirting with the bartender. Blondes. They were everywhere.

I arrived at reception to find another stunning woman with shimmering hair who said she would summon the management.

In my experience, summoning rarely worked, but I kept my mouth shut out of politeness.

Reggie emerged and shook his head. "I'm afraid I have some bad news, my dear. We can move you to another villa, one of the deluxe ones, but not until the day after tomorrow. Are you comfortable staying in your current room until then?"

"No, not really."

"Perhaps we could book you some kind of excursion?"

My phone rang. It was the Redondo Travel number. I looked at my watch. It was ten at night in Bay Ridge. "Would you excuse me, Reggie?"

I walked outside. "Cyd Redondo, Redondo Travel." It was Sister Ellery. Traitor.

Chapter Twenty-four

"What are you doing in the office?" I asked.

"I had to be here for the locksmith. He's changing the lock back."

"I didn't authorize that."

"I know. Your Uncle Ray did."

"At ten o'clock at night? What? Why?"

"You're out of the loop."

"I can't be out of the loop. I am the loop."

"Not today. Even the Catholic Women's League has nothing on the inmate grapevine."

"I don't understand what you're talking about. Uncle Ray called you from prison? Why?"

"He can't make long-distance calls from jail. He heard something and he was worried. Wanted me to get a message to you. There's a bid on two buildings in our block. Ray says someone's trying to buy the whole thing. He heard they're going to demolish everything and build mixed-use high-rise housing or some bullshit."

"What? No! No one on the Avenue would sell up for that. That would ruin the whole town."

"Maybe the buyers lied. Or the sellers don't know that's what's happening. No matter what, it's fishy. So he wanted somebody in the office while you were gone, to keep an eye on things. You're welcome."

"Fine. Who's the buyer?"

"He had your Uncle Guido Jr. do some research. It's a shell company—DD&D. Diana Development and Design."

"Diana?" No! Diana Development and Design, my foot. Dollars to donuts that was Peggy fricking Newsome. That might explain why she was so keen to bankrupt us. Maybe she didn't just want our clients. Maybe she wanted the building too. But why? And how could she afford to buy a whole block?

Sister Ellery cleared her throat. "Any instructions?"

"Don't send anyone else to Bali, period. And thank you, I guess. I'll call you back."

At least I knew where Peggy was, the witch. And she didn't know I knew. I walked back into reception. "Reggie? Do you know of any places to stay in West Bali?"

"There is one private resort near there I could recommend. I'm sure they'd be happy to host you for a night or two. Should I arrange it?"

Reggie sorted out the reservation and gave me the address and phone number.

"Do you need a car?"

"Let me check something first."

Scott had also put his number in my phone. I don't know why I was nervous about using it. I thought about Peggy Newsome's signature hair flip and dialed anyway.

"It's Cyd Redondo, Redondo Travel. Sorry to bother you."

"Cyd? Hi. What happened?"

"It's a long story, I'll explain later. I want to take you up on your offer to fly me to West Bali. Today. Obviously I'll pay for the fuel if there's anywhere to land there."

He said he was tied up until four but if I could get to Ubud, he could meet me at the helipad there and fly me over, weather permitting.

"That's great. Thank you so much, seriously."

Just then, Lu appeared. She took one look at me, and turned to Reggie. "Have you been up to your old tricks?"

"Absolutely not! I gave you my word. Cyd needs to go to West Bali and I've been arranging it."

She shook her head, then looked at me and gestured at her watch. I wondered what happened to *jam karat.*

Reggie came forward. "Would you like to leave your luggage here, in my care, of course?"

"No, thank you. If it's all right with Lu, we'll go straight to the helipad. Thank you, Reggie."

The back of the Kijang was full of baskets. Lu put my carry-on in the spare tire compartment and I kept my Balenciaga with me in the front seat. As we were pulling out I spied the two burglar suspects walking toward reception. I leaned out the window and took a picture of them, then told Lu to step on it.

She did. "Who are those men?"

I told her.

"What else just happened?"

"What do you mean?"

"You have a man glow. It's Reggie, isn't it? Is it Reggie?"

"What? No. I mean he's very charming, but no."

She elbowed me.

"It's not him, stop it. Why?" I saw her blush. "Oh. You like him?"

"We have, well, a history. But he is an inveterate flirt, plus I'm promised to someone else. We must hurry. We'll address your glow later."

"Good, because my archenemy has gone too far and I have to think."

"Your enemy is my enemy."

I grinned. "Is there an offering for that? Or a curse?"

"You bet. But we'll need equipment."

"Great. Also, I need you to get me to the Ubud helipad by four. Will that work?"

"With time to spare."

As Lu navigated the road into Ubud I asked her why the women kept their Tupperware party a secret?

"It began in Jakarta, where many Muslim men do not allow their wives to work. The men were not threatened if women gathered for an *arisan*, for gossip. So the first parties were underground there. In Bali, it is different. Women already do all the cooking and the offerings and run all the food stands and handle all the money, while their husbands lounge around, stroking their cocks."

"I beg your pardon?"

Lu pointed to two men standing by a food stand. Each was petting what looked like a huge rooster.

"Oh."

"Why do they carry chickens around?"

"They are their most treasured possessions."

I just stared at her.

"For cockfighting."

"There's cockfighting here? Wow. It's totally illegal in the U.S."

"But it still happens, yes? Technically it's illegal here, too. That is why they do it in the temples."

"In temples? Holy Toledo." It was her turn to stare. "It's a town in Ohio. I have no idea why we associate it with surprise."

"Ah, *saya tidak percaya itu*!"

"Right." Actually my knowledge of the language hadn't advanced to that phrase, but I was good with context. "So why is it a secret here?"

"Depending on a woman's family situation, it may be beneficial to make their own money."

"Understood. I'm ready to seal in the freshness."

Lu laughed. "Jill said you were all right."

"Nice of her."

"Yes."

After twenty stop-and-go minutes, we pulled in front of a walled compound with bicycles and scooters lined up outside. Lu handed me a few of the baskets from the back, grabbed two more, and locked the Kijang. I took white gloves my grandmother insisted I always carry out of my bag, put them on, and hooked the baskets on my non-purse shoulder. Lu gestured me ahead toward the entrance, just as it started to pour rain.

I went through the opening and promptly smashed into a wall.

"What the hell?" I stumbled back into Lu.

Just inside the entrance was a random piece of wall about the size of a large headstone. Who would build an entryway that ran straight into a mini-wall?

Lu laughed. "It's to confuse demons. Apparently works."

"Ha. Why does it confuse them?"

"Demons can only go in a straight line."

"How can anyone possibly know that?"

She shrugged. "Observation."

"That reminds me, as a card-carrying demon, do I need to cover my hair?"

She regarded me. "Can you?"

I took out my crushable sun hat, uncrushed it, slopped my hair on top of my head and rammed the hat on. With the hat and gloves, I truly was the ghost of Tupperware past.

We negotiated around the obstacle wall and moved toward a shrine already peppered with petals. Lu removed one of her baskets, took several beautiful offerings of palm leaves, flowers, and rice, and placed them down.

Lu gestured for me to follow her around a gargantuan banyan tree and toward an open-aired structure in the middle of the compound. I could see groups of women chatting, perched on benches or pillows, and a few tables with oversized floral arrangements. Like everything else in Bali, the whole scene looked like it had been set-decorated. Even the tropical rain shower was straight out of a movie. At least I wouldn't have to worry about sweat stains.

I could see it was not the Tupperware party of my youth—no Talbott's suits or shirtdresses, no pumps, or pearls—and, to my surprise, no sarongs. All the women seemed to be in Western clothes in what I guessed must be the Balinese equivalent of business casual.

I could hear Indonesian, but no English. I might miss most of what was said, but under the squeal of children and the squawking of birds, I could hear a language I did understand—the reassuring burp of Tupperware. It didn't matter that there were no credenzas and too much rice, these were my people.

Still, as Lu and I climbed the stairs of the party house, I was suddenly self-conscious. The chatting had stopped and everyone was staring at us.

I looked down, out of embarrassment, and saw the arrangements on the table weren't floral. They were plastic, or more specifically, polyethylene slag, a World War Two by-product, bought up and made fabulous and indestructible by Earl Tupper. But this was Tupperware like I'd never seen—unrecognizable shapes in unfamiliar colors—purples and roses and deep turquoise-blues, rather than the pastels and vague fluorescents I was used to. The items were arranged and stacked in a design that defied gravity—until I waved at everyone, careening my Balenciaga into an elaborate, architectural, yet burpable, structure, and demolished the whole thing, sending bowls, cups and covered ice trays flying.

I moaned in horror as I watched one bowl execute a rubbery bounce all the way down the steps, boomerang off the roots of the banyan tree, and ricochet toward me. Then everything went turquoise.

Chapter Twenty-five

When I came to, I was lying on my back in a puddle, my black dress splattered with mud, front and back. Lu, laughing, helped me up, leaving my hat in the mud. Someone gasped. Of course. My demon hair. I rammed the filthy hat back on, making everything worse. I shook myself off, got up, and, shaking my head, met her on the stairs.

Lu took my hand, led me back up and turned to the women, speaking in Indonesian. I caught a few words: "United States, Tupperware Salesperson of the Year. 1987 through 1995!" How she knew this, I'd never know. There was another long speech, including the name "Brownie Wise," which made them all laugh. Then, in English, "Please welcome Cyd Redondo."

"Redondo Travel," I whispered.

"Of Redondo Travel."

There was laughter and applause and many of the women put their hands together in front of their chests and faces and bowed their heads. I did the same.

"I am so, so sorry about ruining your gorgeous arrangement. Please tell them, Lu!"

The women nodded. "Nothing lasts in Bali," Lu said.

I picked up a deep red Slim Drink Container with Pour Safe Seal that had landed upright on the stairs. "Except Tupperware."

"Except Tupperware. Maybe."

"Is there anywhere to clean myself off?"

"I suggest standing in the rain and letting gravity do its work."

"You're kidding, right?"

"No. Think of it as romantic."

It might sound romantic, but in reality it just turned me into a mosquito buffet. Still, I got most of the mud off. After I'd repositioned my hair and hat with my now fawn-colored gloves, I realized I couldn't see my Balenciaga.

Not on the ground, not on the steps. It was bad enough that it must have gotten drenched, but gone?

The last five minutes seemed like a sweepstakes win next to losing my purse. Every inanimate object I treasured in life, including my dad's Wilcox Crittenden compass, was in that bag. It had never really been out of my sight in the four years I'd had it, at least while I'd been awake. And I'd never be lucky enough to get another one.

And then I heard a collective "ooohhh" and saw it, miracle of miracles, safe, dry, and sitting on a table in the middle of the room. I almost fainted with relief.

I dripped my way back into the room, dodging children as they collected rolling sippy cups and cookie cutters.

Lu came up beside me and pointed at my bag. "Your bag is worth more than these women make or see in five years."

"I know. Me, too, really. I couldn't afford it. It was a gift."

"Or," Lu said, "for the purposes of today's Tupperware recruitment, it might be something you rewarded yourself with after a couple of good party years." She winked at me and asked the women to bring me my bag. I was instantly surrounded by the swish of silk and the smell of new Tupperware, which beat new car smell, any day.

Lu clapped her hands and we all gathered around a woman who was taller than the rest, with a calm, regal demeanor. I sat next to Lu, hoping she would translate, as the woman moved toward the Tupperware table. She lifted a beautifully carved bowl, and handed it to the woman nearest to her, who took it, put a few rupiahs inside, and passed it on.

Having been a Catholic all my life, I recognized a collection plate when I saw one. I elbowed Lu. "How much?"

"Whatever you can spare. We donate so our newest member can have a full set of whatever they need. We do this every meeting for one of our guests. Tupperware is too expensive, sometimes, for young wives."

"What a great idea!" I put in a large handful of rupiahs as the bowl went past, which helped with some of the women who were still glaring at me. I decided to look at the stacks of Tupperware as the collection plate went around.

The idea of a purple lidded salad bowl almost gave me a nosebleed. I was trying to do currency exchange in my head on several of items, when I heard my name.

"Perhaps before we begin, we can have a few words from our illustrious guest."

"Me?" Even after five years of Toastmasters, I still hated public speaking. And what could I possibly talk about?

Lu shoved me up and said she'd translate.

I took a deep breath. "I believe in Tupperware."

I let that sit there for a minute, scrambling for the next thing to say. I saw a little girl hiding behind her mother.

"I have been collecting it since I was ten years old and I use it every day."

I proceeded to explain that I gave it to all my clients. I opened my bag and pulled out a few of the smaller items I never left home without. Then I talked about some of the games, giveaways, and food we had at our parties. And after Lu cleared her throat, I added that the extra income from selling Tupperware had allowed me a few special luxuries I couldn't have afforded otherwise. It wasn't a lie. Exactly.

"Thank you again for your kind hospitality and apologies for my clumsiness. I am pleased to call you all sisters in the slag." God, I hoped Lu left that part out, it probably sounded even worse in Indonesian.

Then, the presentation began and it was full of wonders, several I didn't completely comprehend, including a mini, three-level Tupperware steamer and, believe it or not, a wok. A Tupperware wok. I can't even.

I managed to get my purple nesting salad bowls, the small stacking steamer in turquoise, and a tiny Little Mermaid sippy cup for Barry and Angela's child. I might have to ship them home, but it would be worth it.

Once everyone had chosen their items, it was time to eat and chat.

Many of the women understood a bit of English and I could catch a few words in their language, but the missing parts didn't matter. It's like I tell my clients—if there's enough goodwill and desire to communicate, you will. When in doubt, laugh.

And laugh I did. Of course, it was easier to connect with women I hadn't had to hide from in the boys' bathroom for most of seventh grade.

Every Tupperware party I'd ever attended at home reeked of embarrassing history and old rivalries. I thought about all the spite at the heart of Angela's baby shower and felt awful. Having a baby was a brave act, no matter how annoying a person she was. And Barry loved her. I should have been kinder, just because of that. I vowed to be a better person when I got home, like most people did at least once while they were on vacation.

Right on cue, I heard a baby gurgle and turned to a particularly adorable specimen on one of the women's laps. He was grinning and slapping his chubby arms against his thighs. "What a gorgeous baby," I said. "How old is he?"

Lu asked the mother, then told me, "Ninety-one days."

"May I?" I held out my arms and the woman handed the baby to me. I saw her give Lu a look. I held him up and for some reason, I thought about Roger Claymore, of the Raisinet eyes. If we ever had kids, which was about as likely as a quick pick Mega Millions win, I hoped they'd have his eyes.

The baby giggled and so did I, as I settled him on my hip. Then my phone rang from inside my bag.

"Lu? Can you see who it is?"

She reached into the bag then looked up. "Says Mom."

I kissed the baby's head and went to put him down on the rug.

Every woman in the room screamed.

Chapter Twenty-six

I gasped as the baby's mother hip-checked me. In one movement, she dove for her wriggling bundle of love, reached under him in the inch between his bottom and the floor, scooped him into her arms, and tossed him up to another woman, who caught him before the mother did a face-plant on the rug. I bent to help her up, but she glared at me and refused my hand.

"Oh my God, what's wrong?" I turned to all the staring women. "I am so sorry! What did I do?"

Lu started laughing, then caught a few looks from mothers and stopped, leaning in to whisper, "Balinese babies can't touch the ground until they are 105 days old on the Balinese calendar. In some communities, even longer."

"Are you kidding me? Why?"

"Many reasons. For one, it keeps demons away from them until they are strong enough to fight them off."

"How do they learn to crawl?"

"They learn once it's safe."

I got Lu to apologize for me, again, saying I didn't understand and that this was a new idea to me. At home, we were always putting them down on the carpet or on the grass in the backyard.

The women looked horrified. "Poor, poor babies," one woman said. "Were you put on the ground?"

"I absolutely was," I said. "Lots."

I heard a collective "Ah," then the child's mother, who apparently spoke English, patted my arm. "We will leave offerings for you."

"That is so kind of you. Thank you. If you will excuse me for a second, I need to call my mother."

"The woman who put you on the ground?"

"Yes. I'm sure she didn't know what she was doing."

They all shook their heads as I walked down the stairs. At least it had stopped raining.

"Mom?"

"Cyd. Hope you're having fun."

"I am. I'm at a Tupperware party."

"In Bali? You know we all think you have a bit of a problem, honey."

"Why are you calling? I thought you didn't want me around."

"Well, I hadn't heard from you about Gerald."

I have to admit, I was a little annoyed that she was pestering me, considering. "That's because I don't know anything yet."

"Oh." It was her disappointed voice.

I went straight from annoyance to guilt. "I'm working on it. I talked to someone who knows people in law enforcement. I'm seeing him in two hours. Okay? Are you three having fun?"

"You bet."

"I'm glad, love you."

But she was gone. I took a couple of deep breaths and tried to imagine my mom diving to the floor or sliding into first to save me from demons. I thought about her in that tall, thin house on 77th Street full of Redondos and realized that's exactly what she'd been doing for the past twenty-eight years.

By the time I got back, the party was breaking up.

All in all, it was a fabulous afternoon and I was sad to leave. It turned out the party's host was Lu's sister, Amisha. She bowed to me as we were leaving.

"I hope to see you again, dear Cyd. You are good for Lu, this is the happiest I have seen her in a while. She has been quite low of late."

"I'm so sorry. Why, if you don't mind my asking?"

"Our family has plans for her and they are not the plans she wants."

"I can understand that. I have a difficult family myself."

"If there is ever any work she could do for you, to create some distance, that would be much appreciated."

I thought of the nightmare of Sister Ellery and wondered whether Lu might want to work in Brooklyn. But why, aside from the humidity, would anyone want to leave Bali?"

"I will think about it."

"That is kind."

"Not half as kind as your inviting me here today. Best Tupperware party ever, and from me, that is saying a lot."

"Yes. In many ways, plastic is ruining Bali. Isn't it strange how, when it's formed properly, it brings people together."

Lu, bowls on her head, gestured to the Kijang. I looked back at all these women who'd welcomed me, and who just wanted to connect and to keep their chilis fresh. I waved to everyone, and got into the Kijang. I felt a bit bereft.

"These women are so lovely. You are lucky to know them."

Lu shrugged. "Most of the time. They were in good moods today. They escaped their husbands and got out of the house. When there is no

Tupperware, the gathering is usually what I think Americans call a pity party?"

"Right. It's interesting that here, it's the way it was in the U.S. in the beginning, women finding a way to work without their husbands realizing it. And how much that can mean."

"We have to be more secret, but it is the same."

We shared a look as she pulled out into the roller derby that was Bali traffic, looking at her watch. "We have an hour. Perhaps a quick look around Ubud?"

I nodded. She parked off the road near a line of shops and stalls, encircled by layers of parked scooters and pedestrians.

First, there were the street markets. Since it was the rainy season, many of the stalls were covered with sunflower yellow umbrellas. Lu pointed out several art galleries I'd have to come back to when I returned.

We passed a used book store. I saw a few books in English in the window.

"Do you mind if I run in here for a minute?"

"I will get us a health tonic and meet you back here."

The bookstore was the darkest, coolest place I'd been yet in Ubud. It had row after row of books stacked floor to ceiling. There was no way I was going to find what I was looking for on my own, so I hoped the owner spoke English.

He did, grudgingly. I asked if he had a field guide for Balinese birds.

He reassessed me. "MacKinnon's guide?"

"Yes!" I was sure that was the one Stu had mentioned. The owner's accent was much like the Dutchman at the Hanging Vines. It gave me pause for a moment, but after all, the Dutch had taken over the island for decades. There were probably a lot of ex-pats here.

He disappeared behind several stacks of books and emerged with a bloated paperback with three painted birds on the cover. It wasn't new and it wasn't cheap, but I wanted to know something about the songbirds before the competition, or at least identify the ones in the trees around me, so I took it.

"Thank you, sir."

"You here for the birds, are you?"

"Partly," I said. "Cyd Redondo, Redondo Travel."

We shook hands, he wrapped the book in brown paper, and I managed to slide it into a side pocket of my bag without too much disruption.

I walked back out into blinding sun, then clouds. Lu emerged out of a sunspot with two plastic water bottles full of a bluish liquid.

"This was made specially for you."

At this point, I would have taken anything she handed me.

"You must shoot it," she said. "One, two, three."

We both shot the stuff, which was syrupy and spicy and almost made me pass out. "Wow, that tastes like a tonic, all right. What's it for?"

"Vagina tightening."

I did a dry spit-take, as the offending tonic was already down my throat and headed for its destination. "What the hell? You're kidding, right?"

"Am I? You won't tell me who the man is, but it's clearly somebody. He'll appreciate it. Or she."

I looked at my watch. "We should go."

"It's not Scott the pilot, is it?"

"Absolutely not. Why?"

"No reason. Watch out for him, and remember, don't mention the Tupperware party."

Chapter Twenty-seven

She was still laughing when she dropped me and my luggage off at the helipad. I watched her drive away. It was hard not to think about Scott and my tonic once he and I were in copilot proximity, flying into more threatening clouds, this time headed west.

To give him credit, the only thing he'd said about my bedraggled appearance was, "Aren't you hot in that?"

"Black doesn't show wrinkles as much."

"Want to tell me why you're on the run?"

"You were right about the ex-pats. Actually, you downplayed it. A couple of them broke into my room."

He swore in what sounded like Balinese. A few times. Then I told him about the conversation with my mom and how worried I was.

"So, have you found out anything about Gerald what's his name?"

"Before I tell you, just remember, it's dangerous to punch your pilot in flight."

"Oh God."

"Do you want to wait until we get on the ground?"

"No, I need to know. Besides," I said, jerking on my seat harness, "I'm restrained."

"I'm not entirely sure you're restrainable."

"Stop it. Tell me."

"All right. It appears that Gerald Browne, not his real name, was a courier."

"I'm assuming not a mail courier."

"No. Drugs. Of course. The detectives think he was killed because he didn't make his delivery. They thought he might have left the drugs, I'm sorry to say, with your mother. Or hidden them in her luggage. That's why they brought her in again."

"Again? She didn't say a thing!" I grabbed my armrest to keep from standing up. "Turn around. We have to go back to Denpasar."

"Calm down. She's fine. They don't really think she's involved, they're just keeping an eye on her, partly for her own protection. Jill's Adventures has a good relationship with the police—they have to—and she's handling it better than you could. This is a country of relationships."

I tried to imagine Jill landing in Bay Ridge and trying to organize last-minute typhoid shots and took his point.

"So do you think those guys at the Hanging Vines were looking for the drugs in my luggage?"

"Well, your name's Redondo, too. Maybe they think she handed them off to you."

I thought for a minute. "Honestly, Scott, if the police think drug dealers are after my mother, I'd rather be in Denpasar. Can we go back?"

"I promised, if there were anything to worry about, I would tell you. She's with her friends, the police are keeping an eye on her, and they've told her to be cautious. There's nothing you could do that's not already being done. Besides, the police are trying to improve their reputation. They're not going to let tourists get hurt if they don't have to." He saw my face. "My friend promised to let me know about any developments."

"Did your friend say there was any evidence? Any clues to the murder?"

"They found an American cigarette in the alley, but that doesn't mean anything. We'll talk more about this, I have to concentrate for a minute," he said, as a gust of wind almost turned us sideways, threatening whatever part of my tightening tonic might still be digesting.

Finally, we were horizontal again and I could see what I figured was the Bali Strait ahead, and a savannah below. "Is that the national park?"

"Part of it. Can I ask you something? Why did you want to come out here? I mean, aside from escaping the ex-pats?"

"My archenemy is here somewhere and I'm hoping to stage a stealth attack."

"In West Bali?"

"Yes."

"Do you know where?"

We were descending. In the distance, I saw a distinctly blonde haircut.

"Shit!" I dove into Scott's lap to keep myself out of sight.

He just looked down at me. "I take it that's her. You know staying at the same place is not the height of stealth."

"If you say she's cute I'm in a position to do you some permanent damage."

"Nah, I hate blondes."

"Bless you. Now, what do we do?"

"She just got into a Land Rover, so maybe she's doing some sightseeing. You might have time to check in while she's gone. Do you have an alias? Do you need help with your luggage?"

"Are you just going to leave me here?"

"Well, I was. Why? Do you want me to stay?"

I nodded. "Can you?"

"You know what that means?"

I thought I knew what it meant.

"You're covering parking costs," he said. I let out a breath. He laughed. "We'd better hurry."

Chapter Twenty-eight

Happily, Reggie had arranged everything and told the proprietor what was happening, so he was fine with my checking in under an alias, as long as Redondo Travel spelled the resort name properly when recommending it. That seemed cocky, but I wasn't in a position to argue.

The porter helped me to the room and himself to a hefty number of rupiahs, while Scott dealt with the whole helicopter situation. Why had I come here? What exactly did I think I was going to do? I sat on the bed, tightened, and half-cocked.

Scott knocked and I let him in. We stood looking at each other in yet another astonishingly gorgeous space made for romance.

"Don't worry, I'll sleep in the tub," I said.

"Don't get ahead of yourself. I ordered some room service. Why don't you tell me what the hell is going on with the blonde before we negotiate sleeping arrangements?"

"Will you check in with your police contact while I call my mom, first? I can't talk or eat if I can't breathe."

I picked up my cosmetics ziplock and headed to the bathroom with more fricking petals, and sat on the edge of the bath to try Mom.

"Hi. What's wrong?"

"Why didn't you tell me the police brought you in again?"

"I didn't want to worry you."

I sighed. "Well, it didn't work. I've spoken to my friend and he says the police think Gerald was a drug courier."

"That's ridiculous. Drug dealers don't wear suits."

"I'm not even going to favor that with a response. They think he was killed for not making his delivery. That he might have tried to get the drugs through Customs by putting them in your luggage."

"Oh. I'm sure that's not true."

"Well, you told me you let him rummage through your luggage to find your aspirin."

"I didn't say rummage."

I held the phone away from my mouth, Tina Turner style, in case I screamed. "Great. Great, Mom. For heaven's sake, you're not supposed to let anyone touch your luggage, ever."

"Yes, well, we all make mistakes, don't we? Like Barry Manzoni?"

"Point taken. All right, please be careful, and as soon as I know anything more, I will let you know. Love to Madge and Bea Ann."

I came back into the main room. Scott confirmed that his friend had eyes on the three women. They'd just had a spa day and were going dancing.

"Dancing?"

He took one of my hands and squeezed it. "Breathe. She's okay."

"Thank you." I squeezed back.

"All right. Sit and please spill the dirt on the blonde."

"This is a story that requires pacing." As I zipped back and forth between the TV and the hemp couch, I told him the longish story. When I got to the part about Peggy and Chip Jessup laundering money through air trays and Peggy giving my mother a trip, then abandoning the three women, he was up and pacing, too.

"Okay, she must be punished. What can I do?"

"I think my plan was just to punch her smug nose, but that's not going to do any good, is it?"

"Not long term."

"I have to take her down for good. First, I have to find out if she's actually here on vacation, or if this is one of her sinister agendas."

"Do you want me to go undercover? It's going to be hard for you. You don't exactly fit in." Suddenly, I felt tightening. Was it the tonic, or Scott? Either way, it was a sign I didn't want Peggy anywhere near my pilot. "Can I think about it for a minute?"

"Of course." There was a knock on the door. "That must be room service."

He opened the door.

It wasn't room service.

Peggy fricking Newsome—in sarong surround—stood in the hall.

Chapter Twenty-nine

"Cyd Redondo! What a coincidence! I thought you weren't a fan of *Eat, Pray, Love*."

"I'm not."

She blatantly looked Scott up and down. "Well, you've certainly managed to find your bit of rough, at least."

I saw Scott ball his fist before he said, "I beg your pardon."

I put my hand on his arm. "This is not my piece of rough. This is Scott."

"I'm her private pilot."

"I bet. Anyway, how's your mother? I was so happy to be able to give her a chance to get out of town. It's so ironic that she has a daughter who's a travel agent and yet she's always stuck in that gothic monstrosity with all those old people. Of course, I guess your uncle makes it out to the track."

This time it was Scott who stopped my balled fist.

"Actually, I'm glad I ran into you, I've been trying to reach you about my mother and her friends—Bea Ann North and Madge Dupree?"

"Doesn't sound familiar."

"Well, you sold them both your 'Eat, Pray, Fall in Love' tour. They traveled with my mother?"

"Did they? So she didn't bring you with her? I guess that's understandable. No one wants a wet rag along."

"No, they don't. And no one wants to arrive in Indonesia without reservations, either. Evidently someone in your office booked the hotels and tours on the Balinese calendar, rather than the Western one, so their reservations were for weeks ago."

"The what? The Balinese calendar? What are you talking about?"

I looked at Scott. "I rest my case."

"They were charged for everything because they didn't call to cancel. I assume since it was your office's error, you'll be taking care of those fees."

"Well, I don't see how that has anything to do with me. Every client is responsible for signing off on the arrangements. And even if it was an error, surely we can sort that out once we all get home."

"Actually, I have an invoice right here." I pulled it out of my Balenciaga. I'd typed it up before I left the office. "I've already submitted an invoice with a complaint to the ATA, so if you don't pay it, you can take it up with them."

"I spoke to Doug at the ATA only yesterday and he didn't mention it."

"Bureaucracy, probably."

"I doubt that. We have a relationship."

"Your blow jobs are irrelevant in this instance, Peggy. I've invoiced Patriot Travel, but perhaps you'd prefer DD&D LLC?"

Her face went completely white. It was the first time I'd ever seen Peggy on her back foot and I wanted to savor it. She tried to restore her face, with moderate success.

"I don't know what you're talking about, but give it here, I'll pay it." She snatched it out of my hand. I had my confirmation, at least. She was the one buying up property on Third Avenue.

"Good. Thank you. I hope you have a wonderful trip." I shoved her toward the door. She looked back at Scott.

"Let me know if want to upgrade," she said, and left.

I turned to Scott. "See?"

"Yeah. What are you going to do now?"

"Find out what she's up to. At least I don't have to waste energy hiding. Any ideas?"

There was another knock on the door. We both sighed.

"Room service, sir."

Scott opened the door. A man in a white Nehru-collared shirt and tan pants stood outside with a tray.

"Thank you. I'll take it." Scott looked at me.

"Oh," I said, handing him an unknown number of rupiahs.

Scott brought the food in. Suddenly, the room was filled with a horrible, "rats dead in the wall" smell.

I opened the window. "Holy crap, what is that?"

Scott laughed and uncovered a plate filled with a huge spikey oval the size of a pineapple. It resembled some kind of medieval torture weapon. "Oh! Durian. Ha! This is great. Reggie must have talked you up, they sent this specially for you."

Scott held on to it with a large fork, then took a knife and split it in two, revealing something that looked like lard. The stench quadrupled.

"What the hell? That can't be a food," I said, backing up toward the open window.

"Oh, it's a food, all right. In fact, it's a delicacy here. Only available a few times a year. It is something of an acquired taste. But you did say you wanted to experience the real Bali, right?"

If it had just been me and the odor urchin, I would have run for the hills. But I couldn't look like a wimp in front of Scott and besides, he was right, I had to take the weird with the beautiful. I nodded and let Scott cut off a small piece of the beige glob. He held it up to my mouth. This might have been sexy, if I weren't gagging. Maybe it would taste better than it smelled. Nope. It took everything I had not to vomit.

He took one look at my face, burst out laughing, and then leaned over and kissed me. Really kissed me, making me swallow the hideous stuff. That only made him laugh harder and I guess all of the tension I'd felt since I arrived let loose and before I knew it, I was laughing and Scott was on top of me on the four-poster bed, smashing the red rose petals into the white linen.

Chapter Thirty

I decided not to worry about the petal stains as my arms went around him. His mouth moved to my neck and I arched backward, pressing myself into him for a few seconds. Too few. Then, I stiffened and pulled away. Roger. What about Roger?

"What is it, Cyd?"

He pulled me up and we both leaned against the headboard. "I didn't mean to push, but your face, trying to eat that disgusting stuff, it was just irresistible."

"Wait, you don't like it either?"

"How could anyone like that?"

I slapped his arm and shook my head. "I'm sorry. I didn't want you to stop. I can't tell you how much I didn't want you to stop. But I have a kind of on-again, off-again beau and I don't know if we're on or off at the moment. I just, you know."

He scooted an inch or two away from me. "Got it. Promise me something? You'll let me know if it's ever off?"

Well, he sure wasn't making this easy.

"I will. Thanks."

He kissed my hand and got up. "Well, now that your cover's blown, want to look around? I could use some actual food."

"Good idea. I am getting a free room to publicize the place, so I should probably see it without a hat shield. Give me a second." I headed into the bathroom to fix my face and douse myself with Avon bug spray. It smelled better than Off! and definitely better than the durian. As I came out, I spotted Scott tossing the torture appetizer out into the garden.

We locked the windows and doors and headed out.

Like the two hotels I'd seen so far in Bali, it was spread over a garden property, with a central building for the lobby and restaurant. In the distance, I spotted a Land Rover, two Kijangs, and a van parked outside. Just past them, was Scott's helicopter.

"It's safe there, right?"

"Of course. It's Bali."

From what I'd seen of Bali, I didn't feel that confident, but as Sister Ellery told me, I worried too much about everything.

I kept my eyes peeled for Peggy as we wandered down the stone walkway to the main building. It was gorgeous, but it also felt like a historic resort that had recently been "spruced up." The more we walked, the more corporate sheen I saw.

According to my clients and travel agent colleagues, it was always the too-perfect floral arrangements, the faux suede "not quite a blanket" at the bottom of each bed, and electronic dance music played a little too loudly in the lobby, that gave away a "boutique" hotel that was actually owned by some behemoth multinational entity. As I'd only stayed in two private properties in Bali, I didn't know all the signs yet—until I accidentally stepped on an offering that didn't squish.

I was horrified. I knew it was super disrespectful to step on offerings, even if they were in the middle of the road. I reached down to restore it to its rightful place and stopped. It was plastic. I held it out to Scott.

"Son of a bitch."

"Is this their version of eco-friendly? More plastic?"

Scott stared at the artificial flower, lifted it as if to throw it into the fountain. He reconsidered and put it in his pocket.

My horror was only reinforced when, once we entered the lobby, I noticed a plaque that read "Paradise, a WOCAM International Resort." I froze.

"What?" Scott put his hand on my back.

"It's just I've had some dealings with WOCAM before."

"Positive dealings?"

"What do you think? Have you heard of them?"

"They built a huge place down near Kuta beach. And they're doing some stuff in Australia, up near the Great Barrier Reef. From what I know, they specialize in sneaking into protected properties in the guise of promising responsible eco-tourism and money to put back into preservation."

"And do they?"

He held up the plastic lotus flower. "What are the odds?"

"That's what I thought." I glanced at the unmanned—or unwomanned—desk. "I just want to wait here a second. I need to introduce myself, even if they're evil. The devil you know, right?"

"Okay, I'll go get us a table. Drink?"

"Whatever you're having. Actually, not if you're having beer."

He grinned and headed toward the sound of clinking wineglasses and forks. I guess the corporate entity wasn't so big on guests eating with their hands.

I wandered around the lush lobby, collecting brochures. I arrived in front of the flat-screen TV on the wall and stopped to watch what turned out to be a promotional film for the West Bali National Forest. Then the film cut to the most gorgeous bird I'd ever seen. The subtitle said it was a Bali starling. The one Stu had talked about.

The starling was a snowy, almost arctic white, with a Lone Ranger mask of cobalt blue skin around its black eyes, an Andy Warhol quiff of white hair—in a good way—on its head, and just a tiny hint of black at the end of its tail. The voice-over noted that there were possibly only seven left in the wild. Seven! What had happened to the other three?

Everything Stu had said was true. There was a bit of hope at the end of the film, though, as apparently it bred well in captivity, and many zoos still had starlings, which they hoped to reintroduce into the wild. There was even a Pre-Release Center near the hotel. But in my experience, once a bird—or a person—could only survive in captivity, it was all over but the shouting. Or in this case, singing.

The film was just restarting on its loop when a thin, fidgety man in a tropically challenged suit returned to the desk. He gave me an irritated look, the kind I'd been trained in my Hospitality 101 class not to give a guest.

"Yes?"

"Cyd Redondo, Redondo Travel."

"I'm the Guest Liaison." His name tag said Franz, but who wanted to say that out loud?

"I just wanted to thank the management for having me. And perhaps arrange something at the National Forest for tomorrow?"

"That requires a guide. You can't enter the forest on your own."

"Well, if it's not too late to arrange it, a guide would be great."

He sighed. According to Brooklyn College's Extension Program, sighing at guests was also discouraged.

I wanted to do two things the next day. Have a meeting with the property manager, and visit the starling Pre-Release Center. The concierge said that the birds moved inland to breed and even the most avid bird-watchers rarely saw one in the wild.

That was disappointing, but understandable, so I thanked him and said I'd still like to do a bit of a tour around the park, preferably not in a heavy snake area. He wrote something down, then said a guide would meet me after my meeting with the resort manager.

Then Franz looked me up and down. "I assume you brought trekking attire?"

"Of course. Palazzo pants."

He sighed, again. How could you be this unhappy and annoyed while you were living in a resort in Bali? Honestly.

"We have some for purchase. I'll see if we have anything in . . ." He looked me up and down. "Your size."

Okay, I might disguise myself and punch him later. "That would be fantastic, thank you so much. By the way, do you know if Peggy Newsome is going to be touring tomorrow as well? We're from the same hometown in the U.S."

He perked up. "You know Ms. Newsome? Isn't she fabulous? So elegant! She's one of our new investors and we're all so thrilled. That must be great, to live in her orbit, as it were."

"Yes. It's divine." I hated him.

"Unfortunately, she has a board meeting tomorrow, so she won't be in the park. We have a host of VIPs arriving."

"That's too bad."

"Should I give Ms. Newsome your regards?"

I stopped myself from suggesting he give her a sip of strychnine. "No, that's all right, we've seen each other already. Thank you again for your help."

"My pleasure. Please be in the lobby no later than nine."

"I will, thanks."

I headed into the dining room, where Scott had secured a table that overlooked the beach. At least the corporate decorator couldn't curate—i.e., ruin—the flicker of moonlight on the waves. That was all Bali. Scott had chosen yet another cocktail that bordered on a performance piece, this one with rum, coconut, floating flowers, and something called mangosteen.

I took a sip of the drink and moaned. "Is that a fruit?"

Scott laughed. "Yep. They have those in Oz and New Zealand, too."

"So, do you live in Australia? Or here?"

"I was born here, went to Australia for school, joined the police there. I'm back because my mother needed some help."

"Well, that's incredibly kind and responsible of you."

"Is it?"

"Isn't it?"

"I guess. It's complicated. Speaking of mothers, have you talked to yours?"

"I'm not allowed to call."

"Why?"

"It's a long story."

"My favorite."

He ordered two more drinks, so I told him. His reaction was the perfect combination of amusement and concern. I was getting more and more nervous about sharing a room and not throwing myself on top of him.

I felt like I was doing all the talking. His turn. "Are you going to tell me about your mom?"

"There's someone she wants me to marry. I haven't gotten around to it."

Chapter Thirty-one

My stomach dropped. "Gotten around to it? Does that mean it's imminent?"

"I mean I haven't gotten around to telling her no."

"The woman, or your mother?"

"Both. I don't want to let either of them down. It's complicated."

"I understand."

"Do you? Have you ever been married?"

"Not anymore, according to the Catholic Church. I mean, briefly, but now I'm what I guess you call an 'annulée' rather than a divorcée. Try explaining that on a date. And I had to move back home. So there's that."

Scott clinked my glass. "To families."

I clinked back. "Any chance you want to come with me to the preserve tomorrow? For some bird-watching? I've booked a guide."

"I have to fly back for a client."

"Oh."

"But I can come get you Thursday morning and take you back to Ubud. Your new room will be ready then, right? Will you be okay here? I mean with that bottle blonde around? Is she a twitcher?"

"That is such a loaded question."

"I meant a bird-watcher. Speaking of." Scott grabbed my hand and nodded at a green bird with a perfect pink neck, drinking from one of the fountains.

"The birds here," I said.

"Yeah."

We charged the dinner to the room. I would have paid for it, were it not a WOCAM property, but I did leave a cash tip for the server, since I didn't trust he would get it, otherwise.

"I'm going to call my office. Meet you back in the room?"

"Sure."

I watched him walk away and took the moment to consider my options. I was crazy attracted to Scott. At least on the surface, there didn't seem to be anything wrong with him. But I'd thought that about Roger too. Roger. Maybe I should try to call Roger and see if we were still meeting in Paris.

I checked my pocket time zone converter, then called his cell phone. A woman answered. A woman who sounded like she had yoga arms. I almost dropped my phone in the fountain. Just as I was hanging up, I thought I heard Roger's voice in the background. I was such a moron.

By the time I got back to the room, Scott was sitting on the couch, a blanket over him, all his clothes on. I put down my purse and saw he'd lit all the mosquito coils. He was the perfect guy. I'd just made another stupid decision.

"No, Scott, let me sleep there, seriously. It's my fault we aren't sleeping in the bed."

"Nope. Don't want to lose my cred if you're ever in an official off period with this other guy."

I didn't sleep at all. I don't know whether Scott did. After tossing and turning for a couple of hours, I arranged a couple of mosquito coils in lantern position so it wouldn't wake him, and took out my *Field Guide to the Birds of Java and Bali.*

Not only was it four hundred pages long, it documented four hundred and eighty-three birds. Four hundred and eighty-three. And those were just the ones on Java and Bali. Who knew? There were gorgeous painted illustrations, grouped by type or species or something. So many of them looked similar or had at least half the same name. There were fifteen flycatchers and twelve bulbuls. I mean bulbuls! How was that for a name? And so many starlings and mynahs, which were apparently two names for the same species. How did Stu Capistranis tell them all apart? Especially in those dark market stalls?

Then I found it. The Bali Starling. And I knew its number now. 445. I could remember that one, at least.

I finally heard Scott stirring. He looked kind of dopey, which made me like him more. We had a room service breakfast together and then I walked him out to the springy helicopter pad. No tar, for once.

He kissed me on the cheek. "Be careful out there."

"I will. Will you check in with your detective friend?"

"Absolutely. See you at nine tomorrow morning?"

"I'll be ready." I stayed to watch him take off. He waved before he disappeared and I couldn't tell whether I felt bereft or relieved. Both, probably.

I went back to the room. Even though I knew I shouldn't, I tried to call my mother. It went to voicemail. I didn't leave a message.

There was a knock on the door. So far, that had resulted in Peggy Newsome and durian. What now?

Something almost as bad. Franz's "gift" of clothes, all of which were hopelessly unflattering. Does anyone look good in khaki anything? At least they might keep monkeys and snakes away, by their sheer ugliness. I needed to wear something more professional to my meeting, so I put the trekking clothes in my purse, along with my sarong, to change into later.

I decided my palazzo pants would be business casual if I paired them with a silk tank top and high-heeled sandals.

It was a gorgeous morning. Until I saw Peggy. She was laughing with a group of men in suits as they headed toward the Land Rover. One of them had a decided limp and looked like he wasn't used to wearing a suit. There was something familiar about him, but I couldn't place it. As he was getting into the Rover, two Indonesian men in shorts ran up to him. He handed them something and they ran off. I waited until the Rover had left the parking lot to head into the lobby.

Happily, Franz was not in sight. Instead, someone dressed like an American executive assistant welcomed me and showed me into the main office. The open windows sported stunning views of the ocean and the savannah behind. There was a model resort on one of the tables, showing a major expansion of the existing villas, plus new pools, a small marina, and a new helipad. It looked like there wasn't going to be much park left.

I was trying to figure out how much when a small man with too much hair and not enough upper lip entered the room. His suit was almost as nice as one of Reggie's, but didn't fit through the shoulders or hips. Monsieur Phillippe, as he asked to be called, welcomed me and offered me a coffee, which, out of politeness, I accepted, though I'd already had five.

"We are delighted to have you here, Mademoiselle Redondo. Franz tells me you are acquainted with Ms. Newsome and her company?"

"We live in the same city, we're in the same business. Everyone knows everyone."

"Ah. You must be an *enfant terrible* if you are in competition with her and are still in business."

"I try," I said. "So she is involved with the new resort?"

He laughed. "She very much wants to be. She is here, I think, on a trial basis."

So for once, Peggy wasn't on top. What did that mean? "Ah. So, if this works out she might relocate here?" And leave Bay Ridge.

"*Oui.* She would come like a rocket. It is an expression."

"*Oui*, it is."

Maybe this was the chance I was waiting for. Peggy out of Bay Ridge? It was awful she might ruin the resort, but better this than Third Avenue.

Unless she was after both?

I walked over to the model resort. "Tell me more about the expansion you and your partners are planning."

He curled what he had of a lip. "It will be the most exclusive resort in Bali."

"And the greenest?"

"Positively chartreuse."

"It sounds *extraordinaire*. Very much a place my most exclusive clients would love. Who are your partners?"

"WOCAM is made up of a series of companies. We have partners from the UK, from Australia, and a series of partners in Southeast Asia, of course."

"Is that the prospectus?"

I reached for it. He pulled it away and put it on his desk. "Oh, it's all still proprietary, I'm sure you understand."

"Of course. Well, then I'd love a tour and of course if there are any renovations or additions you are allowed to talk about, I'm all ears."

He escorted me out into the gardens. He didn't seem to know anything about the plants or flowers, but knew every villa's square footage, amenities, and in terms of pricing, he was a walking currency exchange and, as far as that went, a man after my own heart. He showed me the lovely pool area, rife with carved fountains. It seemed dull compared to the one at the Hanging Vines.

Back at his office, I pled jet-lag and asked if I could trouble him for one more cup of coffee before I left. Happily, I snagged a prospectus and put it in my Balenciaga in the twenty seconds it took him to duck his head out the door.

When he walked me out, there was a man standing there who said he would be taking me to the park entrance, where I would meet my private guide. He basically pushed me into the vehicle, so I had no time to change clothes or question the situation.

We drove a bit further inland, where I could see both dense areas of trees and wide grasslands. It was one of the only places I'd been so far in Bali where I didn't see a rice field.

We pulled up next to the entrance, where the man handed my ticket over and the ranger asked me to wait. I pulled out my travel-size bug spray, since I hadn't really had time to prepare for a trek.

I could already hear fifteen birds I'd never heard before. After I had doused myself, I reached into my bag and pulled out my *Field Guide*, as if that was going to help. I was on the kingfishers when a man in cargo shorts, a pocketed vest, and a backpack exited the gate. I recognized his hat.

Chapter Thirty-two

He stopped. "Ms. Redondo?"

"Mr. Capistranis." I smiled. "What are you doing here?"

"I think I'm your tour guide. What are you doing here?"

I held up my *Field Guide*. "You inspired me."

"I mean why are you in West Bali? Just checking out the island?"

"Partly. For my clients. But just between us, my archenemy is staying here and I'm trying to figure out what she's up to."

He snorted.

"I know that sounds melodramatic, archenemy, but it's really not."

"No. I understand. Archenemies are real. It's just, you sounded like our mutual friend just then."

"Well, that's terrifying."

"May I ask who this enemy is?"

"Not that it would mean anything to you, but sure. It's a woman named Peggy Newsome."

"The ditzy blonde? The WOCAM woman?"

I stared at him. "Yes. How did you know?"

"Our friend warned me to keep an eye on her."

I had told Hazelnut some of the Peggy Newsome stories, but what could she possibly have to do with endangered species? Besides wearing them?

"You've talked to Mr. Alias?"

He nodded. "There's something going on out here. A new influx of poachers. We're both worried about the starlings. And the white-rumped sharmas."

"And the straw-headed bulbuls, right?"

He grinned. "Yes, and the bulbuls. And this company wants to expand onto park land, to 'preserve' it. Which gives them an even less safe habitat, not to mention more jerks tramping through here."

"So they're getting it from two sides."

"Yeah. The weird thing is that Hazelnut, well, he can be paranoid, but he thinks the two might be connected."

"The poachers and the developers? How?"

"Something that happened in London. He just says he's working on it."

"That is weird. Well, I wouldn't put anything past Peggy. Though she's not usually the outdoorsy type. So does that mean you're undercover here?"

"Yes, and no. I do freelance guided bird tours here for money, but I asked for this weekend. There's some kind of powwow about expanding the resort. Plus, with the competition coming up, there are too many buyers in Bali. Some of them are here. There's one Hazelnut is particularly worried about. So it's prime poaching time. Are you up for a bit of undercover work yourself?"

"Of course. What do you need me to do?"

"Follow me. You don't mind walking, do you?"

"Of course not. I dressed for it."

We headed toward a thin trail, one with high grasses that kept catching my flowy pants and nicking my ankles. Were there ticks in Bali? I decided to believe the birds ate most of them. We arrived at a clearing with a view of the sea. The terrain was completely different than the jungles I'd seen near Ubud.

"This looks like Africa."

"You've been to Africa?"

"Tanzania. That's where I met Hazelnut."

"How did you meet him, anyway?"

"He tied me up and threw me in the back of a FedEx truck."

Stu laughed. "Typical."

"I know."

I thought I heard a new kind of bird. My heart leapt. "I guess the chance of seeing a Bali starling is pretty much nil, right?"

"I know where two of the nests are, but we shouldn't get anywhere close. If they feel the nest is compromised at all, they abandon the eggs. This population can't afford that." He must have seen the disappointment on my face. "I have really good binoculars, though."

"Are the birds in the Conservation Center breeding, too?"

"We've let them out in the wild for their breeding season."

"But aren't they safer at the center?"

"Theoretically, yes. But they're much more likely to choose a mate and breed properly in the wild. Captive bred birds keep the species alive, but they're just not the same. It's like comparing a VW Bug to a Ferrari. No offense to Volkswagens, if you have one."

"None taken. I drive a V8."

"So not actually an eco-tourist, then?"

"I'm easing myself in," I said. "Is there a way to keep track of the birds once you let them out?"

"Kind of. We got funding to chip a few, but not all. There's never enough funding for anything that's important."

We both heard the rumble of a vehicle in the distance. Stu sped up. As we moved into an area with denser trees, I heard the trilling and peeping birdsong again. "Is that a starling?"

Stu stopped and nodded upward.

"Where?"

He nodded again.

"Okay, I know it's rude to point in Bali, but in Brooklyn it's like a condiment. Where the hell is it?"

He pointed. On a tree branch above us, a bird was staggering back and forth like someone who'd had four too many margaritas. He wobbled on the branch and almost fell.

"Oh God. Is he all right? Or she?"

"It's a male. Orange-headed thrush. The males go into a trance when they sing."

We watched him. Then we saw him flap his wings and try to fly away. He seemed to be stuck.

"Dammit," Stu said.

"It's bird lime, isn't it?"

He stared at me. "How do you know about bird lime?"

"I'll tell you, but we have to help him, first."

The branch was about eight feet up, which we might just be able to reach if we were Shaquille O'Neal. Stu looked around for anything that might serve as a ladder.

Having been stuck in bird lime myself, I couldn't bear the idea of this poor thing weaving around like an inflatable tube man outside a car wash. "Between us we could reach it."

Stu considered the situation. "Think you could hold me up?"

I snorted. "No chance. I think I have to be on top. What do you bird guys use to dissolve it? There's an antidote, right?"

"Not really. We just try to pull them off as gently as we can."

I looked up at the tiny bird. I was so afraid I would hurt it. I reached into my Balenciaga and found my travel-sized tub of Vaseline, hooked my bag over my shoulder, and looked at Stu. "How do you want to do this?"

"You can leave your purse down here. It's not going anywhere."

"That's what you think. The bag stays with me."

"Okay. Your choice. I apologize in advance for any awkwardness."

"It's okay, it's an emergency."

He squatted on the ground, holding on to the trunk of the tree. "Climb on," he said.

At least I wasn't wearing a sarong.

I put my legs on either side of Stu's shoulders. Once I was situated, he grabbed the tree to stand up, then gripped my thighs to keep me stable.

"You feel pretty strong."

"Kickboxer. Three-year champion Fort Hamilton and Bay Ridge. Not afraid to use my skills and you are right in the middle of my danger zone."

"Message received."

I used the trunk for balance, then put my hands on the branch as he moved me up and closer to the thrush. The poor bird was frantically trying to get away, but the bird lime held. I felt like a monster. The closer I got, the more he started crying out in unmelodic panic. His tiny, pumpkin-latte-colored head shook back and forth. He wasn't going to let me get near him. I wanted to punch whoever had done this.

"Stu! How can I calm him down?"

"Since you've got your bag up there, do you have anything you could put over him? Any kind of fabric? That sometimes works."

Well, of course I had fabric. Who did he think he was dealing with? I always had two scarves with me.

"Cotton or silk," I asked, hoping he'd say cotton.

"Silk, it's lighter."

"I need to be a little bit closer." He moved me down the branch.

I steadied myself with my left hand and reached into my Balenciaga with my right. I finally located the only Hermès silk scarf I'd ever owned—85% off at Loehmann's 2001 Blowout Sale—and lowered it down over the frantic bird.

It seemed to calm him a bit, at least long enough for me to rub his tiny feet, or claws, or talons, or whatever they were, with Vaseline. I was just about to try to grab him when he detached and flew away. With my scarf.

I watched it flutter and land somewhere in the grasslands beyond—I hope on top of something that would appreciate the craftsmanship.

Sid gave a whoop.

"Great job! What was that?"

"Vaseline. It works on beach tar, so I thought it was worth a try. Will he be okay? Won't he try to come back here? Is it his territory?"

He thought for a minute. "Probably."

"Should I cover the branch with Vaseline while I'm up here?"

"Better for us to cut it down, it's evidence. Plus, we may need that stuff again. If there's bird lime here, it's probably all over the forest. How flexible is the branch?"

I gave it a shake. "Not very. Not at all."

"Got anything sharp in that red bag of yours?"

"A pair of cuticle scissors and a nail file. How about you?"

Even though I was still balanced around his neck, he managed to reach into his backpack *à la* Indiana Jones and whipped out a metal case about five inches long. He snapped the case open and shook out a collapsible ten-inch saw.

"Holy crap! I need one of those!"

"Be prepared."

I laughed. Somehow he managed to hand it up in a "safe scissors" way, so I grabbed the handle and tried to remember what my Uncle Ray had told me about the smartest way to cut wood. I missed him. And I still wanted to do him proud, so I whacked the teeth hard into the branch and started to saw. It was going to take a while and Stu was going to have to hold pretty tightly on to me to keep me stable. Otherwise it would be me falling onto a ten-inch saw.

Stu didn't let me, or the saw, down. After three long minutes, I had cut through enough of the four-foot branch to break it off myself. "Incoming," I yelled as it fell to the ground.

"Hey, Cyd?"

"Yes?"

"Good job."

"I try."

He was just about to lower me down when I heard a gunshot.

Stu fell to the ground, taking me, ass backward, with him.

Chapter Thirty-three

"Stu? Oh my God, Stu, are you okay?"

I could see blood, but I couldn't tell where it was coming from, because I was upside down. Happily, I hadn't landed on the saw. Just when I was about to sit up, another shot flew over us and shattered a branch about ten feet away. There were animal cries. Then silence. Finally, we heard that rumbling motor start up again.

I helped Stu shuffle behind the tree. The rumble got fainter. Who had done this? Were they gone?

"Why don't you tell me what the hell that was while I check your leg?" His thigh was bleeding, but not as hard as it would be if they'd hit the femoral artery. Still, in this climate, not good. At least my bag hadn't been shot. I pulled out my Jack Daniel's, my Band-Aids, a small bungee cord, and my cotton scarf—this was why I always carry two. I pressed the scarf, hard, until it seemed like the bleeding had slowed a bit.

Stu looked pale.

"Can you lift your leg a little?"

"Ow!"

"I know, sorry. Here." I hooked the bungee cord around his thigh a couple of inches above the wound, as it was the closest thing to a tourniquet I had.

"This looks like a flesh wound, through and through. You don't feel a bullet in there, do you?"

"No."

"Okay," I said, as I screwed the top off the airline liquor bottle. "This is going to sting."

I was careful to use only half of the whiskey, as, given the way the morning had been going, I might need the rest. He winced, but didn't squeal. I used a tiny drip on my finger, then I pulled out my emergency Neosporin, an Always mini pad, which I knew from experience could absorb a lot, and anchored it with three of my biggest Lion King bandages.

He hadn't said a word the whole time. I finished cleaning everything up and replaced what was left in my bag. "What now?"

"What about you?"

"What about me?"

"You're bleeding from the head."

I felt my forehead. It was wet. "It's nothing. Head wounds always overbleed."

"At least let me put one of those Band-Aids on it." He did.

"What are we doing?"

"They're after the starlings. We need to go."

"Can you walk?"

"Of course!"

I offered my hand. He grabbed it so hard I almost fell down. He gave a loud groan and sat back down.

"You need a crutch. Don't move, I'll find something." I dug around and the only thing that was even close to long enough was the branch I'd just cut down. The one covered in bird lime.

"This is the best we have, but you're going to have to be careful. Should I Vaseline it?"

"No. I'll be fine. But if I'm using a crutch, you'll need this."

He took out a tiny gadget with latitude and longitude points, almost like a living map. He programmed something in, then handed it to me. "We're headed for that red dot," he said. "Just in case I pass out or something."

Of course, his underarm immediately stuck to the branch, but at least that kept it stable. I collapsed the saw, put it in my bag, and led the way, heading toward the red dot. The little machine alerted me when I got off course.

I had to hand it to Stu, he kept up a pretty good pace for someone in a world of pain. I would have been sucking down aspirin like Tic Tacs.

We were both listening for the rumbling motor and I jumped at least once at what Stu said was probably a wild pig.

Finally we got close. Stu pointed to a stand of trees and we moved there for cover. He leaned against the tree, reached into one of his vest pockets and pulled out a pair of binoculars, then pointed to a tree about thirty feet away. I kept listening for a rumbling that wasn't porcine, but only heard a *Living Planet*–esque soundtrack.

"Listen," he said. I did and, after adjusting to the baseline of birdsongs, I heard it. A different song. I pulled up the binoculars and finally caught sight of it. The starling.

The bird sat on a high branch doing possibly the most adorable hop up and down—accentuated with a rhythmic quiff lift—I had ever seen. It seemed to be answering another bird.

How lucky was I? I was one of the few people in the world who'd actually seen a Bali starling in the wild. I looked at Stu and grinned. I could see that his bandage was getting more bloody. I would need to change it soon.

"It's okay, right? The starling?"

"That's the male. The female is probably in the nest. Or out getting food." He leaned back and took a deep breath. "I was really worried the poachers knew where the nest was."

Another birdsong started and I watched the starling answer it. It must be the female. Then I saw it. A flash of cargo short. I panned up to see a hand holding a cheap cell phone. The starling jumped down a few branches. I zeroed in on the hand, which punched a button and the second song started again. It was a recording. No! I grabbed Stu's hand.

The bird hopped down once more and I heard him squawk as a net grabbed him.

"No! Stu!"

Stu looked up. "Bastards. If it's not bird lime, they play a mating call to lure them out."

The poacher, with a bowl haircut worthy of Moe Howard, put the bird in a small cage and stashed it in the back of the ATV we'd failed to see. Then he headed for another stand of trees.

I jumped up.

Stu pulled me back down, whispering at the top of his lungs, "These guys are armed. You can't just run out there."

"I could pretend I was lost. Men always believe women when they say they're lost."

"Yeah, but they probably already saw you with me, and dressed like that, you're not exactly unnoticeable. Plus, you're a redhead. Everybody notices that here."

"My head was up in the branches. What if I put on different clothes?"

"It's still too dangerous."

I thought about Roger and Grey Hazelnut, and what they would do if they were here. I opened my Balenciaga and started pulling unflattering items out.

"Cyd, don't. Seriously."

"Look, not to put too fine a point on it, Brooklyn girls are not endangered. There are millions of us in the wild. There are only seven Bali starlings and they just grabbed one of them, which is going to make it six if I don't do something. Plus, the gear is kind of camouflagey. I can sneak up on them." I took a quick, binocularized view of the periphery. "Okay, close your eyes."

In the end he looked away while I traded my tank top for an army green

T-shirt, which was too tight, and then some army-issue cargo pants. My hair. "Can I wear your hat? It might help." I grabbed it and my bag. Which looked very red. "Give me your vest." It was just the right size to drape over my Balenciaga.

"Stay here."

"Cyd, please be careful."

"Don't worry. There is no way in hell I'm dying in this outfit, with a Lion King Band-Aid on my head."

"At least take off those shoes!"

"No way! I might have to run."

Happily, as it was the rainy season, there weren't a lot of crackly leaves. My heels sank into the mud, silently. Still, I was pretty exposed, so I did quick trots from tree to tree as I got closer to the ATV and its captive. There were a few birds in cages on the back, but I'd kept track of the starling cage. I was seven feet away and in the open when a Kiki Dee and Elton John Top 40 duet burst from my bag.

Chapter Thirty-four

I reversed behind a tree, and turned the phone off, but it was too late. The bowl-cut poacher jumped in the driver's seat, while the other man, a bit taller, with straight black hair and a cowlick, shot twice in my direction. Then they were on the ATV and gone. Dammit. Why hadn't I remembered to turn off my phone? I looked back at Stu.

His feet were sticking out from behind the tree. He wasn't moving. If he was dead, it was my fault. Or Debbie Pinkowski's fault for convincing me to put our standard duet at Yo-Yo Ma Karaoke as the ringtone on my phone.

I came around the tree. Stu was flat on his back. I couldn't see any blood. I squatted down and checked for a pulse. I almost cried when I felt one. I rubbed his hand.

"Stu? Stu? What happened?"

Nothing for a moment. Then he shot up. "What? Did I pass out? I must have passed out."

"I thought you'd been shot again."

"There was shooting?"

"You didn't hear the shooting?" He shook his head. "Or anything?"

"No. Are you okay? What happened?"

After I told him what had happened, he asked me to help him up.

"Did you see the mother? The mother bird?"

I shook my head.

"We need to check on the eggs."

"Let me change your bandage first."

"No, there's no time."

I helped him hobble toward the starling's tree. His hobble seemed worse. We stopped about twenty feet away.

Stu pointed. "See that hole about a foot below the biggest branch? That's it. That's the nest. We need to stay here and see what happens. Most likely when she sees her mate is gone, she'll take off."

"And leave the eggs? Why would she do that?"

"Most birds do this if anything's been near the nest—bees, geckos, rats. Starlings especially. They're 'flight or flight.'"

"But what about the chicks?"

"They need two parents, one to guard them, one to get food. Even in the best circumstances, out of three or four eggs, usually only one chick survives."

"That is pretty much the saddest story I've ever heard. Do they know they're endangered?"

"Do we?"

"Good point."

I made sure he was settled against the tree and finally convinced him to let me change his bandage while he kept watch. Suddenly, he straightened up.

I turned to see my second ever Bali starling. She flew around the tree and neared the nest, where she hovered for a minute. Then, with a loud peep and a frantic flap of her wings, she flew away.

"Damn." Stu sighed.

"She's not coming back?"

"No, Cyd. She's not coming back."

I insisted we wait for a bit, just to see if she might return. But she didn't.

I couldn't believe the starling could abandon her eggs. I hated when animals died or ate each other on PBS. My Uncle Leon mocked me, but I wasn't big on the whole circle of life thing. I thought about how lucky I was that my mother, who was only twenty-two when my father died and could have easily left me with the Redondos and gone off to have a real life, had stuck with me. I hoped she was okay.

I took the binoculars from Stu. "Can you feed them by hand? I mean, they must do that at the Conservation Center."

"Sometimes. It's tricky, but possible."

"But we have to try, right?"

"How do you propose to get the eggs out of the nest without breaking them? They're really fragile, you know." He gestured to his injured leg. "And I can't hold you up this time."

"There's got to be a way. Provided I can get them down in one piece, what do we need?"

"Some kind of padding." He looked down at his leg. "I'm guessing your scarves are gone."

"Yeah, well, I usually don't need more than two in one outing. Will cotton balls do?"

"Maybe."

I laid my collection of cotton balls and makeup pads aside.

"But we have to find something to keep them in. They'll need to keep a consistent heat. About ninety degrees Fahrenheit."

I pulled out my new mini Tupperware steamer. "What do you usually do to keep them warm when it's not ninety degrees outside?"

"I usually put bean bags in the microwave, then put them under the nesting material."

I mentally added bean bags to the "things that must be in my Balenciaga" list. "I could turn on my phone and put it under the cotton. If it's enclosed in Tupperware, it should stay warm enough."

"This is all moot unless you get them down."

"I know. I'm thinking."

The banyan roots were the size of a Smart Car, not that I had ever seen one. There wasn't a car in Bay Ridge that couldn't eat a Smart Car for brunch.

I was assessing how high up the hole actually was when I saw movement in the tree. Slinky movement.

"Stu? Do snakes eat eggs?"

Chapter Thirty-five

"Snakes?" He looked up and saw it. "Shit. That's a blue krait."

It got closer. "But it's black and white."

"Semantics. Venom is venom. Do you have anything in there you could throw at it?"

I hated to lose my new *Field Guide*. Could I survive without my phrase book? Well, if the snake landed on me, I wouldn't need it anyway. I knew from my research that fifty percent of blue krait bites were fatal and they didn't have any antivenom on Bali.

I grabbed the phrase book out of my Balenciaga and ran toward the tree, where the snake was in the process of unfurling, too close to the nest.

I had spent so much of my youth being chastised for throwing like a girl, that I had, much to my brousins' shock and chagrin, gone to softball camp. I lifted my arm, sighted my prey, and hurled my entire collection of facile and overused Indonesian phrases at him. I heard a loud thump and then a more alarming scramble in the leaves near my feet, along with an extended hiss reminiscent of Ska in *The Jungle Book.*

The snake regarded me. I stayed completely still, but tried to give it the look Sister Ellery had given me when I talked in algebra. It inched forward. I made my eyes as dried up, bitter, and sex-deprived as I could, which, frankly, wasn't that hard. It curled backward and eased away from the banyan tree and from us. I removed my shoulders from the top of my head.

By that time, Stu had hobbled his way over. He looked even more pale. I thought we had stopped the bleeding. It must just be the pain.

I patted his arm. "I think it crawled the other way, but keep an eye out while I'm climbing. Your crutch is your weapon."

Once I couldn't see or hear the snake, I went back to get my supplies—which included my emergency tube skirt. There was no way I could do what I was going to do in pants, however loose. I told Stu to close his eyes again and changed. Then I took off my shoes.

"Okay, ready."

"What exactly are you going to do?"

I held my stilettos up. "Who needs better crampons than these?"

I couldn't just throw, I'd also learned to climb trees to get away from the men in my family and a few neighborhood German shepherds. I put my bag over my shoulders, gripped the shoes and used the heels to hook into the knots of the banyan tree. At least Stu was on the other side of the tree, so no one but insects and snakes were below to be flashed by my turquoise Cosabella thong. I had hoped, in paradise, someone other than warrior ants might see it, but at least I was wearing one.

I footed my way up the tree and neared the nest hole. I tried to wrap my legs around the trunk, but it was too fat and the wood was more slippery than the oaks and sycamores of my youth. To get to the nest, I was going to have to approach it from above. I cramped my way two feet higher, threw my legs up, and landed most of me on the branch.

I looked down at the hole where Stu had said the nest was. Would the mother bird really not come back? Was there a snake in there already? It didn't matter, my new motto was "no starling left behind." I'd seen my brousins crack too many boiled eggs with a knife to trust my stiletto heel as an exploratory device, so I edged the rounded part of the sole on the end of the hole, in hopes it would coax out anything inside. Then, I waited.

Finally, I shone my mini-flashlight into the hole. It was filled to the brim with layers on layers of tiny twigs and, nestled on top of what looked like sprigs of green grass, there they were. Four turquoise eggs, just a shade lighter than my thong. I gasped.

Stu rallied below. "Are they in there?"

"Yes. They look okay to a non-starling expert."

"Do you see any grass in the nest?"

"Yes."

"That means they're almost ready to hatch. The parents bring the grass in to regulate the humidity right before they're born."

"Is that your passive-aggressive way to say hurry?"

"If possible."

But how the hell was I going to get them out, intact? If I could lift out the nest, that might work. I gave it a tentative tug. It was wedged tight. I was going to have to find a way to get the eggs out on their own. While balanced on a branch.

I needed something I could edge the eggs onto, then lift up and out. I briefly considered my thong, but it was the mesh kind and I was worried it wasn't substantial enough.

Then, I had an idea. My padded balconette bra. Two eggs each side.

"Stu? Could you close your eyes one more time?"

"What is this, *Showgirls*?"

"Animal activists watch *Showgirls*?"

"Lots of nights in cheap hotels. What's coming off now?"

"Padding."

"Let me do a snake check first." He beat his crutch around. "Okay."

You never knew when you might need to do a *Flashdance*-style bra removal in a tree, so it was good practice.

Eventually, I got it off. It was a lilac Chantelle with pink trim. I would hate to lose it, but as long as the eggs didn't break, it was hand washable.

I put the straps around my wrist and tried to lower the cups into the hole. I had to put them inside each other to fit. I was going to have to put all four in one cup. At least I was a 32 E in European sizing. I had to squinch myself up against the branch to try to get one hand inside. I felt for the eggs. They were warm. As slowly and carefully as I could, I lifted them one by one into the fabric cup, trying to make sure they were side by side rather than on top of each other. Oh God, were they going to break before I even got them out? When I had all four, I took a firm hold on the straps and lifted the bra out, quarter inch by quarter inch, until it was free of the hole. I didn't realize I'd been holding my breath the whole time. I looked down. They looked intact. I let out a huge sigh.

"What's happening up there?"

"I don't want to jinx it, but they're out. The question is, can I get them down?"

I was too afraid to climb down the way I'd come up. If Stu had been mobile, I might have risked a short drop, but not in this situation. What I needed was some kind of pulley that could lower them down. What did I have?

I had a sarong.

Holding the eggs against the nest and gripping the branch with my legs, I wrangled the long piece of silk out of my bag, put the ends around the branch, and tied them together. The fabric sling hung within about five feet of the ground.

"Stu?"

"Yep."

"Do you think you can stand up and lean against the tree?"

He hesitated just long enough for me to know he was nervous about it. "Yep."

"Okay. I am going to safety pin the delivery system to the sarong, and then lower it down."

I saw him lean on the crutch and get himself to the tree. He was really pale and it was clear the tree was the only thing holding him up.

I dug around for safety pins and found enough to anchor the bra straps to the sarong. I tested it, and it seemed to hold.

"Ready?"

"Yep." Only a person in excruciating pain would use the word yep three times in a row.

"Okay, here goes nothing."

I took one end of the sarong and inched it up, which inched the bra down on the other side. This seemed to take about two hours. Finally, it was at the other end of the loop.

"Can you reach it to unpin them?"

"Just about." I couldn't look. "Got them!" Stu started laughing. "Four! This is the best Easter egg basket ever."

"Are they okay?"

"So far, thanks to you."

I untied the sarong, refolded it, and put it back in my bag, then began my braless, tube skirt descent. Thankfully, Stu was looking at the eggs instead of my thong. I reached the ground.

He managed a smile. "That was impressive."

"Extinction is the mother of invention," I said, pulling my new Tupperware steamer and my complete supply of cotton balls, half of the remaining mini pads, and two clean emergency thongs out of my bag. I put all this padding around the bra in the middle section of the three-piece container. I turned on my phone as a possible egg warmer. It dinged twice.

Both calls were from my mom.

"Stu? I have to make a call. Stu?"

He'd slumped away from me. That's when I saw the other bullet wound.

Chapter Thirty-six

The hole in his back was bleeding like crazy. He hadn't said a word. Had it gone through his lung? I ran over, grabbed the rest of my mini pads and put pressure on the wound until it started to clot a little. His leg was bleeding again, too. He needed an emergency room and the nearest one was back in Denpasar. This was exactly why I was nervous sending clients to Bali. I was just reaching for my phone when he came to.

"Oh, thank God. Why didn't you tell me they got you twice?"

"Tour guides are as common as Brooklyn girls."

I shook my head. "Should I call the hotel to send someone?"

"They'll never find us. Reach in my pack and get my phone?"

I did and handed it to him. He made a call and said someone would be here soon.

I held up my bra. "What do I do with these? Do they need more grass? Is my purse humid enough?"

"Don't worry. You just need to get them to the Conservation Center, where we met up. Ask for Juk. He'll know what to do. He's raised a few clutches there."

"And what if they hatch on me in the meantime?"

Stu shifted, then winced. "They won't, but if they do, they are usually okay for about twenty-four hours, while they're absorbing the egg yolk, so they're getting pretty good nutrition on their own at first."

"They eat their own yolk?"

He was rolling his eyes when we heard an ATV. And froze. I lowered the Tupperware into my bag. Then there was a high whistle and Stu relaxed. "It's my vet pal."

The veterinarian, Pauley, an overly tanned Aussie who had to bend down to give me a finger-crushing handshake, squatted to take a look at Stu. I liked that he didn't ask any stupid questions.

He stood up. "They're through and throughs. Didn't hit anything life-threatening, but you've lost blood and we need to get them cleaned out and pump you up with antibiotics. Is she coming with us?"

"We're dropping her off at the Conservation Center."

I gathered my things, and Stu's. "What if you need blood? I'm a universal donor."

"We have blood there."

"Human blood?"

He laughed. "Yes. I'm O negative, too."

I looked at the ATV, then at Stu. "Is that vehicle going to be safe for, you know?"

"Ah. Probably not. Do you think you can walk back?"

"If you tell me where I'm going."

"Here." He handed me back the red dot gadget and reprogrammed it, so there was a new dot. "Just follow that, it's only about a half a mile down the trail."

"Okay."

"Hey, Cyd, watch out for blue kraits."

"And cobras," Pauley added.

"Great, thanks a lot." I touched Stu's arm and put another business card in his pocket. "Will you call me later, just so I know you're okay?"

"Sure."

They headed off. I watched until they were out of sight, then followed the red dot. I only suffered about fifteen bug bites and faux-sighted about thirty blue kraits and five cobras, which turned out to be sticks, before I got back to the dirt track.

Finally, I saw the Conservation Center in the distance. When I got about a hundred yards away, I stopped, spooked. Did I still have Stu's binoculars? Yes. In all the confusion, I'd left them around my neck. I used them to zero in on a man with a cowlick who looked familiar. It was the poacher who'd shot at us—now in a ranger shirt. Waiting by the entrance.

Chapter Thirty-seven

Now I didn't know who to trust. Was Stu in cahoots with this guy? Surely not. He might take one flesh wound for the team, but not two. So, either the poachers had broken in and taken over the place, or they actually worked for the center and Stu didn't know about their felonious, pardon my language, asshat moonlighting job.

It didn't matter, really, because none of those scenarios made it safe for me to leave the eggs there. Like it or not, I was a starling stepmother for the foreseeable future. At least they hadn't hatched yet. I didn't know which made me more nervous, eggs or chicks. I could accidentally kill either. I backed into the brush until the poacher went back inside. I considered calling the hotel for a ride, but car plus pothole plus eggs seemed like a bad idea. I'd have to walk back. Carefully.

At least the weather had been dry so far, but it was still the rainy season and that could change any minute. I started back, not understanding why anyone went braless, ever, especially in a climate that made every day a wet T-shirt contest. I tried to stay on stable ground and mostly out of sight. Finally, I spotted the resort. I checked the parking lot. The Land Rover was back. I couldn't think about that now.

I was happy to see the room had already been serviced. I put the Do Not Disturb sign on the door and locked it.

I was about to put my Balenciaga down, when I remembered that babies weren't supposed to touch the floor. I knew these weren't born yet, and they weren't human, but I didn't want to even come close to jinxing them. I was terrified to open the Tupperware steamer, but I needed my phone. I checked the eggs for cracks, eased out my phone, grabbed a few blades of grass from my back patio to add to the padding, and closed the steamer. It had been an hour or so. I tried my mom. No answer. Just to be safe, I called Madge. She was not pleased.

"Your mother is a grown woman. It's so selfish of you to try to monitor her like this."

This was the second time I'd been called selfish in a week. Was I? "Look, it may seem selfish to you, but I missed two calls from her. I'm a travel agent and I know that Bali isn't a safe place. Did Peggy tell you they have a huge, and I mean huge, drink spiking problem?"

"Don't be ridiculous. Besides, it's about time she had a fling."

"A fling? With who? I mean whom? First she meets a stranger on a plane, who's murdered, and now she's going out with someone else? That doesn't sound like her."

"How would you know? Don't you understand, that's why she's here! To be a little bit irresponsible. That's why we didn't let her tell you, so she could just have some fun. Your mother is only fifty-one. Just because she had early menopause doesn't mean her life is over. In fact, it makes it easier to have a fling, because there's no chance of another accidental pregnancy."

We were both silent for a minute.

"Another one? Are you saying I was an accident?"

"Do you know anyone who's eighteen who really wants a baby?"

"The Virgin Mary, for one. Look, will you tell her I called if you see her?"

Madge sighed. "Fine."

I hung up. I really didn't feel a goodbye was in order. I knew Madge was bitter, but seriously, calling me unplanned at that moment was low, even if it was true. I needed some coffee, but I didn't want to leave the eggs unattended, or lug them around anymore. I was terrified they would break. So I ordered lunch via room service, then took a quick cold shower and sweated into the terry cloth robe on the back of the bathroom door.

I hoped Stu was okay. And Peggy was not. I didn't like knowing the Land Rover was back. But I did want to know which man had spoken to the poacher. Just then, Bea Ann called.

"Cyd? I heard Madge talking to you. I don't want you to worry. I'm sure your mother is fine and was just saying hi. The man she went to Ubud with is named Alistair Brush."

"The British guy?"

"I don't know. Do you know him?"

"He was in the room at your hotel when I arrived, removing a snake."

"Well, it's encouraging that there's someone who does that. So, just have fun yourself."

"Are you having fun?"

"Let's just say I haven't had to 'lower or shift my conceit of attainable felicity' yet."

I laughed. "Yeah, go ahead, go all *Moby Dick* on me."

"I'm a librarian in paradise, what did you expect?"

"Love you, Bea Ann. Talk soon."

I figured she wouldn't lie to me, but I still hated being on the other side of the island if Mom needed me. And I figured it wasn't that safe to keep the eggs here, with poachers only limping distance away. So I tried Scott.

I loved that he picked up right away.

"Hi. Any chance you could come pick me up sooner?"

"I wish I could. I'm in the middle of a private hire. Are you all right?"

"Yes, of course. Oh, I'm sorry to bother you. No problem. If I find another way back, I'll let you know."

"Okay. Just so you know, the police are moving away from your mom as a possible suspect."

"Well, that's a relief. Now she can have a real vacation. Apparently she went to Ubud with the snake removal guy for the island. Hilarious, right?"

"She's with Don?"

"No. Who's Don? She went with Alistair Brush."

"Who the hell is Alistair Brush?"

"He was checking our room for snakes when I got to Denpasar."

"Cyd, there's only one snake guy on the island. Don. Everyone knows him."

"Well, maybe he's got a new assistant."

"Don works alone. I've known him since I was a kid."

"Could Brush be a competitor?"

"No way. I'll make some calls. Did you get to see any starlings?"

"Two."

"That's amazing."

I didn't really want to get into the whole shooting thing with him when he was working.

"Okay, bye."

"Look, if there's any way the job ends early, I'll call."

"Thanks."

I looked at the clock. Was it really only noon? It had been a pretty intense half day. I needed coffee. And food that didn't smell like a morgue. I hoped room service wasn't on complete Bali time. I put on a light blue La Perla bra and an electric blue linen dress. As I picked up my purse to get tip money, I felt movement.

I was just starting to open the purse when there was a knock on the door. At least there was a peephole. I asked the man to please leave the tray outside. I would tip him later.

Once he was gone, I pulled the tray inside, took a swig of coffee, and, with dread, undid the snap on my Balenciaga. What would be inside? Scrambled eggs? I took off the top layer of the steamer and finally, after praying, which I was horrible at, lifted the lid.

There was a big crack in the egg on the top. Oh no. The one beside it had a crack, too. Great, I had made the world worse. I noticed something sticking out of the third egg. Oh God. Then it moved. It was a beak. Something was breaking itself out. A chick. Three of the eggs were hatching!

I watched as three tiny pink beaks pecked and pecked until the eggs cracked in earnest and they splayed out of them, releasing some liquid that might make the Tupperware unusable for broccoli in the future. I assumed this was the yolk Stu had said they would eat, so I tried not to think about it. Three of the chicks were alive, at least for now. I didn't know what that meant about the fourth egg. Was it just shy or behind, or had it not made it? I centered it in the most padded section, hoping its brothers or sisters wouldn't knock into it.

The chicks, probably no more than two inches long, were a deep wine color and featherless—except for a few tiny white "sticks" the width of dental floss sticking out. The babies' heads were almost as big as the rest of them, and defined by exaggerated V-shaped yellow lips inside their beaks. Or were the lips the beaks? Why didn't I pay attention in tenth grade biology? Their necks seemed to be made of a gelatinous substance incapable of keeping anything still. The wobbling made bobbleheads look rigid.

Then, all at once, they opened their mouths, pointed them up and began a tiny, high-pitched trill that went straight to the center of my heart. Stu had said they would be okay for a day without my feeding them, but would they? No way they were dying of starvation on my watch. What on earth did they eat besides afterbirth? I tried Stu, but no answer. I didn't have a number for the vet clinic. And of course, he thought I'd left the eggs at the center. Who else might know what I needed to do with these chicks?

Well, there was one person.

Chapter Thirty-eight

As much as I hated the idea of asking that traitor incarnate—Sister Ellery—for help, she was the only one who actually knew Grey Hazelnut, aka Ron Brazil, etc., and might have contact info for him. The tiny, head-forward chicks were peeping. I had to try.

I girded my thonged loins and called the apartment that should be mine but was currently occupied by Sister Ellery. No answer. What time was it in Bay Ridge? Was she at Strip Bingo? In desperation, I tried the Redondo Travel number.

"Redondo Travel, Ellery Redondo speaking."

"What the hell are you doing?"

"Cyd Elizabeth Madonna Redondo, watch your language!"

"No. I repeat, what the hell?"

"It's Redondo Travel. It doesn't look good if there aren't any Redondos here. How's your mother, by the way?"

"I don't know. I need something from you right now."

"You're not with her?"

"She banished me. Seriously. I need your help."

"Okay. Okay." I could feel her crossing herself. She still did it out of habit, I guess.

"Since you were friends and fake-engaged, I was wondering whether you have Ron Brazil's contact information."

"You know Ron Brazil doesn't exist, right?"

"Obviously I know that. I want to find him under whatever name he's using at the moment. Didn't you have a phone number for him? On the cruise? Just to let him know you were going to be late to break dancing or something?"

"No. He always just found me."

"And you have no idea whatsoever about where he might be or who might be able to reach him? Or his real name? Or any other names?"

She hesitated. "Nope."

"I'm going to have some dead baby endangered birds on my hands. It's a long story, but you know how hard it was for me to call. Come on. Please, this is all your fault."

"It's not all my fault."

"I wouldn't be here if you hadn't kept things from me. And some things have happened here that are not great." I took a breath. "Please. He's the only one who can help me."

"Okay, he once told me his real name is Bob Tibbet."

"Bob Tibbet! That's not a real name."

"None of his names are real names."

"I know that, but even he wouldn't use Bob Tibbet as a real, real name. It isn't even nut-related."

"That's what he said. His email is bobtibbet at gmail.com. All lowercase."

"Do you have a phone number?"

"He's going to be mad."

"No, he's not. Not when he hears what's going on." She was in the middle of the number when I lost her. I tried to call again, but my bars were gone.

I heard trilling. I looked at the baby starlings. I was about to close up the steamer and put them in my purse when I remembered they weren't eggs anymore. They might need air. It wouldn't be the first time I'd mutilated Tupperware for an endangered animal, but it would be the first time I'd ruined a piece I hadn't used yet. Then I flashed back on that cowlicked bastard jerking their father out of the tree, and used my cuticle scissors to take out my rage, *Psycho*-style, on the defenseless purple three-in-one steamer, cutting enough slits so the darling things could get some air. I'd just have to have Lu send me another one once I got home. Did they have Media Mail in Bali?

I cleared space for them in my Balenciaga, since there was no way I was leaving them unattended. I'd already had one hotel room broken into. I put on some lip gloss for courage, secured my bag on my shoulder, and headed to reception, for directions to their business center.

Franz seemed hesitant.

"Travel emergency," I said. After I threw around Monsieur Phillippe's name, the snippy receptionist caved and let me into the tiny space, which consisted of a beautifully carved desk dominated by an ancient cement-colored IBM desktop. I used the Redondo Travel account, subject "Bird Emergency—I'm with Stu," then typed in my cell number and asked him to call me as soon as possible, preferably in the next three minutes. As I seemed to have reception in reception, I reached Sister Ellery again and she re-gave me the cell number. Happily, the requisite fountain in the lobby was drowning out the occasional trill from my purse. I remembered I should erase the history from the computer. When I brought up the "recently visited" sites, I found a series of previous Google searches. They were all about Bay Ridge.

And me.

Who had been researching me? Peggy? It must be Peggy, because not all of the searches were just about me. There were searches for the deed to Redondo Travel and the date of transfer, but also about the ownership of the defunct Pet World and name of the executor—Robert B. Barsky—as well as the ownership papers for the Andersons' Dry Cleaning business at the end of our block. They were both, apparently, zoned for business and residential properties. I was just taking pictures of the searches when I heard voices bouncing off the sandstone. One of them was shrill enough to be familiar. I erased everything for the last three days and tried to log off.

"Yes, well, the model for The Glen should arrive today. You're going to love it. If it gets here, of course. That's one thing we are going to have to decide on—what delivery service to contract for here, if we're going to be in business together. Everything is so backward."

That was just like Peggy Newsome to walk into a place she didn't understand and slag it off.

Then, I heard a man's voice. "Don't I know it. The couriers are frickin' half-wits too." The voice had an undercurrent of South African, but some Jersey, too. Although I could have handled Peggy, I now had an overwhelming, starling-esque desire to flee or flee.

Of course, that damned little color wheel was still spinning. I knew if I didn't log out completely, whoever was researching me would have a little treasure trove waiting for them, including Hazelnut's information. It might even put the starlings in danger. The voices got closer.

The man raised his voice. "I lost a shipment three days ago. Still unaccounted for. Halfwit gave it to the wrong American woman."

Peggy laughed. "Well, that isn't hard to do. All these lumpy divorcées everywhere, dripping in Chico. Most of them were lucky they were even married long enough to be divorced."

I really hoped there was a special place in hell for travel agents who had nothing but contempt for their clients. Or just a special, especially flamey one for Peggy fricking Newsome.

She was still talking. "Of course, at least they got divorced. Not annulled like some people we know."

They both laughed. The spinning circle finally stopped and disappeared. I grabbed my notes and my purse and slinked to the door.

When I opened it, Peggy was right in front of me. Behind her was the man I had seen talking to the poachers this morning. The man with the limp.

The man in the suit that didn't fit. The man with the ski-jump nose who belonged in a bad wife-beater undershirt and low-slung cargo shorts, to show off his gut and putty-colored leg adornment, or whatever the current politically correct term was for peg leg.

It was Bunty Barsky. International endangered animal smuggler, born in Bay Ridge, ruined in Vietnam, and currently wanted by Interpol for, among other things, attempted murder. Of me.

Chapter Thirty-nine

I don't know which of us looked more surprised. Although Peggy must have told him I was here, he still looked shocked—about a fifth as shocked as I was. Half the estate lawyers in Bay Ridge, not to mention a host of Interpol agents, had been trying to trace him for months. Agent Graham Gant emailed me once about a spotting in Jakarta, but it had been a different leg-challenged animal poacher. I guess it was an occupational hazard, depending on what you were poaching. Frankly, I'd figured he was dead, since the last time I'd seen him, he was on his way to becoming a leopard/Komodo dragon sandwich. I'd love to hear how he avoided that luncheon meat situation, but not from him and not now.

It didn't matter. He was clearly up to his old tricks. Peggy, of course, dressed in a sheath dress the cost of Monticello, gave me a huge smile. "Cyd! We were just talking about you."

I was crazy aware of the chicks in my purse and willed them to be quiet. If birds had a second sense about when they were in danger, it should have been on overdrive.

Peggy grinned. "I forgot to ask. How was Angela's baby shower?"

"Lots of chocolate," I said. "I'm afraid I need to go. Lovely to see you."

"Don't be silly. You're on vacation. I don't believe you've met my associate, Mr. Tibbet."

I have to admit, I wobbled for a second. What? Wait, could this be Hazelnut? Not even he, the master of disguise, could gain ten inches of height and duplicate Bunty's mug. And if it wasn't Hazelnut, how could Bunty know about the name? What was going on? Had I just sent a bird poacher an email about starlings? For the love of God. At least, growing up with ten brousins, I had thirty-two years of screaming on the inside, while smiling on the outside. In that moment, it probably saved my life, as well as the chicks'.

Bunty held out his hand. "Robert Tibbet. Entrepreneur."

Franz, obviously eager to get in on the party, entered and moved to join us. "You look gorgeous as ever, Ms. Newsome. Miss Redondo, Mr. Tibbet is also one of our investors. In the resort expansion."

"Ah, are you? Yes, Monsieur Phillippe showed me the model this morning."

This was a battle of wills, but we probably would have joined forces to kill Franz.

I could feel the tiny trilling vibrations of Dewey, Hewie, and Louie, which was, happily drowned out by my phone. I'd put it in the side pocket, so I didn't have to do a Tupperware reveal. Unknown number.

"Client emergency, I'm sure you all understand. Nice to meet you, Mr. Tibbet," I said, backing out the door.

"Yes, I imagine you want to freshen up, too," Peggy shouted, as I headed out toward the garden. I got far enough away not to be overheard, but I was afraid if I went to my room, I'd lose reception again.

"Cyd Redondo, Redondo Travel."

"How did you get this number?"

"Your former fiancée."

"Which one?"

"The nun?"

"Ah. AntiChristine?"

"Yes, of course it is, you nitwit. Look, there's a lot going on, so I need to spit this all out and then you can talk. I'm in Bali. Stu Capistranis and I were checking on the Bali starling nests in the national park. We saw two poachers get the male, the female abandoned the nest and flew away, and the poachers shot Stu. Twice. He's going to be okay, but he's indisposed. He told me to take the eggs to the Conservation Center, but I saw one of the poachers in a ranger shirt there, so I took the eggs back to the hotel and they hatched about an hour ago. And, Bunty Barsky is here, he just saw me, and he's using the name Bob Tibbet, so I don't know what to do with that information."

"Son of a bitch."

"Exactly. First things first. These chicks. Stu said they'd be okay for twenty-four hours, but now I only have twenty-two and change. What do I feed them and where do I get it?"

"What's the bird again?"

"Are you even listening? The Bali starling. The Bali mynah. The only bird that's indigenous to Bali. The bird that's so important, it's on their fricking money. Up until this morning, there were only seven left in the wild. That bird!"

"Got it. How many eggs?"

"There were four. Only three have hatched. At least last time I checked."

"Three? That's amazing!"

"It's going to be amazing if they live. Help me. What do I need?"

I could hear him scrambling around. "I guess it would be too much to ask if you know the *Field Guide* number? All my files are organized around those."

"445."

"Are you just making that up?"

"No. I bought the MacKinnon *Guide*."

"Well, I am absolutely plussed. Okay." I could hear him scrambling again, but this time there were a few growls and squeaks in the background.

"Where are you?"

"Okay. I've got the info, have you got a pen?"

"Give me a second."

I inched the purse open to hear the trilling, thank goodness, and pulled out my tiny notepad. I balanced it on the top of the bag and moved my phone to my left hand.

"Go ahead," I said, licking my Putt-Putt pencil.

"For the first couple of days, bugs only. Crickets are best, but you have to pull the legs off or they get stuck in their throats."

"The crickets will be dead, right?"

"No, alive. Everything they eat has to be alive."

"I have to pull the legs off live crickets?"

"They have a high pain threshold."

"Really? And you know that, how?"

"I wrote a paper on it. The chicks eat mealworms, too, but for the first few days they can't handle the exoskeleton of the adults, so you'll need to sift through the worm basket to find the molted white ones."

"I'm not sure I heard anything after worm basket."

"Don't tell me you're one of those prissy girls. I thought you carried snakes in your bra."

"I was hypnotized, and who says prissy anymore? How old are you, anyway?"

"Old enough to know that Bunty Barsky is both smart enough and stupid enough to use one of my identities. I was hoping he was dead, but at least this way we can keep track of him. Does he know you have the chicks?"

"I'm not sure. I hope not, but I did see him talking to the poachers yesterday, so they know I was around. I think they were gone by the time Stu and I got the eggs down."

"Well, it's not safe for you to stay there. Get to Ubud. You'll be there in plenty of time to get crickets and worms. The songbird competition starts tomorrow, they'll be on sale everywhere."

"I don't have any way to get there until tomorrow morning."

He gave a long sigh.

"I'll be there in an hour."
"What? Where are you?"
"If I told you I'd have to kill you. I won't be myself."
"Yeah, well, I was expecting that. Will there be a safe word?"
"Heep."

Chapter Forty

Although any enterprise with Hazelnut was risky, I was relieved to be getting out of there, both for the sake of the chicks and for my sake, too. Of course, I couldn't go back to the Hanging Vines yet, could I? I'd have to call Reggie. And Scott. And could I manage to check out of here without alerting Peggy and Bunty to my whereabouts? I didn't want to be charged for rudeness. Heaven knows what those two had said about me to Franz or Mr. Phillippe.

First, I headed back to the room and made sure nothing had been messed with. Then, I checked on the babies.

The three that had hatched were alive and trilling. The other egg was just sitting there. At least it hadn't cracked. Maybe it had never fertilized. Hazelnut would know what to do. For all his faults, the one thing I could depend on was that he would do what was best for the birds, whatever that might cost him. Or me. But he was a realist and definitely had a stronger stomach than I did. After all, he'd once worked in a slaughterhouse for three months to get evidence of their cruel practices. I would have lasted about three minutes.

And he definitely had a kind of fatalism about people—something I guess Stu had, too.

Stu! How was Stu? He hadn't called me. God, he had been so brave, I really hoped he was okay.

And Hazelnut was in Bali. Or at least Indonesia. What were the odds? Just as I was thinking about him, he called back.

"I need photos of the resort model. From a few angles."

"I stole the prospectus. Isn't that enough?"

"Sometimes, AntiChristine, you are not unintelligent."

"Gee."

"But no. I need pictures for my government contact to prove they're going to violate national park rules."

"They're having their resort board meeting in that room right now. I can't get in."

"There are plenty of ways to interrupt a meeting. Are most of the people Balinese? If so, your hair might be enough."

"Very funny. No, they look Western."

"You'll think of something."

While I was thinking, I took the time I had left to go through all my stuff and make sure it was there. Everything was damp. I didn't know how anything ever got totally dry in this humidity, but I guess that's why all the Balinese people I'd met had the most gorgeous skin I'd ever seen. I'd just have to look at my time here as one extended, super-moisturizing spa day. Although nothing, including my "health" tonic, had done much to relax me so far.

I didn't know whether the palazzo pants would ever be the same, but I wasn't ready to throw them away yet—not if there were worms in my future. They were the closest thing to farming clothes I had.

I packed everything up as neatly as I could. The chicks might be jostled around less if they were surrounded by all the clothes in my carry-on, but they also needed to breathe and, though it had been months ago, I still remembered the horror of those parrot sausages rammed into my clients' Samsonite. At least in my Balenciaga I could give them occasional oxygen and keep hold of them at the same time. I checked the ticking chick clock—twenty-one hours and counting before I had to start on a feeding ritual.

I left Scott a message that I'd gotten a ride back to Ubud. I would call to confirm once I got there, just in case it fell through. Then I tried Reggie.

"Cyd! How lovely to hear from you. I was just about to call. We've had a cancellation and if you'd like to return this evening, your new, anonymous villa will be waiting. Well, not completely anonymous, Ms. Upright."

"That's such good news, Reggie, I cannot tell you."

"How have you enjoyed the Paradise?"

"It's a gorgeous spot. I'm a bit sad they are going to remodel and expand."

"Yes, I'd heard that. Pero would turn over in his grave, I imagine."

"The original owner?"

"Yes."

"Well, we'll have a talk about this when I see you."

As I hung up, I could see that someone was trying to open my door. I picked up a lamp and moved closer. Finally, the knob stopped turning. Had that been Hazelnut? Or Bunty? Or one of the poachers? I knew Bunty wouldn't want to blow his cover by acknowledging how he knew me, but he always had awful henchmen working for him, and I'm sure they wouldn't mind being recognized. You've seen one henchman, you've seen them all.

I went to the window to make sure they weren't outside. I was struck again by the heart-stopping beauty here and wondered how anyone could try to ruin it. Then I saw three large birds fighting over something on the ground. I knew how to get everyone out of the conference room.

Chapter Forty-one

I had four durians delivered by room service. Happily, I always had surgical grade face masks in my Balenciaga, since I needed the five-layer protection to get near them. I'd asked for a large knife, which I washed and sterilized with Jack Daniel's after use.

I was going to take advantage of the open windows in the conference room, which would not only allow me to place a series of stink bombs just outside, but also allow me to crawl in after the attendees fled. If they fled.

I was glad I'd kept Franz's "camouflage" gear, as well as my crushable hat, both necessary if I was going to place the fruits strategically. The smell would permeate everything. I couldn't lose another bra, so I was going to have to flop to the main building. At least I already knew which windows were nearest the table and the buffet. I donned a second layer of face mask, so as not to give myself away by gagging.

Where could I leave the chicks? I was going to jostle them too much. I had no choice. I always carried a flattened Tampax box in my purse, as no one wanted to go into that. Reconstructed, it just fit over the babies. I placed both in a drawer in the bathroom, after having done a thorough snake check. I taped a piece of my red hair over the drawer, locked everything, and headed out. It only took me about two minutes to distribute the pieces of durian. Now, I just had to hunch under the one window that had palm frond coverage and wait.

It didn't take long.

I have to say, it gave me some satisfaction to know Peggy caved first. "Oh. I'm sorry, I'm going to have to take a minute." I heard the door open and slam. That was followed by some coughing, a few more moans of horror, and chairs being pulled out.

Monsieur Phillippe went into full damage control mode. "I am so sorry, I have no idea what is happening. Please, please follow me, there's another room we can use across the lobby."

I heard a general exodus and finally, the uneven thump of a prosthetic foot. I thought everyone was gone, but I had to be sure.

I was about to ease up to look, when I saw a hand reach out the window and search for, then find, a piece of the durian. The man groaned in pleasure.

What could I do? I took a chance that he was Balinese, jerked off my hat, and jumped, growling, face masks, unfettered breasts, and red hair forward, right into his face. He screamed, dropped the fruit, and flew out of the room.

I scrambled in the window and took three quick pictures of the model. As I turned to leave, I saw another model labeled The Glen at Third Avenue. I felt some kind of horrible dread. I snapped pictures of that, too, jumped back out, and sped back to my room.

It was still locked and my hair was still in place. I unfolded the Tampax box, put the babies and the egg back in the steamer, and took another shower. After I'd put my dress back on, I threw the clothes I'd been wearing as far as I could get them into the underbrush. A flock of birds headed right toward them.

I checked on my own chicks again. The fourth egg had broken with no chick inside. I had to stop myself from sobbing. What kind of mother was I? Just then, my phone rang.

"Parking lot."

"What company are you with, sir?"

He sighed. "Heep. Heep Transport."

I double-checked the room, looked under every piece of furniture, shook the covers, and checked the drawers. I gathered my bag and carry-on and exited the patio door.

I was nervous I couldn't get to the parking lot unseen, but for once, there was no one there. Then, I saw Bunty walking toward me.

Chapter Forty-two

The old, animal trafficking Bunty. I wanted to run, but to where? So I froze as the bad shorts, balding pate, and oversized, ski-jump nose came toward me. I couldn't hit him with my purse, the chicks were in there. I reached for my pepper spray, then stopped as he got closer. This man didn't have a prosthetic leg. In fact, he was as bowlegged as William Peterson in *To Live and Die in LA*.

Hazelnut.

I grinned. "How's Howard?"

"Still only functionally extinct."

"Let's keep it that way. And what's with the outfit?"

"If he's going to steal my identity, I'm going to steal his." He held out his hand. "Bunty Barsky at your service."

"Well, at least I can call you something now instead of 'Hey, you!'"

He shrugged toward a helicopter, which looked like Scott's. It was. My heart did a little leap. He waved from the cockpit.

I turned to Hazelnut. "You and Scott know each other?"

"I hired him for the day for something else. He didn't seem to mind coming here." He raised his eyebrows. "You know Claymore is having a baby with his old girlfriend, right?"

I almost crumpled to the pavement. "No. That can't be right. He can't be. He asked me to meet him in Paris next month." Hazelnut shrugged. Oh God. A woman had answered his phone. Would he ever, ever be straight with me? About anything? And I had turned down Scott for him. Some vacation this was turning out to be. I looked at my watch. I was on a mealworm deadline.

"Let's go."

Hazelnut looked back at the resort. I turned, too, and saw the suited group gathered in front of the main building. Hazelnut hurried me toward the chopper.

"Hey! Slow down! I have precious cargo. These poor things," I said, "they aren't even five hours old. Are they going to survive the shaking this thing is going to do?"

"The road would be worse. And takes a lot longer. Let's get in and we'll figure it out."

He helped me up. There was Scott, grinning. "Of all the choppers in all the resorts in all the world, you climb into mine."

I blushed. Hazelnut rolled his eyes.

"Enough with the Romeo stuff, we have a physics problem." He turned to Scott. "Find me a bike helmet."

"You know I'm a certified pilot, right?"

"They aren't for us."

Scott nodded, jumped down and ran toward the hotel.

Hazelnut leaned in. "Can I see them?"

I opened the Balenciaga and lifted the steamer out of the inflatable neck pillow I'd been using to try to keep them padded and still. I eased the container open. They started to trill. They were alive. All three of them. I had placed lots of fabric and cotton pads around them along with mini pads and a hand towel from the hotel bathroom. One of them was still on his tiny back, flailing a little. Hazelnut righted him with the gentlest touch, ever. He looked up at me. "You're not really supposed to touch them, but I couldn't leave him like that."

"I would have done the same thing."

He surveyed the setup. "Not bad, AntiChristine. Not bad."

He reached into his own duffel and pulled out what looked like a World War Two helmet. "These are made to withstand a lot," he said. "If we can put them in a bike helmet, inside this, with the padding you already have, they might be okay."

"Might is not good enough."

He looked back at the resort. "There aren't going to be any birds if we don't get a head start. We're just going to have to do our best. You know this creature-saving thing is not for the faint of heart?"

I looked back and saw the two poachers from this morning, in ranger gear. Talking to Bunty and Peggy. They started toward our chopper just as Scott hopped in with two bike helmets.

"Get us up," Hazelnut yelled, taking the bike helmets. We did everything we could to create an unshakeable pod for our trio as Scott started the rotors. Hazelnut got into the jump seat.

Scott turned to me. "What's going on?"

"Just act like we're carrying nitroglycerin," I said.

"*Wages of Fear*. Got it."

At least Tupperware was unsquishable. I loosened the seat and shoulder belt a little and put the helmet pod under it, then held it to my chest. The poachers were running toward us. And then, with a soul-shuddering jerk, we were up and over the trees.

"Nice try, you avian thieving bastards," Hazelnut said, as we headed east.

• • •

Scott and Hazelnut were talking through the headsets. I couldn't hear them. I couldn't hear the chicks either. God, I hoped they were okay.

We lowered quickly at one point, way too close to a volcano for my comfort.

Scott grinned. "Just avoiding some turbulence 'cause of, you know, the nitro."

I smiled at him and my stomach went all wobbly. Thank goodness it was a short trip. Eventually, we landed on the hotel helipad we'd used before. I could see another helicopter on the edge of the helipad, and tons of scooters and Kijangs in the distance. Scott headed for the paved parking lot and landed there.

I was going to lose another pair of shoes to the tarmac. I couldn't let Scott do a fireman's carry this time. I might drop the chicks. And I would never hear the end of it from Hazelnut.

By some miracle, I hadn't used the airsick bag. I tore it in half. One of the ground crew arrived to help me down. I asked him to put the two halves of the bag on the ground before I stepped down. It kind of worked. These might be Vaseline salvageable. Scott shook his head.

I stepped lightly, dragging the paper bags like mutant squares of toilet paper, to safety, then jerked them off and put them in the nearest trash can. Hazelnut was staring at me.

"Your nose is melting," was all I said.

He reached up and pulled off the now witch-shaped wax.

"I'll reshape it inside."

Words failed me.

Scott was dealing with the helicopter, so Hazelnut and I walked on the grass toward the exit. There seemed to be dozens of people milling around the grounds. We dodged a few scooters as we walked.

Hazelnut swore again. "Songbird competition. Plus Nyepi is two days after."

"Nyepi is the day planes don't fly, right?"

"Well, if you want to reduce a sacred religious holiday to an arrivals and departures board, yes."

"Is that what I just did? I'm such a jerk. Sorry." I stared at him. "Since when are you culturally sensitive?"

"Since always."

"You can tell me about it on the ride. Are we waiting for Scott?"

"Should we?" He waggled his eyebrows again.

"Stop it! If you hired him for the day, don't you want your money's worth?"

"That's an interesting way to put it."

"Look, I just want to get these babies somewhere safe, with crickets and molted mealworms, where no one is shooting at us, okay? He's pretty good in a crisis. Frankly, better than Roger."

"Okay, wait for him. I had one of my friends drop off a Kijang. I'll go get it."

I stood there. Several people stared at me as I embraced what looked uncomfortably like a Nazi war helmet, with my Balenciaga on my shoulder and my carry-on at my feet. A statuesque woman walked by with my exact purse. I did a double take.

"Excuse me," I yelled. "Lovely Balenciaga." I shrugged mine up.

"Ha! Thank you," she said. "Best knockoffs ever in Bali, right?"

I didn't have the heart to tell her mine was real. "Where did you get yours?"

She stopped, reached into her bag and gave me a card. "They have some Kate Spade and Marc Jacob copies, too. Have a great vacation!"

Everyone loved a bargain.

Scott ran up. "Hey. I don't know what's going on, but you know I want to help, right?"

"If I weren't weighed down, I would hug you right now."

"I'm going to cash that in, you know that?"

"Yeah. By the way, it looks like things with my on-again, off-again just turned off."

"Really?"

We were about to kiss when Hazelnut screeched up in yet another dark blue Kijang and honked.

Chapter Forty-three

He jumped down and turned to Scott.

"Do you know where the nearest bird market is?"

"I think so."

"Great, you drive."

Hazelnut helped me and our progeny into the back.

Scott started the vehicle. "I assume it's still a delicate situation? Because this is pothole central."

"Just be as careful as you can. Give me one second."

I watched as Hazelnut reshaped and replaced his "Bunty" nose without a mirror. The man was a genius, in moments.

"Okay, ready."

Hazelnut and I held the helmet between us, trying to keep it still through the jolts in the road.

Then, suddenly, we were in the middle of Ubud, which seemed five times as crowded as before. Dozens of scooters blew by, balancing large objects with cloth coverings. Hazelnut started swearing in languages beyond the twenty-six I knew.

"Wow," I said, as a pagoda-shaped lump went past. "Are those bird-cages?"

"It's the competition. I'm sure the birds love traveling like that."

"We don't have any talking room when it comes to bird travel at the moment," I whispered.

"That's different. These people are doing it for sport. It's a damn hobby. I wonder how many of the songbird jerks realize that every time they buy an orange-headed thrush or a straw-headed bulbul, they're wiping them out? Or if they did, would they care?"

"They must not know. I'm sure they think they're getting them from legitimate sources."

"There are no legitimate sources."

Scott pulled into what was clearly not a parking spot.

Hazelnut turned to Scott. "You're still on the clock. We're going to put this helmet on the floor back here. Guard it with your life."

"No, I can stay here," I said, my birdternal instincts kicking in.

"I need you with me. Scott, I'm serious. Get these windows up. No people, no monkeys, nothing."

"Got it."

I still felt awful leaving. I looked at my watch. The chicks had only hatched a few hours ago. It seemed like two days. We got out of the Kijang and the sounds of honking, mixed with the smell of diesel and cigarettes and bird droppings, almost slapped me senseless. I stumbled.

Hazelnut, obviously familiar with Balinese custom, nodded ahead and moved over to my left side so he could jerk me along with his right rather than his left hand.

"How are there no legitimate sources? Aren't there any real breeding centers?"

"Like the one where you saw the poachers?"

"Obviously not that one."

Hazelnut grabbed my arm and pulled me out of the way of a scooter with two massive birdcages hanging off either side. The driver ripped sarongs and scarves from market stalls on each side as he passed.

"The real ones are constantly being robbed, and then those birds are trafficked."

"So there's nowhere the birds are safe?"

He stopped me in front of a smallish stand at the end of the market.

"Ah, here we are."

The overflowing pet food stand provoked a sense-surround flashback of my first herpetology convention. The smell. The egg cartons. The squirming. Which of course made me think of Roger. That was where he'd first asked me to have a drink with him. Oh, screw Roger.

Hazelnut spoke quickly in real Balinese. Not being able to point made markets like this a lot harder, so I was glad he was fluent. He turned to me. "You have money, right?"

Of course I was paying.

I gave the seller tens of thousands of rupiahs while Hazelnut hooked a basket covered in cheesecloth over his arm and handed me two egg cartons with a few cricket legs sticking out of them. Just looking at the legs made me a bit faint, but not nearly as nauseous as the basket. Since when was cheesecloth secure? Hazelnut moved us down the aisle and back toward the car.

"Did you get the pictures?"

"Yep. Took pictures of the prospectus, too. Is it safe to email them to bobtibbet?"

He gave me an alternate super-secret site address, which he told me to erase immediately. Obviously, I didn't.

"We'll drop you off while I figure out exactly what Bunty is up to. Where are you staying, again?"

"The Hanging Vines." I told him what had happened there and why I'd been in West Bali. "Reggie's given me a new room under a fictional name. Is it going to be safe, do you think?"

"Probably not, but nowhere will be while you have the chicks."

"Wait. Aren't you taking them? You should take them. You know what to do, at least. Didn't you tell me you went to vet school?"

"Vet school! Who didn't go to vet school? They're safer with you. Someone's always after me. And Reggie's one of the good guys at least. He's helped me before. Any idea what those burglars were looking for?"

"No idea. I guess they always think Americans travel with valuables, though I'm not exactly Kim Kardashian."

"Yeah, you're shorter."

"I beg your pardon! We're the same height."

"No way. She's statuesque."

"Hello? Photoshopping! I might even have a half inch on her. Look it up. Anyway, there is this other thing going on." I told him about Gerald's murder, the possible drugs, and Mom's being questioned by the police. "I was wondering whether the burglars thought I had the drugs?"

"It might not be about drugs," he said.

Chapter Forty-four

"If not drugs, what?"

He shook his head and started in on the feeding instructions. When Scott jumped out to help us in, I almost impaled the chicks by forgetting they were on the floor, but stopped just in time. I put the crickets down, picked up the helmet, and put it in my lap.

Scott looked back at our purchases. "Got everything you need?"

We nodded.

"Hanging Vines?"

"Please." At least the road out of town wasn't quite as crowded.

Hazelnut had the baskets on his lap. "Where was it your mom was staying?"

I told him.

"Anything else weird happen while you were there?"

"Well, there was a snake removal guy when I arrived. Apparently that's the guy Mom went to Ubud with today."

Hazelnut nodded. "Don?"

"No."

Scott swerved to miss three dogs. "I told her Don is the only one."

"He said his name was Alistair Brush. English, with unflattering longish hair. He had a blue Kijang too, with 'Brush Your Reptiles Away' on the side."

Hazelnut snorted. "Smuggler."

"How can you know that?"

"Scott's right. Don is the only reptile wrangler here. And he'd never let anyone else work for him. So that guy is absolutely using snake removal as cover for something else. He might be one of your burglars."

"What does that mean? What is he doing with my mother? Is she in danger?"

I closed my eyes as we headed toward a truck filled with empty birdcages teetering on the back. We pulled into the resort to find Alistair's reptile van parked near the entrance.

"Look! That's it. That's the van. The snake removal guy. I told you I wasn't making it up." Hazelnut and Scott looked at each other.

Scott turned to Hazelnut. "Should I stay with her?"

"No. You're not staying." Hazelnut turned to me. "We have to go. AntiChristine, you know what you need to do?"

"Yes."

"And how often?

"Every two hours."

"Do you have an alarm on your watch?"

"Have you met me? Should I start now, or wait the full twenty-four hours?"

"I'd start in the morning, just to be safe." He held out the helmet. "Hey."

"Yes?"

"They're counting on you. If you can handle this for a couple of days while I get through the competition, I'll find a way to get them out to Nusa Penida—there's a sanctuary there."

"Are you going to be at the competition?"

"I will, but undercover. Don't talk to me."

Great. I hoped I didn't have a mynah emergency.

Scott jumped out and grabbed the bird food before Hazelnut could object. "I'll just help her down."

The woman at reception gave "Ms. Upright" her key and we headed to the funicular.

Scott stopped short. "I've never been on one of those."

"I know, isn't it the best? Wayan taught me how to operate it."

"Yes, I did." Suddenly Wayan was beside us. I squealed. Just a little.

"Sorry to have startled you. Lovely to have you back. Where to?"

I could tell Scott really wanted a ride. "Third level, please, Wayan."

"Would you like to drive?"

"Yes! Yes, I would."

"Remember you engage the weights, push the start button for up or down—"

"And then disengage the brakes. I remember." When you've had ten brousins teaching you how to drive, you pick things up quickly, just out of annoyance.

I started the machine. I remembered the timing of the brakes—there were tiny lights that marked the place you started to engage them on each level—and especially because of the chicks, I made sure we glided to a gentle stop. When I saw Scott's face, I was glad we'd done it.

He saw me to my room. "I don't know how late I'll be, but if you don't have dinner plans, I could come back when I'm done. I think there are a few chilis you haven't tried." There was definitely one chili I hadn't tried. "Be sure to lock your door."

He gave me a quick—too quick—kiss on the lips and left. I unlocked the room and thought about Roger—having a baby with his old girlfriend. Roger. Barry and Angela. Did every person in the world have to be having a baby right now? Cripes.

Once I was inside, I locked everything that would lock and pulled the wooden shutters closed. I put my carry-on and my Balenciaga up on the counter, for bedbug and demon protection, while I figured out what to do with the crickets and worms. I couldn't put them outside, they'd just scatter into their natural environment. Refrigeration seemed like a bad idea.

It still grossed me out that the chicks ate live things. Did I eat anything alive? Was lettuce alive? Bean sprouts. Bean sprouts were alive. I hated them, so at least I hadn't come anywhere near massacre status with those. I eased the cheesecloth off the worm basket. The pinkish mass was roiling like a deep-fat fryer. But so far, it was a contained roiling.

How high could crickets jump? How could I keep them from making a jail break? I found a small trash can, put the basket and egg cartons inside, then closed them behind the carved doors of a cabinet in the main room. It was a cut above a roach motel, at least.

I finally took the chicks out of my purse and opened their travel compartment.

Their wobbly heads wriggled against each other and the way they looked up at me almost broke my heart in two. I knew what it was like to grow up without a father, but not without both. I had to do right by them until they got the expert help they needed. Which I hoped was soon, for their sake. I put their polyethylene condo near the back of a shelf in the wet bar, far above the floor, when I heard the doorknob turning.

Chapter Forty-five

It might be Reggie, but given the day I was having, what were the odds?

I moved to the wooden shutters and peered through one of the slits. The Dutchman was trying to use lock picks on the door. How he could manage with such bulbous fingers, I didn't know. There was a tall man behind him, facing the other way.

Who had betrayed me this time? I needed to get out, but didn't want to run with the newborn chicks. They'd been through enough for one day. I gave myself twenty seconds to think, then banged hard, on the door, just by the knob, and heard the satisfying clink of lock picks hitting the tiled walkway.

I grabbed a candlestick holder, anchored my Balenciaga over my shoulder, and moved to the back entrance, hoping the psychos hadn't covered both, and looked out. The coast was clear, for now.

I threw the candlestick—sorry, Reggie—down toward the level below, to make them think I'd gone that way so they wouldn't come inside for the chicks. Thank God I'd hidden them behind the glasses. Unless they peeped, no one would look twice at Tupperware. That was the great thing about it. Everyone took it for granted—until they needed it and realized they'd left it at the bingo potluck.

Meanwhile, I moved to the most jungly part of the walkway. I hoped there was enough echo, with the tiled steps, that they might not know where the sound of heels was coming from. I couldn't run without them.

By some miracle, the funicular was on my level, but unmanned. Where was Wayan? I didn't have time to waste. I jumped in and started the machine, sending it up and away from the thugs, who'd followed the candlestick down two levels. I ducked down, thrilled it had worked. I'd forgotten how torturously slow the car was, especially ascending.

I heard yelling. I poked my head up for an instant to see where the men were. They were, against all rules of Balinese courtesy, pointing in my direction. Dammit.

They started running. How much time did I have? What could I do? While I was thinking, I grabbed my phone and shoved it in my bra, then took off my shoes and tied the sandal straps around my wrists, hoping they'd work as modified nunchucks. I hooked my Balenciaga on my shoulder and looked for the men. They might not be in great shape, but a lifelong couch potato could beat this railway.

I was only one level ahead now. I was grateful they hadn't started shooting yet, as I was currently the poster child for sitting ducks. At least the next stop was sheltered by a few frangipani trees.

I only had a few seconds if I was going to make this work. I needed something long and flexible. Was Stu's saw still in my bag? It was.

I could hear the men smashing branches on their way up. I was grateful the lush plants hadn't been horticultured to death the way they were at home. I set the brake, but put the car in gear to go up. Then I climbed up on the small bench seat, grabbed onto the top of the car and threw the saw up.

I started to pull myself onto the roof of the railway car, grateful that kickboxing had given me a working core. It didn't guarantee a dignified ascent, though, as I made my second official thong flash of the day. Finally, I was on top. I had one more thing to do.

Losing my Balenciaga to a purse snatcher was one thing. Losing it to gravity was another. I took out one of my bungee cords and hooked it twice to the steel rings at the top of the car, bungee-ing Stu's camouflage jacket around it so the red didn't show. Then, I lowered myself, facing downward to keep track of my pursuers. I shook out the saw, used its tip to disengage the brake, and held on as the car started to move up. At a glacial pace. It got one level up before it came to a stop. Someone had summoned it. Wayan?

"Stromme kut? Where is the *trut*? Where's the *Godverdomme* driver?"

Not Wayan. Of course, when I learned a language, I learned a few swear words. The Dutchman was going down next time I was in kitten heel proximity.

"He's taking his fuckity time."

I almost fell off the roof.

That was a voice I recognized. It was Henrik, one of Bunty's henchmen from Tanzania. I guess he qualified as an international henchman, now. I'd shot him once.

This meant Bunty knew where I was. The fake name and different villa had been pointless. And, if he and the Dutch guy knew each other, and my burglary had been about the drugs, Bunty might also have something to do with Gerald's murder. And my mother. None of this was good. I rammed myself flatter, glad the railway car didn't have a moon roof.

"She can't be far."

I heard panting and another man arrived. Who?

"Any luck, Chim Chiminey?"

I smelled the Brut and heard the Dick Van Dyke-esque Cockney accent. Alistair Brush.

Where had he come from? Had he found the chicks?

I gripped tighter and lowered my head farther, my heels digging into my forearms.

They lowered their voices. It was the first time since I'd been in Bali when I wished the birds and monkeys would just shut the heck up. Were the ex-pat Three Stooges faking me out and about to shoot through the ceiling? I hoped they didn't permanently damage it. Killing endangered birds would be hard enough to explain to St. Peter without desecrating pieces of art.

"Did you go through the new fuckity room?"

"Of course, mate. Same old shit. Too many sodding shoes. She must have given it to that pilot."

Were they going to go after Scott, too?

The Dutchman chimed in. "I think she still has it." Alistair made some incomprehensible comment that was clearly lewd, given the laughs afterward. If this were just about me, I would have sliced him senseless with Stu's saw. I still might.

"Fuckity it. I'm not waiting."

What did that mean?

I felt the three men climb into the railway car. It jerked. I grabbed back on just in time to hear grinding. The car started downward. Fast, then faster—and finally, free falling.

Chapter Forty-six

I really wished I were facing the other way, so I didn't have to witness my impending death. My family flashed before me. And Roger. And the chicks. And strangely, Hazelnut.

And then, just as it looked like the whole contraption was headed right over the pools and into the ravine, there was a horrendous screech. The car stopped dead, and I flew off instead.

It's hard to describe what it feels like to be thrown into deep water when you don't know how to swim. Most people equate swimming pools with vacations. I equate them with death. Water is the enemy. It goes up your nose and into your eyes, but if you close them, you're just sinking and it's impossible to get your bearings. Flying off the top of the funicular was traumatic enough without landing in what was, for me, a tropical extinction cocktail.

Okay. I'd survived falling off a cruise ship. Granted, I'd had a life jacket that time, but this was a pool, not the Tasman Sea. It must have a shallow end. I peered through the water in vain for the silvery ladders that abounded in every American motel pool, however humble. Nothing. I was blowing bubbles out, but needed a non-water substance coming in as soon as possible.

I assumed Henrik knew I was in here—I had ejected right past him on the way down. Would there be a gun trained on me when I came up?

Just as I started to flail my arms toward the surface, someone grabbed my arm. I whipped around and whacked my attacker with my sandals, then heard a blubbery "Hey!"

I opened my eyes to aim better and saw a soft belly above a rubber duck–themed speedo. I stopped hitting the stranger and hung on to him instead, as he hauled me to the surface and I gulped in mouthfuls of hot, humid, precious air. We were at the very far end of the first infinity pool. I reached for the slippery edge and tried to hold on, without looking at the thirty-foot drop to the one below.

The man appeared to be standing. Was this the shallow end? He rubbed his forearm. "What the hell?"

"I'm so sorry. I thought you were trying to kill me."

"It's okay, I guess. You didn't break the skin. Wow, you came off that car like something out of a James Bond movie. I'm going to put a warning about that on Tripadvisor, for sure."

Then I spotted my assailants, running down the pool steps. Henrik was pointing again, which was especially culturally insensitive when you did it with a gun.

"Duck!" I pushed my cranky Samaritan under and tried to pull the gunfire away from him by scrambling up on the edge of the pool.

Then the Dutchman yelled and executed the most unattractive cannonball in history, sending out a shuddering wave that swept me right over. I windmilled my arms for what seemed like an hour, then hit the water in a Coyote vs. Acme splash and waited to die.

I didn't. It just felt like it. I reached with my feet for the bottom. This pool didn't have a shallow end, which was good, but also bad.

Just when I was trying to figure out where I was, a current swept me forward toward a large grate at the jungle end of the infinity pool, then smashed me up against it. This must be how they kept the water circulating instead of going over the edge all the time. Maybe I could use it to crawl up to the surface. I got about halfway there when I felt a vibration and found Henrik treading water beside me, in his suit. I guess Bunty paid him well.

I aimed my Stuart Weitzman heels at the arm I knew I'd shot before, hoping they would break the skin this time. He shoved me up against the edge of the pool, the edge that poured out into the ravine. I tried to hold on to the grate, but that meant I could only fight back with my unarmed legs, which was exhausting and ineffective. I imagined this was why water aerobics promised to burn so many calories.

I made one core-splitting kick, and slipped off the grate. Henrik took that opportunity to grab me around the knees, jerk me up, and toss me over the edge.

Chapter Forty-seven

I screamed, which seemed pretty standard in the circumstances, since the ravine looked about twenty-five stories deep with rocks and shallow water at the bottom. At least this time, there were trees to break my fall. I reached for anything I could and managed to get a one-hand hold onto a substantial branch.

But my hands were wet, so when I tried to get my other hand on the tree, the first one slipped and I kept bouncing, holding on to something for two or three seconds, then falling farther, like a Tarzan intern on his first day.

I grabbed on to a frangipani tree for just long enough to notice the bridge I'd spotted from my room, the one I could now see was just three bamboo poles tied together. Before I could formulate a plan, the branch broke. I threw out my "sandal grapples" and, by some miracle, one shoe/wrist caught long enough for me to grab on to the bamboo pole crossing with the other.

The bridge had the fortitude of al dente spaghetti. There was no way to climb up. It was short, though. If I could get into the jungle underbrush across the way, it would be awhile before the thugs could get to me.

I put a vision of those three little birds at the forefront of my brain and started, hand over hand, across the bridge. I didn't look back. I didn't look down. I didn't think about how wet and slippery my hands were. I would have given anything for a dry towel, a shot of Jack Daniel's, and Indiana Jones at this moment, but all I had were my Stuart Weitzmans and my kickboxing muscles. They were going to have to do. As long as I could hook one heel in between the bamboo poles for a bit of security, I could keep going.

Finally, the bank was only about five feet away. Of course, there was a monkey sitting there. He started bouncing up and down. Just what I needed.

Surely he was afraid of humans. I just had to keep going and he would move. He didn't.

I stared him down from about a foot and a half away and reached into my PBS *Nature* brain files. What repelled monkeys? They were afraid of snakes, but, for once, I didn't have one handy. And hot peppers, but I was fresh out of Tabasco. Loud noises might work, but then Henrik might know I was still alive.

I looked the monkey right in the eye. He wasn't budging. And I needed to. Then, there was a gunshot. The monkey shrieked and ran and I almost lost hold of the bridge. I gripped harder and threw myself onto the edge of the ravine.

I could only imagine the gunshot had been for me, so I lay there until all I could hear were birds. I knew there was a temple up the hill just across the way and, if it was anything like the temples I'd seen, there would be plenty of places to hide. I donned my heroic sandals and went to tighten my Balenciaga on my shoulder. It wasn't there.

This was only the second time in my adult life I'd not had my purse. The first time, it was confiscated by Interpol and I had to live without it for a day and a half. Then, and now, it felt like I'd lost an arm. I should have learned that time to carry more things in my bra. Oh, my bra. My phone was in my bra. I pulled it out, but it had been underwater too long. At least if there was a chance of reviving it, I was in the rice capital of the world.

I hadn't heard any more shots and I could see the temple above me so I started up. The sun was getting lower in the sky, casting wavy shadows all around. What day was it? Had I just been in the West Bali National Park this morning? Talk about *jam karat.*

Still, the magical thing about Bali was, whatever you were doing and no matter how much trouble you were in, the place still overtook you. When I got to the temple, even though henchmen were after me, I still stopped for a moment, amazed at how beautiful it was.

Lu had told me before how most of the carvings were in sandstone, which deteriorated quickly. So even if they were covered in lichens and looked ancient, they were probably only a few years old. Local artists recarved or replaced them on a regular basis. Can you imagine anyone doing that with the Sistine Chapel?

Today, the gods had kept me alive. I looked for a frangipani tree and picked a few flowers, then laid them on top of a palm leaf I found on the ground and placed the offering on a shrine at the entrance. Then I looked for a hiding place that might be the least sacred. Did they have bathrooms in temples?

I finally found a small building at the back that looked like snake central. I'd just turned around to keep looking when I heard a moan, then something that sounded like "Help!"

I tried to follow the sound, keeping behind columns as much as I could. I stumbled into a small alcove with a large column overgrown on the front with lichens and vines. Tied to the other side, was my mother.

Chapter Forty-eight

Her long reddish hair was matted and her best sundress was covered in mud. She'd managed to partially wriggle off her handkerchief gag. When she saw me, she smiled, then fainted.

Of course, my emergency water, smelling salts, and sanitary wipes—i.e., Jack Daniel's—were in my purse. I was just going to have to untie her and rub her hands until she came to. Had Alistair Brush done this? If he hadn't been in my homicidal sights before, he was now.

Finally, she started to come to. "Cyd? Cyd! You found me!"

"Yeah," I said, deciding, since I had crossed the three-inch bridge hand over hand, to take the credit. "Are you hurt?"

She shook her arms and her head. "Just scared, mainly."

I grabbed her hand and helped her up. Nothing seemed broken or sprained.

"Thank you. I'm okay. It's mostly my pride that took a hit, I think."

She did have a cut on her arm that looked nasty, though. "That must hurt."

"It's nothing. Forget about me. What happened to you? Have you put on Bactine?"

She looked around. "Where is your Balenciaga?"

"It's part of a long story. And it's almost sunset, which is not good. I don't know whether it's better to stay here where there's shelter, or try to get back to the hotel. Damn, I wish my phone wasn't wet."

"I have mine."

"How did they let you keep your phone?"

"He didn't find it. I always keep it in my bra, like you said to do in your travel instructions."

"You read my travel instructions?"

"Of course I read them. I've read everything you ever wrote in your whole life. Even your book report on *The Peter Principle*."

Damnit, I was not going to cry.

"I didn't know that."

"There are a few things you don't know. Not many."

"Ha! You have no idea. Give it here and let's see if I can remember the hotel number."

I realized I didn't know who at the hotel was in on the conspiracy. Hazelnut and Scott weren't available. Who could I call?

"Any chance you have Lu's number in here?"

"Of course. She put it in when she picked us up."

I dialed. Please answer, I thought, while trying to look confident to Mom.

"Bridget?" It was Lu.

"It's Cyd, I'm with her."

"Are you all right?"

"Kind of."

"Good, Reggie called me. I was afraid I was going to have to tell her you were dead. Where are you?"

"We're at the temple across from the Hanging Vines. Where are you?"

"Twenty minutes away. Stay there."

"Thank you." I hung up and handed the phone back. "She's on her way."

Mom put it back in her bra. "I guess Madge let you know I was missing?"

"No. She didn't. She told me you were on a date and to leave you alone."

"Hmmm. Well, I did tell them not to call you. That I could take care of myself."

"Well, you did. You already had your gag off, you would have untied yourself eventually, and you had a working phone. Perfect tourist."

She grinned. "Not completely perfect. Apparently I have a weak spot for lying men."

"So who was it, who left you here?"

"Al. Alistair."

"Alistair Brush? The snake removal guy?"

She nodded. "He asked me out, suggested a day at the markets in Ubud. Madge and Bea Ann had other plans, but they thought it might cheer me up. Madge said she got a good feeling."

"Yeah, well Madge said that about Gerald, too, didn't she?"

Mom raised her eyebrows, then shrugged. "I was a little nervous about it, but Al was actually a gentleman until he got a phone call. Come to think about it, he gave me a water bottle just after that and I don't really remember anything until I woke up. Could it have been one of those spiked drinks you warned us about in the instructions? I was only being careful about cocktails." She smiled. "I can't believe you're here. Thank you. You know it's strange, he asked about you, actually, asked where you were. At least I didn't know."

"I'm glad he didn't hurt you to find out. He found me anyway—that must have been the phone call. Did he say he was coming back?"

"He just told me to be quiet."

"Well, I'm glad you weren't."

He had clearly gone from here to the hotel, so Henrik or someone else must have called him. Who?

Mom took my hand. "How did you find me, anyway?"

I told her. Well, I told her most of it.

"So, the chicks are in your room. Do you think they're okay?"

"I can't even think about it until I get back. Mom, do you have any idea at all what these guys have been looking for? I didn't get the chicks until this morning, so it wasn't that."

"Probably the money."

Chapter Forty-nine

"I beg your pardon? What money?"

Mom shrugged. "Well, when I first arrived, I knew from your pamphlet I needed to hydrate and put on sunscreen—you know how I burn. I'm so glad you got your father's skin. I reached into my carry-on and found a paper bag with something in it. I was afraid it might be an animal, you know, like with the Andersons. But it didn't feel like that. So I opened it, and inside, wrapped up in plastic, were two zippered bags like you use to do a bank deposit, those fake leathery ones?"

"Yeah. And?"

"At first I thought it might be drugs, but instead, it was a lot of cash."

"Rupiahs?"

"American dollars. I figured Gerald must have put it there and I didn't know why. I had already gotten through Customs, so I didn't think anything could happen to me, and I figured he needed it, but I didn't want it lying around the room. Madge was on a bit of a tirade, so I went out for a walk."

"And took it to the police?"

"No. I buried it."

"Wait, you still have it? You didn't tell the police about it? Why not?"

"Well, once I knew Gerald had been killed, that would have made me look guilty, for one thing, and from everything I've read, and everything Gerald said, there's a lot of corruption in the Denpasar police department, so that didn't seem smart. Besides, finders, keepers."

"Finders keepers? Really? Mom, why did you keep the money?"

"I thought you might need it. For the business."

"So you withheld evidence? For me?"

"Who else?"

My mind was spinning in so many directions I didn't actually know what to do. Who needed to launder money? Drug and arms smugglers. And animal traffickers. And maybe they would try to invest it in another business to clean it. Like a resort. An eco-resort would be even better.

"You said Gerald was in real estate, didn't you?" She nodded. Bingo.

Then Mom started to tear up. "I really did like him. I thought he liked me, too."

I didn't think that was the case, but it wasn't the time to speak ill of her dead money launderer.

"Where's the money now?"

"Still there, if someone hasn't dug it up."

"Are your fingerprints on it?"

"No, I used the plastic gloves from the emergency pack."

I took a breath of relief. She grinned. "I know you think you get all your skills from your dad, but careful—you got that from me."

Then, the chick alarm on my watch went off.

We both jumped. "Sorry. I put in a preliminary chick feeding alert, just to make sure it worked. At least my waterproof watch is actually waterproof." Mom grinned at me. Then she stopped.

There was Alistair Brush, standing under a coconut tree. With a gun.

He swore unintelligibly in what I assumed was bad Cockney. "Henrik said he finished you."

I moved in front of Mom. "Henrik's a halfwit."

Mom shoved in front of me. "Alistair Brush! How dare you treat me like some S&M blind date? You are not handsome or smart enough to get away with that. I don't care if I am middle-aged."

"I'm smart enough to find you both."

Geez, I guess we were kind of a Redondo bonanza.

I thought I could hear a vehicle shaking the jungle. It might be Henrik.

Brush moved closer. "The tourist board will make sure there's not too much print about the mother and daughter found at the bottom of the ravine, after hiking without a guide."

Mom made a fist and started forward and, again, I tried to get in front of her. We both tripped over each other and wound up in a pile too close to Brush. I'd landed half on top of Mom, so I pushed her down and sat up as he raised his gun. I grabbed Mom's hand. She squeezed back. I closed my eyes. One second. Two seconds.

I heard a tiny rustle and then a tremendous crack. A gunshot? I opened my eyes just in time to see Alistair Brush drop like a stone.

I was still for a while, to make sure he wasn't moving. What had just happened? Was there another gunman?

"Stay here." I got up and kicked the gun away. Brush had a large wound on the top of his head. I took his pulse. Nothing.

Mom sat up. "Is he dead?"

"I think so. Let me try CPR." I did. Nothing. What had happened? I looked around. A few feet away I spotted a bloody coconut. The fake snake remover/mother kidnapper had been conked out, literally. I'd read that coconuts could be dangerous, but what were the odds? I went over to help

Mom up.

"What happened?"

"I know you're not going to believe it, but I think it was a *deus ex coconut*."

I heard a snort of laughter, then breathed a sigh of relief. Lu.

She came from the same trail where Alastair had appeared, and nodded. "It happens. Jill says it's thirty times more common than shark attacks, but it's rarely this poetic."

"I am so glad to see you."

"You as well, and you, Bridget. Bea Ann called me an hour ago saying you should have been back."

"I was detained."

I looked down at Brush. "What should we do? I don't want some tourist to stumble over this."

"I will take care of it. I know someone."

I knew what that meant. "Can I ask a strange question?"

"Yes, you can check his pockets. And the van."

"He brought the van?" She nodded. "Great."

I pulled a phone, keys, and a few pieces of paper out of his pockets.

"Take it," Lu said. "The phone. Like I said, I know someone."

The second phone evened out my cleavage, at least. I folded the papers, hoping there would be something in the van to put them in.

I went to retrieve the gun. It was gone.

Lu helped us back down the trail and I braced myself for another scooter ride, but she had found a place where the Kijang could get through. It was parked beside Brush's van.

I opened the back of the van and found, among other things, National Park Ranger shirts and something that looked like part of a prosthetic leg. I gasped.

"What?" Mom asked.

"Nothing. I'll explain later, we have to get back."

Chapter Fifty

We had to go the long way around to find a real bridge across the ravine. Mom and I just stared out the window, while Lu concentrated on what wasn't really a road. When we were finally nearing the hotel, Mom's phone rang.

She retrieved it and answered. "Bridget Redondo." She smiled and mouthed to me, "It's Bea Ann."

I tried not to listen in and distracted myself by wondering whether Mom, me, or the chicks were safe at the hotel. We had to go back to retrieve everything either way, so I just tried to breathe in the frangipani and diesel.

We made it back in twenty minutes, just as the sun was going down.

As we pulled in, we saw a police vehicle and a Balinese man in uniform talking to Reggie, who looked, for the first time, ruffled.

He turned, saw us, and ran over.

"Cyd! Oh, I am so glad you are all right!"

"Thank you, Reggie, me too." I helped Mom out. "This is my mother, Bridget Redondo."

"Honored, I'm sure," he said, kissing her hand. Lu had gotten out too. She didn't offer her hand, but she and Reggie shared a look.

I turned to him. "Is it safe for us? Did they catch everyone?"

"It is safe at present. After you fell, the gunman aimed at you, but Wayan ran at him and threw off his aim. Instead he hit his associate."

"The Dutchman? Is he dead?"

"Wounded. The police are arranging for his treatment."

I bet, I thought. "What about the gunman?"

"He hijacked a vehicle and left. There is much to tell the police, as you can imagine. I suppose they will want to talk to you."

"And to me." Mom waved at the policeman. "That's Lieutenant Rika."

I leaned in and whispered, "The one you lied to?"

"One of them. He's a bit of a stickler."

Oh great, what next?

Reggie turned back. "If you want to leave, we will understand, but we would love to show you how much we value you. I've arranged for guards at both doors, all night, to be sure you are safe. They are my cousins. I trust them absolutely."

But should I? For all I knew, Reggie might run this whole operation. I wasn't sure.

"Either way, we wanted to be sure you got this most vital item back." He gestured down the stairs and there came Wayan, a sling on one arm, and my Balenciaga on the other.

I ran to hug him and realized I might hurt his arm. Instead, I stopped, put my hands together in front of my chest and bowed. "Wayan! Would it be very impolite for me to kiss you on the cheek?"

"If Mr. Reggie will allow it."

Reggie nodded. Wayan endured the kiss, blushed, and handed me my bag.

"Honestly, I don't know which I appreciate more. Your saving my life, or your saving this."

"Beautiful things are important."

"They are."

It looked all right. Then I had an awful thought. "Is the railway car all right?"

"The son of a demon stripped a gear, but I have made repairs. She will be fine. It is not the first time a tourist has stolen it with bad intentions."

Or good intentions, I thought. This was all my fault and they had saved my bag. I couldn't leave now. "Mom? I'm going to stay. I'm sure Lu will take you somewhere you'll be safer."

Lu nodded. "Without question. My family will welcome you to our home."

"See? You should go. I'll be fine. I know you wanted to have this vacation on your own."

My mother took my hand. "No, sweetheart. I'm sticking with you."

I really was going to cry now.

Lu promised she would stay in Ubud and accompany us to the songbird competition tomorrow.

The police officer headed our way.

Chapter Fifty-one

"Mrs. Redondo," he said, bowing slightly to my mother.

"Officer Rika, this is my daughter, Cyd."

I bowed my head. "Cyd Redondo, Redondo Travel."

"Ah, the corpse."

"The almost corpse," I said. "Thank you for coming. Any news on my attackers?"

"Ah, but was there an actual attack?"

Was he serious?

"Several witnesses said you were on top of the rail car. How did they throw you off?"

"By slamming on the brakes," I said.

"Perhaps they braked to avoid an accident."

"Well, Henrik did shoot at me and throw me into the ravine, that counts, doesn't it?"

"You know this man? An acquaintance? A romantic entanglement? A lovers' tiff, is that the word?"

"No!"

"Well, were you shot?"

"No." I pointed to torn clothing. "I was hurtling down the cliff so fast, he missed."

"We will look into it," he said. "Please do not leave Ubud."

"I won't." Not yet, anyway. I had scores to settle.

He spoke once more to Reggie and then got into his vehicle and drove away.

"I told you," Mom said. "It's impossible to get a straight answer out of them."

"I can see that. Ready to clean up a bit?"

"More than ready."

Reggie, armed with the bag of dry rice I'd requested, insisted on accompanying us to our villa and introducing us to our guards, both solemn, tall, and dressed in camouflage gear.

They would cost me hundreds of thousands of rupiahs in tips if they actually kept the chicks and my mother alive.

Finally, we shook off all the hospitality overcompensation and actually entered the villa.

Mom almost squealed. "How can we afford this?"

"There's no we. It's on me." She didn't have to know it was technically free.

She shook her head and started to explore. Meanwhile, I opened the bag of rice and buried my phone deep inside, praying that would resuscitate it. Then I walked to the drinks cabinet. Please, please, please, I thought, please be alive.

"Mom? Will you hold my hand while I check on the chicks?"

She pivoted and headed back. "Of course."

I eased the doors open, and listened. It was very faint, but it was there. That heartbreaking trilling. I squatted down, moved the wineglasses aside, and slid their temporary home out.

Mom was staring at it. "What is that?"

"A mini Tupperware steamer. It was. Now it's a starling RV. I'm so scared to open it."

"Are we going to wake them? I want to see them, but waking babies is never good."

"I don't know. I feel like they might need some air. I didn't punch that many holes in the top."

She took my hand. "You punched holes in that. In a new piece of Tupperware?" I nodded. "I'm proud of you, Cyd."

"Let's turn down some of the lights and just check."

Stu and Hazelnut had told me most of them didn't survive, but I wasn't sure I was tough enough for that to happen on my watch. I told Mom what they'd said.

"If it weren't for you, a snake or a rat would have eaten them already. We can't control everything, sweetie."

"No shit," I replied. "Sorry. Here goes nothing."

I lifted one side of the lid. I had to be careful not to burp it by habit, and suck them to the top. There they were—all breathing, two of them conked out and one wiggling a little on top of them. He, or she, gave me a tiny trill.

Mom laughed. "They're so adorable and kind of ugly, just like human babies."

"I beg your pardon."

"It takes a while for babies to be cute. You were quicker than most."

"It's hard to tell now, but you won't believe how gorgeous they are when they grow up." I didn't put the lid all the way down, just to give them a bit more air, at least while I was sitting close enough to make sure they stayed inside.

"How old are they?"

I looked at my watch. Was it only eight thirty?

"Almost nine hours."

"And when do you need to feed them?"

"My bird expert said they can live on the yolk for a day, but to try first thing in the morning. He said they actually sleep at night." Then I shook my head.

"What is it?"

"I'm one of the only people in the world, ever, who got to see a real Bali starling in the wild. Right now they think there are only seven. Or six—the poachers got one. I mean, I saw two of them and now I have these. It's such a privilege, but it's so sad at the same time."

She squeezed my hand and got that look on her face she always had on Valentine's Day. Mom had always said she was so lucky to have had my dad at all. Beyond that, we had never, ever talked about it. It had been a taboo subject for both of us, or at least for one of us at any given time. Was that good or bad? I wasn't sure.

I closed the lid, put the steamer back behind the wineglasses, and opened the other side of the cabinet to make sure the chicks' breakfast hadn't hopped or wriggled away.

Mom stared. "What is that?"

"This is what they're supposed to eat at the beginning." I explained about the legless crickets and the molting baby worms.

"It's all very mulchy," she said.

"Yeah, well, you would know."

I heard a knock at the door. What now? I thought.

I peeked out and saw Scott negotiating with our guards. I cracked the door.

"Do you know this gentleman?"

"I do," I said, hoping I wasn't letting in a Trojan date.

"I'm sorry," Scott said. "We talked about grabbing dinner." He looked me up and down. "It looks like there have been a few developments."

"A few," I said. "Come on in. This is my mom, Bridget."

Scott shook her hand. "You've been a hard lady to locate."

"Yes, it took Cyd to do it." Mom looked back and forth between us. "Did you have plans?"

"Well, before everything happened we did." I looked at Scott.

"Please join us," he said.

"No! I think you've earned a dinner out, sweetie."

"I'm not going to leave you alone here."

"I have Frick and Frack outside," she said. "And to be honest, I could sit and just look at those torches and the candles on the water all night."

"There is a pretty good restaurant here, we could bring you something back," Scott said.

"No, thank you. I'm fine.

"Are you sure, Mom?"

"Yes. I would, however, at the risk of being a nag, suggest freshening up a bit?"

Oh my God. I had been in two pools and down a ravine. What must I look like?

Scott grinned. "I wasn't going to say anything, but the restaurant is more casual than casualty."

"Very funny. I'll be quick. Don't drink from the tap," I yelled as I headed into the luxurious bathroom and found yet another gorgeous tub full of petals, which I just couldn't face at the moment.

I did a small scream when I saw myself in the mirror. I had blood on my dress, scratches on my face, twigs and leaves and who knows what else in my hair (better not be ticks), and as I undressed, I found bruises, too, including two hand-sized ones from where Henrik had hoisted me to my almost death. Bastard.

"It's not going to be that quick," I yelled out the door, as I got out my travel tweezers and started a twig search in my hair, which was currently the size and shape of Maine.

After a cold shower and enough hair product to douse three silverback gorillas, I got out my next-to-last pair of false eyelashes. I knew it was risky, but I wasn't going to dinner with Scott bare-lidded. When I'd finally anchored them to my eyes instead of the faucet or my makeup bag, I reached for some perfume, then put it back. The combination of moisturizer, concealer, and Bactine coming off of me was overwhelming enough. Instead, I plucked a few flowers from the bathtub and put them in my hair, brushed off my amazingly resilient sarong/pulley, and paired it with a silk top. I looked at my scratched sandals, which, given what they'd been through today, probably belonged in the Smithsonian, and traded them for some nude stilettos.

I found Scott and Mom in the sitting area, laughing.

"Your mother was just telling me how, when you were little, you used to sleep under the bed. Do you still do that?"

I gave my mom a look. "I might tonight." She shrugged, then when Scott wasn't looking, gave me a thumbs up. It was pretty sweet, actually.

Once we were outside, Scott offered his arm. "Did you want to take the stairs this time?"

"Yes, please, as long as you're on snake patrol."

"Speaking of snake patrol, Hazelnut and I had one of my police friends do some research into your Alistair Brush. Not his real name, of course."

"I'm guessing he's not English, either, with that accent."

"Believe it or not, he is. Used to be a courier."

"Courier for what?"

"You name it. He moved to Bali at the end of last year. Have you seen him again?"

I hesitated. I didn't know what Lu had done and I didn't want her—or me—to wind up surrounded by a cobra field in Kerobokan prison. "He was here, with Henrik and the Dutch guy."

"Who's Henrik?"

"From what I can tell he's kingpin adjacent."

"You know that, how?"

"I don't think I can tell that story without a cocktail."

We arrived at the restaurant, alive with candles and the smell of pork, chilis, and coconut. We went to the bar first. Although I knew the Dutchman was in custody, I was still glad Scott was with me. We had a shot of expensive rum to start, which was probably a mistake, since I hadn't eaten since breakfast.

Scott turned to me. "Another drink?"

I looked at my watch. Countdown to cricket mutilation. It didn't seem like something I should do hungover.

"Can we have some food first?"

"Of course." We moved to a table that overlooked the pools. I took the chair that faced the other direction. It was too soon.

Scott and I talked and ate. I told him a bit about my day, parts of it, anyway. Even though he'd been ferrying Hazelnut, in disguise, I didn't know how much he knew. He talked about going to school in Australia and how he was always torn between here and there. So, for a while I forgot that killers were after me, that Peggy fricking Newsome and Bunty were in cahoots, and that my Tupperware selections and I were responsible for the preservation of a species.

Afterward, Scott walked me back up to our level. Happily, it was only a Three Bat Night. Halfway up, he pulled me into a kiss so heart-stopping, I didn't even scream when he put his hands right on my Henrik bruises—though I did feel like crying when he stopped.

"Figured I would get that in before I turn you over to the paramilitary guys."

"Good thinking."

"What are you doing tomorrow?"

"Songbird competition. Want to come?"

"I have one job. Don't know how long it will take. Can I call you?"

"Yes. No. My phone is in a bag of rice right now." I gave him Mom's flip phone number.

"Good night, Cyd."

"Night."

The bodyguard at the front door winked at me as I went in. At least Mom had obeyed my instructions and taken the four-poster bed. She was asleep with one arm flung out. She looked so young through the mosquito netting.

Leaning on the door looking at her, the whole day finally hit me. I was too tired to even take off my eyelashes. I checked on the chicks, lit two mosquito coils, undressed, set my watch for the dawn feeding, and wrapped myself up in an extra net. The last thing I heard before I passed out was crickets.

Chapter Fifty-two

I woke up to clinking. The sky was just pink enough for me to make out a shape on the other side of the room. I sat up straight and reached for the mosquito coil—the only weapon handy.

"Hey!"

The figure's long hair swirled around. "Oh, honey, I was trying not to wake you." My mother was standing by the counter, in a sarong, with her hand in the worm basket.

"What are you doing?"

"I knew this would be hard for you. Just thought I could find a few non-exoskeleton ones before you woke up." I could see three blood red worms crawling up her arm.

"Mom?" I pointed at her arm. "Worm alert?"

She looked down, pulled the worms off gently and put them back in the basket, then put a few things I didn't want to think about in a coffee cup. "Did you get worm food?"

"Come on. I have to get food for the food?"

"Well, they have to be alive, right?"

"Okay, I need coffee before I can even watch you do that," I said, calling to order room service while trying to locate and retrieve my false eyelashes from the mosquito netting. "Just wait for me and we'll do it together."

"Are you sure?"

"Yes, they're my responsibility," I said, easing the chicks out of the cabinet. "It would be great to have some help, though, cricket wrangling."

"You've got it." I noticed Mom's sarong was almost exactly like mine.

"Did Lu give you that sarong?"

"Yes. I guess she and her sisters make them. We could almost be twins."

I walked over and kissed her on the cheek. "Morning, Mom."

I decided not to get dressed until we had successfully served breakfast. I could sleep naked if I had to, but I couldn't attend the songbird competition that way. Besides, being covered in cricket blood and worm slime might be distracting for the avian performers. I had no idea how developed a bird's sense of smell was. Did they even have one? I'd have to ask Hazelnut.

Once we were caffeinated, we set up the insect and invertebrate smorgasbord—worm larvae in one coffee cup, and a few crickets in another. I hadn't done a great job of containing the crickets, as apparently they could jump higher than I thought. I hoped we'd still have enough. I had no idea how many worm babies or mutilated crickets to feed the chicks, but I figured when they were full they would stop cheeping. I hoped so—I didn't want to create a starling *foie gras* situation.

Finally, I got out the steamer nest and opened the top. The stress of worrying that every time I did this, they could be dead, was getting to me.

Phew. They were still breathing, although one of them was a bit too still for my liking. I hoped that was just from hunger.

Right on cue, they all opened their huge mouths, still half the size of their bodies, and gave a few demanding trills.

I took a slug of coffee, then moved it away from the feeding cups. "This won't be too bad," I said. "First course, larvae?"

After a few attempts, we each managed to grab on to one. But as soon as we were ready to drop them in, the birds' tiny heads would wobble, and the worm would drop into the white, mini-padded bottom of the Tupperware, where it became invisible.

Mom took out another squirming, lice-like creature. "We can't hold their necks still, can we?"

"We're not really supposed to touch them. We just have to keep trying."

The odds of our getting the tiny worms into the circling mouths was about a hundred to one, but eventually we got a few in for each chick. It wasn't nearly enough food.

We were going to have to resort to crickets.

Most of the ones in the cup had jumped out. I took the only one that was left, held it up, and looked at Mom. "Help?"

The only equivalent of trying to hold an angry cricket still while your mother pulls its legs off is probably having your brousins take you, at age ten, to a David Cronenberg triple feature.

"Make sure you don't drop the legs in—they might accidentally eat them."

She gave me a look, but managed to flick the first leg away, successfully.

Of course, once the legs were off, we had to make sure the cricket went longways into the tiny, lurching mouths. When I realized we were going to have to do the same vertical procedure with full-sized, wriggling worms, two days from now, I almost gave up.

We finally got one in and you would have thought the Mets had won the World Series. Of course, by the time we'd managed it, all the other crickets had escaped and I had to crawl around on the floor, trying to retrieve them. While doing this, I was able to more accurately determine how far they could jump. About three feet.

I got up from the floor, four hopping crickets in my partially closed fist. "We're gonna need a bigger mug."

Fifteen minutes later, the birds stopped peeping. Mom brushed her hair from her face. I didn't mention the cricket on her thumb. It was bound to leap off, eventually. Instead, I set the alarm on my watch.

"When do we need to do this again?"

"Every two hours."

"Are you serious?"

"Yes. So, we'll have to be back in two hours, I guess." I thought about how nothing on this trip had gone according to schedule, with the combination of *jam karat* and intermittent felons. What were the odds I could control either of those things and get back in time?

Plus, the poachers would probably be there. They might not know I had the chicks, but they knew I could identify them. And Henrik was still out there. Even if he was out of the picture, I'm sure Bunty had an endless thug supply. If we were delayed for any reason, the chicks could die of starvation. We couldn't go.

I needed to call Lu and tell her. I'd given my phone all the rice exposure I could spare. Would it work? By some miracle, it powered up and dinged with seven texts from an unknown number. They all read: *Bring items to competition ground. Confirm receipt. Heep.*

I swore in three languages, then typed *See you there.* How we were going to manage it, I had no idea.

Chapter Fifty-three

Still, if Hazelnut was going to take charge of the chicks and get them somewhere safe, we had to bring them.

Mom walked in. "Honey, I'm worried about the chicks. I think I should stay here with them."

"Me, too, but we can't."

"Why not?"

I told her. She sighed. "I hope they live long enough to get there."

"We're just going to have to be sure they do."

"What about the feedings? Do we have to bring crickets?"

"We can get them there. It's probably the biggest day of the year for worm merchants."

I tried to think of ways we could stay incognito at the competition, then looked at the clock. "I have to get ready. Lu's going to be here any minute."

I didn't have time for eyelashes. I'd just have to keep my sunglasses on. "Don't forget sunscreen," I yelled out the bathroom door.

"Already doused," my mother replied. I looked back at her in her sarong and a plan began to form. Whether or not it would work all came down to, as usual, Tupperware.

First, I told Mom we needed to double down on the twin thing. We added matching products to our red hair and then both put it up in a French twist. I gave her a pair of my kitten heels. Then I took a card out of my purse and made a call.

By the time we left, it was just an hour until worm time. I'd punched a few tiny holes into two sandwich-sized ziplocks for separate bags of larvae and crickets—I'd watched enough *Nature* not to take the chance one might eat the other. The bags lay on top of the Tupperware steamer, inside one of the bike helmets. As we got into the Kijang, I asked Lu whether her sister had any more of these sarongs and could we stop by and buy some?

"Buy some! They will be a gift, of course."

"No, I'll pay. I need ten. I hope I need ten. Some Tupperware, too."

She stared at me. "Ten?"

I had to trust Lu for this to work. She had gotten rid of a body for us. If that wasn't reliability, I didn't know what was. So we told her what we were trying to do.

"I'll need traditional corsets and blouses. And some red wigs. Do they even sell those here? Is that possible?"

"I know someone," Lu said, and turned her attention back to the road. By the time we'd gotten the supplies we needed and arrived at Lu's sister's compound, my alarm went off. It was feeding time.

We didn't want to expose the chicks to any more germs than necessary, so we went through the worm/cricket routine in the van. Both of the food sources were still alive, barely, which was good, because they were less mobile and we only lost a few into the backseat. In the end, we got into a rhythm, and got through it.

Lu had briefed her sister, Amisha, who helped us carry out the mini-steamers. Then Mom and I went inside and donned our matching tops. Lu changed into an identical outfit, too.

Amisha led us out with a tray of offerings, which was so lovely of her, and we all placed them on the shrine in the middle of the compound. I wasn't great at praying—I could never sit still long enough—but I was an expert wisher, ever since Bea Ann made me read *From the Mixed-up Files of Mrs. Basil E. Frankweiler* and I threw my first quarter into the fountain at the Museum of Art. Today, I sent up thanks to whoever sent me such a good librarian.

"Mom? Have you heard from Bea Ann?"

"No. It's a little odd. Her mailbox is full. I'll try Madge and see what's happening. Go ahead, ride shotgun."

I went to thank Amisha. She said she would bring the sarongs and meet us there.

I seat-belted myself and my charges in and told Lu where we needed to stop on the way into Ubud, then turned to Mom. "Did you reach Madge?"

"Left a message. I'm sure they're just out having fun. Madge needs to let off some steam, I think. She's been weird lately. I've just been writing it off to menopause."

"How do you mean?"

"Well, she threw that fit at the hotel the day we arrived, she keeps disappearing, she says to shop, but then she doesn't bring anything back. And she keeps talking about high school, I guess wanting to relive her glory days."

"Madge had glory days?"

"Oh, yes. Homecoming Queen Class of '69. And Miss Bratwurst."

"Wow. Had no idea." We settled in for the swervy ride, past even more scooters balancing birdcages than we'd seen the day before.

The honking was almost overwhelming and the smell today, for the first time, featured more cage droppings than frangipani. In the distance, you could occasionally hear a wave of bird sounds. Maybe it was laughingthrushes. We passed an exit off the road, filled with tourists.

"What's that?"

Lu looked back. "The entrance to the Monkey Forest. We must go. The monkeys would love your Balenciaga."

I could see tourists—cameras out—and statues, covered in monkeys, as we sped past. Lu pulled in beside a line of stalls and nodded to Mom.

I stayed in the car with the chicks. Suddenly, my birdternal instincts went on high alert. And then, I saw a familiar Land Rover in the sideview mirror.

I ducked down as far as I could, as the Rover passed by and continued toward the competition ground. I edged up just in time to see a cowlick sticking up from the passenger seat and catch a few letters on the license plate.

If Bunty and the poachers were here, this plan better work.

I just wished Hazelnut had given me a place to meet him—his having to find me was the one fly in the ointment.

I checked the sideview again and clocked flashes of red, as Lu and Mom ran across the road and added their purchases to the back of the Kijang.

Lu got into the driver's seat. "Stage one completed."

I looked back at Mom, who was grinning and holding a gold Kate Spade clutch with a bow on the front. I'd created a monster. She leaned forward and put it under the seat, then saw my face in the mirror. "What happened?"

"I just saw the poachers go by." I turned to Lu. "Maybe we should get started?"

"Got it. We're not far from the rendezvous point."

While she drove, I kept my eyes peeled for the Land Rover. Finally, she pulled into a small stand of trees and gave a honk.

Amisha came forward with seven of my Tupperware compatriots, all dressed in the same sarongs and traditional blouses Mom, Lu, and I were wearing. I checked the chicks, lay my Balenciaga carefully on the floor of the passenger seat, then moved to the back to help Mom and Lu put the steamers inside each of the red knockoff Balenciaga purses Lu had bought.

There were a few details a real Weekender tote aficionado would find lacking, but from a distance, the knockoffs looked just like my Balenciaga, right down to the fringe. It was a surreal experience to see nine of them in one place. We distributed them to the delight of the women.

Then we handed out the wigs. These were less popular—partly because Lu had gotten them from a craftsman who made Rangda "demon wigs" for the traditional dancers. I showed them how Mom and I did our updos, and a few minutes later, nine clones stood before me.

I turned to the women and placed my palms together in front of my chest. *"Om Swastyastu."* I started to try to explain the drill in my halting Indonesian.

Lu tapped me on the arm and said something in Balinese that ended in "Pierce Brosnan." All the women nodded. A couple sighed. Lu looked at me. "We've all seen *The Thomas Crown Affair*, we understand. Carry the purses, put one down, pick another one up, keep moving, blah, blah, blah. Right?"

"Right. Exactly right. Please tell them the bags are theirs. I wish I could afford to give them real ones. And I've also purchased the steamers for everyone. If they're lost during the exercise, I will replace them. Make sure they know that if someone grabs for the bag, they should let them have it. I don't want anyone to get hurt."

Lu translated. Amisha came to stand beside me.

I leaned in to whisper, "Do they know it might be dangerous?"

"They do. Only the brave sell Tupperware in Indonesia. They're much more worried about being redheads."

"It's no picnic," I said.

We organized a staggered departure for the competition grounds and hid Mom's outfit and Balenciaga under a caftan, so as not to give the Cyd for a Day gag away.

As we got closer, we could hear the crowd cheering. The competition was about to begin.

"So everyone knows what they're doing? Mom, you've got your watch set, too, right?"

"Yes. Don't worry."

"Lu?"

She held up her phone and nodded.

Mom had to stay near me, since we would both be needed for feeding if Hazelnut didn't find me in forty-seven minutes. Lu pulled up to the grounds.

I picked up my bag. "I want to check on the chicks one more time."

Mom put her hand on my shoulder. "There's the Land Rover. We don't have time."

Lu let Mom off about twenty feet down the road. I saw her struggling a bit on the grass in her borrowed kitten heels.

I opened the Kijang door and was overwhelmed by the astonishing songs of dozens of birds, which was almost drowned out by screaming and whistle blowing. It had a Disney's *Cinderella* meets *Raging Bull* at a referees' convention feel. But the birds cut through and they were something. I caught Mom's eye. She smiled. She felt the same.

At least no one was going to hear Huey, Dewey and Louie. Many of the spectators stood or sat with their own birdcages. Past them on the other edge of the field, all eyes were on a large metal structure, open on all sides, its vaulted ceiling covered by a fabric tarp. It was filled with empty stools. Birdcages on hooks hung above them. Several men were walking inside the structure, going from cage to cage. I still had my mini-binoculars in a side pocket. I focused in on one gorgeous bird with a bright orange neck.

I asked the bird owner next to me who the men were.

"Judges." There was movement in the tent and cheers as one of the men placed a red flag on one of the stools. "Red wins!" the man said.

The crowd went wild. As soon as the cheers died down, a new group of owners moved in with their cages, then backed away and began to shout and blow on their bird whistles.

The new birds all looked similar. In fact, they all looked like Burung's bird, Mitzi. It must be the spotted doves. I wondered if I would see Burung. I wasn't sure I wanted him in the mix of the operation. I had no choice when he saw me and waved.

"Cyd!"

I waved back. He jogged over. "You came!"

"I did! How is Mitzi?"

"She is an angel. Will you listen for her?"

"Of course."

He touched the whistle around his neck, then ran back toward the tent, yelling words and blowing signals only Mitzi the dove could understand.

I looked over. My mom wasn't in sight.

The cowlicked West Bali poacher, however, was. We saw each other at the same time.

Chapter Fifty-four

Being spotted was part of my plan, but not this way. I thought of Stu Capistranis, taking two bullets for those birds without a murmur, sent a quick text saying *Go!* to Lu and Amisha, clutched my Balenciaga to my side, and walked like hell.

The poacher was on the other side of the field, headed straight for me, when a clump of men with cages arrived, forming a brief wall of tweeting and flapping between us.

I ran to the market across the street and ducked into the darkest stall, filled with scarves and tapestries, but that didn't shake him off. I wrapped something aqua and silky around me and held my breath.

Nothing. When I peeked out, he was stopped across the street, looking around. Then he turned and headed back onto the field, following a mini-me, flaunting her Balenciaga, headed toward the tent.

Should I stay here? Given the look the stall owner was giving me, maybe not. I overpaid for the scarf, threw it over my hair and bag and exited, trying to keep an eye on the man until I was sure he was headed in the other direction. Then, I saw the other poacher, the bowl haircut one, at the edge of the field. Just then, two more Tupperware compatriots entered the grounds from different sides. They passed each other in the middle of the field and exchanged purses. The bowl haircut guy looked in both directions, then followed one of them.

Henrik followed the other.

Damn. I'd hoped he'd left the island. He started running, then flew through the air and landed facedown in the mud. I saw a "I Support the Right to Arm Bears" hat above a pair of crutches. Stu! Stu was here and had tried to save the woman he thought was me.

Henrik struggled up and spotted Stu. There was no way he was outrunning Henrik on crutches. Then I saw a slightly taller me, Balenciaga swinging, walk between the two men. On shaky kitten heels. Henrik followed her.

Stu crutched after both of them. I couldn't chance it. I couldn't let Henrik get my mom, no matter whose existential nanny I might be.

I texted Lu *Headed to field*, put my phone in my bra, and rammed myself into a largish tour group headed for the tent. I caught sight of another Balenciaga on the other side, being followed by the cowlicked poacher. At least he was handled for the moment.

I couldn't see Mom, but I spotted Stu's hat and followed that. Had they gone into the temple? At least I was wearing a sarong and didn't have to stop and buy one to enter.

I heard a scream. For a second I thought it was my mother. Then I realized it was me.

Someone had picked me up around the waist and was carrying me backward. I could smell American cigarette smoke. I kicked back into their shins as hard as I could. Then something damp and sickly sweet covered my mouth.

When I woke up my Balenciaga was gone.

Chapter Fifty-five

Where were the chicks? Where was my mother?

I was on the ground in some kind of crumbling lichen-smeared structure. It wasn't the temple where Alistair had left Mom, as the carvings were different, and there were more banyan trees. The sounds were different, too—fewer songs, more buzzing and screeching.

I assessed my situation. I was gagged and my hands were tied behind my back, with something that felt like a bungee cord. Had I been hoisted by my own pursetard? My fingers couldn't quite reach the fasteners. I scooted around to look in the other direction, just in case my purse was there, and saw about fifteen monkeys, of all sizes, staring at me. One of them was wearing sunglasses.

I was in the Monkey Forest.

Okay. I remembered monkeys were ruthless about stealing things from the tourists, and would look everywhere for food if they could find it. Then, I spotted a half-peeled banana lying under a palm frond, about four feet away. It would probably be compost by the time I assed my way over, but it was worth a try.

I finally got hold of it with my hands, rubbed it all over the bungee cord, and squished the rest in one fist. Then I scooted around with my back to the monkeys and waved it as much as I could. Come and get me, you little bastards, I thought. Please.

They did. In seconds, I had about six monkeys crawling on me, plus an audience. Let's just say, what they lacked in hygiene, they made up for in enthusiasm. And dexterity. In what seemed like two hours, but was probably thirty seconds, they'd unhooked the bungee cord, grabbed the banana, checked my hair for mites, and scampered away.

I flexed my fingers, took out my gag, wiped my banana-hands on it, and tried to stand up. I was still groggy from whatever my kidnappers had given me, but after a few minutes, I got my jungle legs.

I pulled my phone out of my bra. No reception.

I remembered from my research that the Monkey Forest was west of the city, so I just had to go east. I reached for my father's compass and remembered that my bag was gone. Which reminded me my mother was gone. The chicks were gone. I had failed everyone and everything.

I wasn't going to cry. I couldn't help Mom or the chicks if I couldn't get out of here. Then I saw a flash of red through a green archway and followed it. The monkeys were throwing my Balenciaga back and forth.

"Put that down!" I didn't swear, since they had just saved my life. Instead I went primal scream and threw sticks at them until they finally dropped it and backed off.

Oh thank God, I thought. I picked the bag up. It was empty. Completely empty.

Then I looked closer. The hardware was fake. This was one of the knockoffs.

Was it Mom's? Was she around here, somewhere? I shouted for her and tried my phone again. Still no reception.

I tried to figure out where the sun was, and which direction was east, but there were too many trees in the way. I saw something that looked almost like a trail leading away from the crumbling temple and headed down that, calling for Mom about every five feet.

I'd gone about fifty jungly yards when the beeping went off. It was the worm alarm. That didn't decrease my stress. Then I stopped. I smelled Virginia Slims.

"Cyd? Cyd! Thank goodness. We have been looking all over for you."

"Madge?"

Madge Dupree stood there in her Chico sundress and jeweled flip- flops, smiling at me.

"Where's Mom. Is she okay? There were people after her."

"Bea Ann's looking after her. She sent everyone to look for you. I've got a car."

I almost collapsed with relief. She reached out her hand and helped me over the banyan root. I'd been much closer to the road than I realized. Scooters were going by and there was a Kijang with a driver waiting. Madge opened the car door. "You get up front where it's comfortable."

I said hello in Indonesian to the driver and got in. "Thank you, Madge. I don't know how long I would have wandered around out there."

"Don't be silly." She placed her purse in between the seats. "Do you know what happened? Your mother said she saw some man carry you away?"

"I guess. I don't know. They knocked me out."

"So you don't know who might have done it?"

"A lot of people might have. Who actually did it, no."

Madge nodded at the driver. We pulled off the road into a driveway.

"Where are we? Is this where Mom is?"

"Yes, I just need to make a call and let them know it's us."

She climbed out of the car and moved to the back. My banana-drenched hands were sticking to everything. I hoped Madge might have a packet of Handi Wipes and pulled her purse onto my lap. I didn't find any Handi Wipes. What I did find was dead Gerald Boynton's passport.

Chapter Fifty-six

Had the driver seen my reaction? Had Madge?

Scott had said Gerald's killer tried to make his death look like a robbery gone wrong. Had Madge killed him? Was that possible? I'd been so relieved to see her in the jungle, I hadn't even wondered how on earth she'd found me—unless she'd been there when someone dropped me off. And if she was the killer, where was Mom? I grabbed a set of keys and a couple of other items out of her purse and tried to rearrange my face as the driver got back in the car, followed by Madge.

"Mom's okay, right?"

"Your mother is always okay, Cyd. She has a charmed life."

Normally, I might've begged to differ. "Have you and Bea Ann had fun?"

"I'll let Bea Ann tell you about it."

We arrived at a large open house, surrounded by fountains and frangipani trees.

The driver parked, then came around to "help me out." Madge gestured me up the stairs. At least I still had my phone in my bra and my almost empty Balenciaga.

I entered the room, filled with a huge flat-screen TV, to find Bea Ann tied up in the corner, her reading glasses askew. It was all I could do not to punch Madge in her smug face in that moment, but I stopped myself, for Bea Ann's sake, and played dumb instead.

I ran over to her. "Holy crap, Bea Ann! What happened, who did this to you?" As I hugged her, I tried to loosen the ties around her wrists. They were already loose. She winked at me.

I looked at Madge. "What's going on? Where's my mother?"

"What difference does that make? She doesn't want your help, she told you."

I hung my head and put my hand over my heart/phone. I hoped I'd hit the right button.

I moved toward her. "You killed Gerald Boynton, didn't you?"

She looked shocked. "I don't know what you're talking about."

"Let's just say I have proof. I just don't have the why."

"He was an asshole! And a moron. That's why." Madge put her hands on her hips. "He had one simple job. He was supposed to put the money in my carry-on. Simple. You know what he said?"

"No idea. What?"

"He said all middle-aged American women looked the same. How was he supposed to tell the difference? Can you believe that? And when I went to collect the money from him he lied and said Bridget had it. I'd gone through her luggage and the whole room. It wasn't there. He'd stolen it, all right. And I was going to have to explain."

Explain to whom?

"Then, I asked Gerald why he sat by your mother instead of me. What was it about her, if we all looked alike? You know what he had the nerve to say to me? That at least your mother still had a waist. A waist! That bastard. Everyone goes through menopause."

"That's pretty brutal."

"Yes, it is. So I shoved him and he fell backward and hit his head. He deserved it."

"And you took a few things to make it look like a robbery?"

"Of course."

"Still, that wasn't my mother's fault. Where is she?"

"Bunty is taking care of your mother until you tell him where the money is."

Bunty. How many times had Mrs. Barksy reminded me her son was Homecoming King, Class of '69? Had this whole damn trip been orchestrated by him? The idea of Bunty anywhere near my mom made me hysterical. Hysterical enough to put Madge's keys between my knuckles and shove them into the driver's face when he got close, throwing him off balance long enough for me to execute an inside kick, cross, and left hook, which knocked him out.

Madge ran at me with a huge vase. I dodged to the right and shot her in the eyes with her own Binaca. She dropped the vase and threw her hands up long enough for Bea Ann to stick out her leg and trip her. I jumped on Madge's back.

Bea Ann threw me her used restraints.

"How did you get loose?"

"Remembered a few tips from *How to Survive an Abduction.* Simon and Schuster, 1976. Madge is not a reader."

"Screw you, Bea Ann, I read *Men Are From Mars, Women Are From Venus* five times!"

"Self-help doesn't count."

We tied her and the driver up. I found a gun under the driver's jacket and pocketed it.

"Madge. Where is Bunty keeping my mom?" And the chicks, I hoped. At least Bunty's poachers knew how much the birds were worth. Surely they'd be trying to keep them alive?

"I'm not telling you that. I promised Bobby. We're engaged."

"Madge. He is not Bobby anymore. He's Bunty. You're engaged to someone who's wanted by Interpol and is responsible for the death and torture of probably thousands of endangered animals."

"It's a misunderstanding." We both just stared at her. "Nobody's perfect."

"Madge, I babysat for your kids. Is this really the stepfather you want for them?"

She didn't say anything, but I saw her face shift a little. I pulled out the driver's gun. In the end, I figured she was a coward. I was right.

"They're at Bobby's compound." She told us where it was.

"Thank you," I said, and gagged her.

Bea Ann and I ran to the driver's Kijang and jumped in.

"What happened to her, Bea Ann?"

"If I may paraphrase Ms. O'Connor, she'd have been a good woman if she'd had a decent husband—or somebody there to shoot her every minute of her life."

After I made a few calls, we pulled out and headed to the rescue, we hoped.

Chapter Fifty-seven

Thankfully it wasn't far and the two quick stops I needed—Western Union and a cricket stand—were on the way. Bea Ann and I discussed our strategy. We had an empty Balenciaga, my kitten heels, a gun with six bullets, Madge's phone, most of the knowledge housed in the Bay Ridge Branch of the Brooklyn Public Library, and a half-full Binaca.

We slowed as we approached the driveway. I had been to one of Bunty's "compounds" before and just the thought of it made me feel faint. I remembered Mom and the chicks and tried to look brave.

Bea Ann patted my shoulder. "Courage is fire, and bullying is smoke."

"Who said that?"

"Disraeli."

"Thanks, Bea Ann. For everything. Except for *The Yearling*. I still haven't recovered from that."

"Malarky. You've always been tougher than you think."

I took my eyes off the road for a second to look at her and almost hit three monkeys.

"Road!" she said. "You have to promise to forget this if we both live, but you were always my favorite."

We heard the place before we saw it. If there were such a thing as a birdsong tornado, we were in it. We stopped the Kijang and got out to case the place on foot.

"Ready?" I said.

Bea Ann nodded and popped the top off the Binaca. We edged our way closer to the cacophony. Unlike Bunty's other compound, which had dozens of different animals, this seemed to be an aviary only—cage after cage of gorgeous, imperiled birds.

Bea Ann looked the way she did when Barry spilled a Slurpee on Volume D of the *Encyclopedia Britannica.* "Should we just open the cages?"

"No. These birds could be from all over, not just Bali but Sumatra or Java. They need to go back to their natural environment."

"Okay."

I searched for any guards, but the coast looked clear, except for the Land Rover, which was parked in front of a house straight out of *The Brady Bunch*. Only Bunty would build a split-level ranch in the middle of Bali. He even had American air conditioning units at three windows. Damn. I couldn't see in.

I handed Bea Ann the Kijang keys. Much of our plan was based on a book about prosthetics Bea Ann read when she was stuck under the river on the R train. "Once you get to the car, wait three minutes, rev it like crazy, then pull up and park behind the cages. I don't think they'll want to shoot through the birds, but duck anyway."

Bea Ann actually kissed me on the cheek. "David Morrell would be proud."

She hurried back into the trees. I ran to the back of the house and found the one window without a cooling unit. I glimpsed a sarong. Mom.

I crept back to the side of the house, took out Madge's phone, found "Bobby" under her Favorites, and texted *Got Cyd, but need help. Turning in now.* I sent another text from my phone. I wished I had an offering.

The air conditioner was too loud for me to hear Bunty's phone ping, but it must have, since he walked out on the porch, still in his suit, followed by Henrik, in a muddier one.

I ran back to Mom's window, waited until the Kijang revved, and smashed the window with the butt of the gun. I climbed inside, kissed her on the head, and undid her wrists and legs. I wondered whether hostage release was an actual profession, as by now I should be certified.

I helped her out the window and we edged around the corner in time to see Bunty and Henrik headed toward the Kijang. Just on time, we heard a chopper approach, flying low and sending all the trees shuddering. Bunty and Henrik looked up.

"Stay here!" I said to Mom, before I ran forward, gun out. I saw Bea Ann and the Kijang headed right for the men. Henrik dodged right and I shot him in the leg. The Kijang was still headed for Bunty, but it slowed down to a crawl. Bea Ann knew that someone with a prosthetic leg had a hard time going backward. As soon as Bunty tried, he fell over.

Bea Ann jumped out and kicked him in the balls. "Bobby Fred Barsky, you should be ashamed of yourself!" Then she sat on top of him to keep him still.

I turned to Mom. "I need your sash. Can you help Bea Ann deal with Henrik? I need to talk to Bunty."

Bea Ann and Mom tackled Henrik. It took all my kickboxing strength to drag Mrs. Barsky's errant son to the nearest tree, where I secured him with the sarong sash and kept the Binaca at the ready.

Bunty cradled his privates and sent up a wail. "Where is Madge? Is she all right?"

"Why do you care? You were just using her as your mule, right?"

"No! No! She offered. She wanted to help. Is she okay, Cyd? We just found each other again, after all these years."

"Christ on a bike, Bunty. You know she killed Gerald Boynton because he said she didn't have a waist?"

"She does! She will! Menopause doesn't last forever."

Seriously? "She's okay, she might need an eyewash. But I recorded her full confession. And you know what happens to murderers in Bali."

He went white. "No, you can't. I'll turn myself in. I'll confess. She still has a child at home."

"He's twenty-nine!"

"Cyd. Please don't do this to her! It was an accident."

I looked back. Bea Ann and Mom had Henrik trussed like a Christmas goose and were laughing. Mom's sarong had half fallen off.

Were Bunty and Madge really in love? Was there a real person in there somewhere who just got screwed up by the war? I didn't know what to do. So I just thought for a minute. Then decided.

"If you want my help, there are a few things you have to do. First, where are the starling chicks and is someone feeding them?"

"What chicks?"

"The poachers didn't tell you I had the chicks?"

"They told me you could identify them. And I knew you would tell Agent Gant and Interpol where I was, so we had to grab you. Madge thought you had the money."

"So where are the chicks?"

He shrugged. "I hope you didn't kill them. Do you know what they're worth?"

"Okay, what was the money for? The money Gerald was carrying?"

"After you totally screwed up my business, I switched to straight songbirds. Much easier to falsify documents for those. Tons of money, huge market."

"What were you doing at that resort, then? Poaching?"

"No. Laundering. It's a conglomerate with a real estate division. It's perfect, because it's an eco-resort, no one is going to object when it takes over part of the national park and we can grab birds whenever we want to keep the hotel going. After Madge and I got back together, I figured I could ease out into real estate and go legit."

"Do you realize how evil that is? You don't even deserve Madge."

"Hey! No one knows what goes on inside of a relationship except the people in it."

"So you're in league with Peggy Newsome, she's part of the smuggling thing?"

"Peggy Newsome? She wishes. I heard she lost the real estate conglomerate about ten million dollars on a development a few years ago. They put her into some bullshit travel division and she's been trying to get back into their good graces. They said they'd give her a shot if she could put up seed money for this property from some mixed-use thing she's doing in Brooklyn."

"Bunty! Don't you know that mixed-use thing is Third fricking Avenue? That she wants to knock down your mother's building? That's why she's been sucking up to you."

"She said it was in Red Hook. She actually came on to me. I should have known."

"She's a witch. It doesn't matter. You know we can't let her do that. For your mom's sake."

"Yeah, Mom, who left you the building."

"You knew?"

"Yeah. It really hurt."

"I'm sorry. I didn't know about it until after she died. That's why I came to Africa. To tell you. I think she did it because she didn't believe you'd ever come back and she wanted to make sure it was safe. She made you executor, so you'd have to approve. She loved you to pieces, you know."

"Did she? After everything?"

"Yes. She did." I looked at that familiar, ski-jump nose and thought of all the hours I'd spent listening to Mrs. Barsky talk about "her Bobby," and how Madge's kids let me win at *Operation*.

"Look, I'll make a deal with you. I will not turn Madge or her confession over to the police. And I will give you a few hours head start to get away, if you do three things."

"Yeah, what?"

"First, you promise to stop smuggling animals. Period. Not even a pygmy chameleon. Seriously. Second, you tell me what you know about Peggy Newsome, including who she works for."

"And?"

"Third, as your mother's executor, you sign off on giving me the Third Avenue building. I promise to keep it safe and sell it back to you if you ever come home." We looked at each other for a moment, then I held out the faxed documents I'd picked up from Western Union. "Well?"

"And you're sure Madge is okay?"

"She is."

"Why should I believe you?"

"Scout's honor." That still meant something in Bay Ridge. "But just remember, if I hear you are smuggling any animals or helping anyone who does—and you know I will—I'll give the recording of Madge's confession to the police."

We looked at each other for a long time.

Finally, he gave me the dirt on Peggy, then put out his hand. "Give me the papers."

I gestured to Bea Ann, who ran over. She had her purse. And a pen.

I put on my most official voice. "Bea Ann, as a notary for the borough of Brooklyn, will you please witness the transfer of 3500 Third Avenue from the Barksy estate to Cyd Elizabeth Madonna Redondo? And Bunty, you better use your real name!"

Bunty signed all the papers. As Robert Fred Barsky, Jr.

I figured Bea Ann would postdate the notary seal when she got home, but I guess I wasn't the only one with emergency supplies in her purse. She whipped out her notary seal and the building was mine.

I was elated and relieved. For about three seconds, until I remembered the chicks.

First, though, I had to get Bunty out of here. "We'll give you three hours' head start. Go now, before law enforcement gets here."

Bunty suddenly looked tiny in his suit. "Cyd? Thanks for having tea every day with her."

"You're welcome."

He limped to the Land Rover and we watched him careen down the driveway.

Hazelnut was going to kill me.

Chapter Fifty-eight

Mom stared at me while she hitched up her sarong. "Why did you let him go?"

Before I could answer, both of our watches started beeping their worm alarm. And I started to cry. Mom turned to Bea Ann. "Can you drive?"

They bundled me into the Kijang and lay me down on the backseat, where I did that kind of hiccup-level sobbing that wears out your abs. I felt Mom patting my leg. I don't know how long we drove, but when I sat up, we were pulling up in front of Amisha's compound. There was an ancient *bemos* parked outside.

Mom jumped out and navigated the anti-demon wall, while Bea Ann gave me a handkerchief. My eyes were hopeless, but at least I was cried out.

We walked in. There were Lu and Amisha and several of the Tupperware women, who all pressed their hands together and nodded to me and Bea Ann.

Mom came down and put her arm around me. "You have to prepare yourself, sweetheart, okay?"

Oh no. For what?

I entered the big room to hear a faint trilling. There Stu Capistranis, complete with baseball cap, held a basket in his lap while Hazelnut, still dressed like Bunty, had a vertical worm between his fingers, swinging it back and forth, trying to get it into what looked like Huey's rotating mouth. I inched closer, as I was sure I was dreaming. There, in their Tupperware nest, were Huey and Dewey. But not Louie.

Mom pulled me in close. "He didn't make it, Cyd, but his brother and sister are fine."

Stu looked up. "It's a miracle! Two. After everything that's happened you still saved two! We usually throw a party if we get one past the first two days. I would hug you, but we're occupied."

"I can see that. It's fine. I think a worm basket incident might push me over the edge."

Hazelnut looked over and nodded. There was a grin beneath it. "AntiChristine." Then he looked at my mother and both of them froze. Like Romeo and Juliet froze. Oh, I did not see that. I couldn't have.

Thankfully, Lu distracted me. "Cyd?"

She was holding up a Balenciaga. My Balenciaga, complete with the bullet hole repair. It was still full of everything I needed to keep living. I collapsed on one of the floor pillows and looked around. "Could someone please tell me what the hell happened?"

It turned out that Lu and Mom had decided that I might do something stupid, like try to save them or one of the Tupperware Cyds for a Day, and that the chicks were actually safer away from the competition grounds. Hazelnut would have to wait. Mom also didn't think I could handle losing my Balenciaga again.

So, when we were loading up the Kijang at Amisha's, she had swapped my real bag for one of the fake ones and left it and the chicks with Lu's sister, with full instructions on how to feed them. How everyone had been abducted, and saved, and how Hazelnut had found Amisha's house, would have to wait for another day. My brain was exploding as it was.

"Does anyone have an offering I could use?"

Lu handed me a particularly intricate rice figure, balanced on its bamboo leaf. I headed out toward the sacred banyan tree and placed it on the shrine. I thanked the gods, or demons, or whoever had gotten us all back here. Then I said a prayer for Louie.

Suddenly Mom was there. She added an offering, then put her arm around me and we just stood there for a moment, in the shade of the tree. "It happens, sometimes. I never told you, but I had a miscarriage right after your dad and I got married. We were desolate. And so scared. But he said we couldn't lose hope, we had to try again, right away. And it worked. We got you. And look how you turned out. I can't imagine how proud he is of you, wherever he is."

"You mean I wasn't a mistake? I mean an accident."

"An accident? You were the furthest thing from an accident. Who said that?"

"Madge."

"Damn that woman. Where is she, anyway?"

Damn her was right. But she was tied to Bunty for life. That was punishment enough.

"No idea. Let's go back in."

We met Hazelnut on his way out. He was carrying a bicycle helmet with him. It was trilling. "This time, you're coming with me." He looked at Mom. "That is, if it's all right with you, Mrs. Redondo?"

She blushed. "It's Ms."

"Great! I'm ready!" I said, just to get those two away from each other.

I held the chicks while Hazelnut drove, and in minutes, we were at the

Ubud airport.

"Are you going to tell me where we're going?"

"No. But the pilot said if I brought you, I got a free ride."

Scott was running toward us. Hazelnut took the chicks and Scott lifted me up and carried me over the melting tar. He held on a bit tighter this time. "Did it work, the flyover?"

"It was perfect. Thank you."

"You're welcome."

We flew down from Ubud over rice fields and then over beaches, where local fishing boats sat like giant spiders on the tides. And to the island of Nusa Penida, where Scott made an unorthodox, but gentle landing.

After a few vehicle changes, we arrived at our destination—the year-old Bali Starling Sanctuary. On the drive Hazelnut explained that the conservationists had made a mutually beneficial deal with the islanders, who'd made a vow to keep the birds safe. They even had release ceremonies at the local temple when the birds were ready to go back into the wild. I wished I could see one of those.

The volunteers were ecstatic about the two chicks. They were prepared with worms, crickets, and pieces of papaya all laid out in a perfect starling buffet. I finally let go of the breath I felt I'd been holding for three days. If Huey and Dewey had a chance of survival, it would be here.

After a tour, where I was lucky enough to see a few gorgeous, full-grown birds who were being rehabilitated, I had to say goodbye to my temporary charges, who wobbled and trilled their farewell. The volunteers let me leave an offering and send up a prayer, to demons, gods, and the Holy Trinity, for the chicks' safety. When they closed the cage door around their clean new nest, Scott squeezed my hand.

Then, Hazelnut told us to go on ahead, he was staying.

"Regards to your mother, AntiChristine."

"In your dreams, Hazelnut," I said, and kissed him on the cheek.

Scott didn't say much as we flew back over the cobalt waves. He was taking me back to Denpasar, where we saw snaky lines of color and trailing smoke below.

I turned to Scott. "Cremations?"

"It's for Nyepi."

When we landed, he took off his seat belt and turned to me. "How long are you staying?"

"I'm ticketed to leave in a week. It will depend on my mom, I think."

"I have to go back to Australia tonight. But I'll be back tomorrow night. Any chance I could be your local guide for the most sacred day in Bali?"

He'd said guide, not date. I figured it was permissible, on a technicality.

"Yes. Yes, I would love that."

"In the spirit of full disclosure, there is something you don't know about me. It might make a difference."

Oh God. Although I was sure I'd heard worse, considering Roger's impending embryo-hood. "Go ahead, hit me."

"I'm Jill's son."

Suddenly so many of Jill's comments made sense. And now made me nauseous.

"Oh no! How old are you?"

He laughed. "My mum is a bit older than she looks. Don't worry, it's not a felony."

"But what about Jill? She's my friend. And colleague. It seems unprofessional."

"I was afraid you'd say that."

"Plus, didn't you say she wanted you to marry someone else?"

"Yes. I did."

"What about her? Who is it?"

"It's Lu."

Chapter Fifty-nine

Great. I'd finally found a man who told the truth, and he was not only a colleague's son, he was betrothed to my new best friend, and Tupperware associate. Could I never get a break?

He took my hand. "I think Mum just wants the business to stay in the family. She's worked so hard, for so long, and in terms of carrying on, if we were married, Lu would be official family and run it, even if I still spent time in Australia."

"She must think you love each other, though. Do you?"

He snorted. "She's like my sister. We've known each other since we were kids. We are great friends, but there's no spark, never has been. Besides, she's in love with someone else, some fancy hotel guy, she won't say who."

Reggie. She was in love with Reggie.

"But neither one of us wants to break Mom's heart, or make her worry. So we've just kept up the façade for her sake."

I hesitated to even consider what a kettle of worms this was, especially since now I knew what one actually looked like.

"Will you let me think about it?"

"Absolutely."

We might have kissed, but an airport employee popped his head in the cockpit. He'd brought a set of stairs and a golf cart to deliver me to the terminal. Scott winked.

I splurged on a car to Burung's hotel. On the drive, I went over the plan Mom, Bea Ann, and I had figured out and called to say I was on my way.

As my ride veered around the sacred banyan tree, I spotted two pastel dresses through the frangipani leaves. It was my job to distract Burung long enough for them to sneak in and dig up the money.

I asked the driver to honk, overtipped him, then headed up the reception stairs.

Burung beamed. "Cyd! I looked for you after the competition but you had disappeared. Mitzi won! Did you know? Come and look!"

He reached for the shiny new trophy and held it aloft in a *Rocky* pose.

"Burung! I am so excited for you. And Mitzi!"

I moved to the birdcage and Mitzi started hopping, which I hoped wasn't because she'd spotted Mom and Bea Ann slipping down the path. "What about the other bird, her coach?"

"Ah, he has taught Mitzi all he can teach. I sold him and bought another."

"Oh, that's too bad. He was wonderful, too."

Burung put the trophy back on the shelf. "Papaya?" He held up a plate with slices fanned out like rays from the sun.

"No, thank you."

He shrugged and ate a piece. Mitzi squawked a little.

"Burung, I wondered whether I could walk around the property and take some photographs so I could include them in my brochure. I think many of my clients might love your place."

"I would be delighted. Should I accompany you and show you the best bits?"

"No, I think I will just wander. I know my clients and what they're looking for." I felt guilty lying to him, but it was for Mom's sake.

"As you wish, take all the time you need." He slurped another piece of papaya and the juice ran down his fingers and forearms. "Are you sure you don't want any?"

"All right. Thank you," I said, taking a bamboo leaf and placing several pieces on top. It seemed impolite not to.

I bowed to him, took out my camera, and headed down the pathway toward our old lodging.

My pals, the fruit bats, were hanging in the trees near the room. I rolled up the papaya in the leaf, afraid they might notice it. They must have been deep in REM sleep, as for once, they stayed put.

I found Mom and Bea Ann on their knees with a garden spade. I tried not to think about snakes or bugs and focused on the package they'd uncovered that looked like a brick of heroin.

Mom held it up, triumphant. "Cyd!"

"Mom! Give that to me and get up off the ground."

"Sorry, you're right." She handed me the package and brushed off her knees. Just as I was putting it in my Balenciaga I heard a click.

"Ah, you've saved me a lot of trouble. You might give me the money, Cyd."

Burung stood blocking the path, right under the fruit bat tree, a small pistol in his hand. "When Alistair didn't find the money, I suspected one of you had it. He was always incompetent."

Not anymore, I thought. What could I do? I looked up at the bats above Burung's head. A few of them were rustling a little. I still had the papaya.

"Now, I can buy any bird, compete anywhere. International! Mitzi is just the beginning."

Mom was hanging on to my arm. "Be ready to run," I whispered.

"I understand, Burung. You want to collect more birds. We don't want the money. Here."

I went as if to toss it. When he reached forward, I leveled him with a roundhouse kick, rammed a stiletto on his chest and smashed the papaya onto his head. Then I picked up his gun.

"Run!" I screamed, then I shot a round into the air and a horror movie number of bats flew off the trees and dive-bombed for Burung's ripe, pre-peeled papaya hair.

I could hear high-pitched squeaks and human screaming as we hightailed it to reception. The scooter was still there, with two helmets. I popped them on Mom and Bea Ann's heads and the three of us took off. If we could just get down the long driveway and onto the busy street, we might be okay.

As we got to the end of the drive, a Kijang stopped, blocking our way.

It was Stu, with an officer of the Indonesian Wildlife Crime Unit, coming to arrest Burung for illegal trafficking. It turned out that, due to Stu's efforts, a few of the conservation starlings had been chipped. Huey and Dewey's father—the bird we'd seen the poachers kidnap—was alive in Burung's back room and had led them there.

After that, it wasn't hard to convince Mom to donate half the money for Stu's work and half to the sanctuary on Nusa Penida, especially since it would be illegal to take it out of the country. There was only one condition—Stu had to send me an "I Support the Right to Arm Bears" hat.

Then, I called Reggie.

Chapter Sixty

After that, I managed to find a computer with internet and hacked into Peggy Newsome's server, before I made a call to her parent company, Heep International.

I offered Mom and Bea Ann the option of spending their last days on their own, but even they didn't want to give up the chance to have Scott as a tour guide. Or to stay with me at the Hanging Vines. Now that Mom and the chicks were safe, I could fully, completely fall in love with everything about Bali. Even the belief in making offerings to demons and gods alike was beginning to make sense to me, though I had so, so much more to learn before I could even begin to say I understood the culture and the place.

Much of it was still foreign, with incense and frangipani rather than sausage and garlic forward, but there were plenty of things that felt familiar—families living on top of each other in one large compound, everyone knowing everyone else's business, the fact that women did most of the work but still weren't respected. So it wasn't perfect. But for me, at that moment, it was pretty damn close. As much as I hated to admit it, *Eat, Pray, Love* had changed my life, just the way Elizabeth Gilbert intended.

On the night Scott returned, we all stood at the top of the Hanging Vines and looked down on the trail of candles that Reggie had placed in Lu's honor. He asked for her hand by the infinity pool and we all cheered. Sometimes true love needed a little shove. I hoped that, eventually, Jill would forgive me.

Afterward, we all danced in celebration. I watched my mother. In her sarong, she looked younger than I'd ever seen her. Had I spent my whole life looking at things through a ten-year-old's lens? It was time for a grown-up perspective, whatever the cost. Which is why I vamoosed the moment an extremely bow-legged man in a linen suit took her onto the dance floor. I was old enough to know I was never going to be old enough to handle that.

Our first Nyepi was everything beautiful and chaotic and sacred, all rolled into one. In the days before the official Balinese New Year, Scott taught us as much as he could about all the rituals and celebrations, including showing us the huge papier-mâché Ogoh Ogoh figures the Balinese created and paraded through the streets the night before the Day of Silence to attract the attention of evil spirits. According to Scott, they believed by the time the demons arrived, on Nyepi itself, the island would appear deserted and the spirits would pass over, leaving the island evil-free for another year.

Of course, to make that work, every single person—including tourists—had to stay indoors, with no work, no sound, no lights. I knew the airport would be closed, but I didn't know that any planes that might fly over were rerouted, so as not to disturb the silence. It was to be a day for meditation and cleansing yourself for the future. That was the short, totally inadequate, Americanized version, anyway.

Scott asked if I'd spend the holy day with him.

He took me to his little house in Ubud just before the beginning of the curfew, so I could see where everything was before the lights went out. It was like him, a mixture of Bali and Australia, with open spaces, gorgeous carvings, and silk pillows, but also a cappuccino maker, jars of Vegemite, and, wonder of wonders, screens on the windows, and a cuckoo clock.

It was still dark when the clock struck six in the morning. He turned off all the lights, stood in front of me, and placed his finger over my lips. "No talking," he said.

So we spent the day not talking, as quietly as we could. I took the idea of the new year seriously. It was about new beginnings, and letting go of the past. Scott had never lied to me and he had shown up every single time I'd needed him. Plus, he was gorgeous and funny. So when I fell in love with Bali, I fell in love with him a little bit, too.

Around midnight, when the moon was just a sliver overhead, he blew out our single votive candle, wrapped me in a sheet, and took me to the window. For someone whose entire lifetime sky was Manhattan-adjacent, this level of dark was inconceivable. It was even darker than the night Roger and I had spent in an African village, when I thought I'd seen as many stars as were possible.

Not even close. The smear of stars, spread across the entire sky, surpassed any Carl Sagan special Uncle Leon and I had ever watched on PBS.

It was silent except for the sound of buzzing insects and the occasional monkey, but at dawn the birds woke up and I truly understood why Nehru had called Bali "the morning of the world."

Once we could move about the island, Lu and I saw my mother and Bea Ann off at the Denpasar airport. Lu was sporting a huge engagement ring. Knockoff or not, it was stunning.

At the last minute, I told them I wasn't coming with them. My mom looked shocked.

"Everybody deserves a vacation," I said, as I hugged them both and watched them walk to their gate. I stayed in Departures for a while until

Peggy fricking Newsome—who'd been booked on the same flight, but whose luggage was now full of bestial pornography, illegal in Bali and provided by one of Hazelnut's dodgy compatriots—was dragged off by several Customs officers. I made sure I took a few photos for the *Bay Ridge Sentinel* and for the Heep International newsletter.

Scott was waiting for me at the curb. My phone pinged with a text. I held up my hand for him to wait a second.

We have four nights at the Hotel de Crillon in Paris. Work your travel agent magic and I'll see you there in three weeks. Can't wait. I love you. Roger.

About the Author

Wendall Thomas teaches in the Graduate Film School at UCLA, lectures internationally on screenwriting, and has worked as a film and television writer. Her first Cyd Redondo mystery, *Lost Luggage*, garnered Lefty and Macavity nominations for Best Debut, and the second, *Drowned Under*, was nominated for a Lefty for Best Humorous Mystery and an Anthony for Best Paperback Original. Her third Cyd Redondo mystery, *Fogged Off*, was a Lefty nominee for Best Humorous Mystery 2022. Her short fiction appears in *LAdies Night*, *Last Resort*, *Murder A-Go-Go's* and *Crime Under the Sun*.

Printed in the USA
CPSIA information can be obtained
at www.ICGtesting.com
LVHW041332111123
763410LV00022B/109